"With this set of stories, gay m[...]
literary mainstream. . . . Who [...] [...]mbone
will become the gay Updike, the gay J. F. Powers?"
                                            —*Booklist*

"Finely wrought . . . These are stories whose content
has rarely been handled quite so gracefully, so artfully,
before."   —*Bloomsbury Review*

"*The Language We Use Up Here* exposes vulnerabilities,
prejudices, and fears that seem endemic to the
mainstream of gay life. . . . It's surprising that more gay
writers don't don their pith helmets—or their crash
helmets—and head straight for the perilous territory
that Gambone explores."   —*New York Native*

"Gambone exhibits that all-too-rare combination in a
fiction writer: a mastery of craft so pure and absolute it
appears effortless . . . and a rich sensibility about the
complexities of human psychology that alternately
delights and skewers to the core."   —*Bay Windows*

PHILIP GAMBONE has published stories in over a
dozen magazines and anthologies, including *NER/BLQ*,
Christopher Street, *Tribe*, and *Men on Men 3*. He is also a
contributor to *Hometowns: Gay Men Write About Where
They Belong* and to *Contemporary Gay American Novelists*.
A former fellow at the MacDowell Colony, he currently
teaches at the Park School in Brookline, Massachusetts,
and in the expository writing program at the Harvard
Extension School. He divides his time between Boston
and Provincetown, Massachusetts.

PHILIP GAMBONE

THE LANGUAGE WE USE UP HERE

AND OTHER STORIES

A PLUME BOOK

PLUME
Published by the Penguin Group
Penguin Books USA Inc., 375 Hudson Street, New York, New York 10014, U.S.A.
Penguin Books Ltd, 27 Wrights Lane, London W8 5TZ, England
Penguin Books Australia Ltd, Ringwood, Victoria, Australia
Penguin Books Canada Ltd, 10 Alcorn Avenue, Toronto, Ontario, Canada M4V 3B2
Penguin Books (N.Z.) Ltd, 182-190 Wairau Road, Auckland 10, New Zealand

Penguin Books Ltd, Registered Offices: Harmondsworth, Middlesex, England

Published by Plume, an imprint of New American Library, a division of Penguin Books
USA Inc. Previously published in a Dutton edition.

First Plume Printing, May, 1992
10 9 8 7 6 5 4 3 2 1

*Some of these stories have previously been published, sometimes in an earlier version, in the
following magazines:*
"Fatherly" in The Greensboro Review; "Salon" in San José Studies; "The Summer of the
Daiquiri" in Chattahoochee Review; "Losing It" in New England Review and Bread Loaf
Quarterly; "Body Work" in Quarry West; "The Words" in Apalachee Quarterly;
"Babushkas" in Kansas Quarterly; "The Language We Use Up Here" in The Gettysburg
Review; "Pallbearer" in Tribe; "Too Much" in Sequoia.

"Enrollment" first appeared in Men on Men 3.

(P) REGISTERED TRADEMARK—MARCA REGISTRADA

LIBRARY OF CONGRESS CATALOGING-IN-PUBLICATION DATA
Gambone, Philip.
  The language we use up here : and other stories / Philip Gambone.
    p.   cm.
  ISBN 0-452-26816-8
  I. Title.
  [PS3557.A455L36   1992]
  813'.54—dc20   91-43730
                                                                  CIP

Printed in the United States of America
Original hardcover design by Steven N. Stathakis

BOOKS ARE AVAILABLE AT QUANTITY DISCOUNTS WHEN USED TO PROMOTE PRODUCTS OR
SERVICES. FOR INFORMATION PLEASE WRITE TO PREMIUM MARKETING DIVISION, PENGUIN
BOOKS USA INC., 375 HUDSON STREET, NEW YORK, NEW YORK 10014.

For Bill

▽

ACKNOWLEDGMENTS

ALONG THE WAY, many people have given me support and encouragement. Early on, the members of my first writing group, The Red Line Writers, read and critiqued the early drafts of some of these stories. Colleagues and friends in two other writing groups have also generously given time and serious attention to my work. I am grateful to them all, especially to Pamela Painter, my teacher, fellow writer, colleague, and friend, who often said to me, "One day you'll have a book."

I want to thank Sydney Lea, former editor of *NER/ BLQ*, who published my first story; and The MacDowell Colony for a month's residency during the summer of 1988.

George Stambolian deserves special mention. He brought my manuscript to the attention of my future editors and has lent a keen eye and a discerning ear throughout the editing process. His helpfulness to me—and to many new writers—has been invaluable.

I owe my editors at New American Library/Dutton

ACKNOWLEDGMENTS

many thanks as well: Gary Luke, who initially accepted the book for publication; and Rachel Klayman, whose love of this book and diligent efforts on its behalf I deeply appreciate.

Finally, I want to give loving thanks to my parents, and to Glenn Seberg.

CONTENTS

THE LANGUAGE WE USE UP HERE

LOSING IT

ALAN IS HOME. HAS been home a while, Peter figures. When you've lived with someone five years, you get a sense for these things. It's the living room—picked up—even though it's Peter's week to clean. Alan is being considerate, knows Peter is having trouble with the new score.

Peter takes off his scarf and jacket. He drops them on the Yamaha baby grand. Late February afternoon sunlight, a swatch of orange on the smooth ebony top, ripples up and over this bundle of clothing. He hides his portfolio with the working manuscript underneath. Peter doesn't want Alan to ask how it's going. Still, he goes to the hall landing and calls out *hello* toward Alan's study upstairs. He has already turned toward the kitchen when Alan calls back: *Down in a minute*.

The hallway is dark, with the comforting, light-mellowing darkness of every hallway built during the brown decades. This apartment, the one Peter and Alan have rented for their entire time together, occupies the right half of a modest Victorian house a few blocks from the Square. Three rooms down and three up, it is part scholar-artist's den (Peter's doing), part high-tech functional (Alan's). Peter can even tell—even before he hears the clackety-clack of the computer printer—what Alan is doing upstairs. Alan is sweetly predictable.

In the kitchen, he puts on the kettle for tea and pulls down a mug from the shelf. He opens a cupboard and surveys the tin canisters: Earl Grey, Lapsang Souchong, English Breakfast, Russian Caravan. As he reaches for the Earl Grey, Alan walks in.

"Let's have Russian Caravan," he says, coming up behind Peter and wrapping his arms around him.

Peter looks down at the hands clasped around his middle.

"Let's not and say we did."

"What?"

Peter laughs. "Didn't you ever use that expression when you were a kid: 'Let's not and say we did'? You said it when you wanted to let the other person know you weren't very enthusiastic about his idea. Like a friend would say, 'Let's play Redlight!' and you'd say, 'Hey, let's not and say we did.' I can't believe you never used that expression." Still in Alan's embrace, Peter swivels to face him directly. "No wonder you're so boring. You led such an impoverished childhood." Then he moves to kiss him.

Alan feigns disgust. "Ugh, let's not and say we did."

"Creep," Peter says, pushing him away.

"So what do *you* want?" Alan asks.

"I was fancying Earl Grey," Peter says.

"Well!" Alan draws out the word as he raises his eyebrows. "Fancying the Earl, were we? And when did we start hankering after the nobility?"

Peter calls this their tea 'n' tease time. He thinks of it as a kind of verbal manicure—filing down the nails of bitchiness that, every four or five days, seem to need attention. At breakfast this morning they were both in foul moods. This teasing about the Earl is Alan's way of announcing a settlement.

"Look who's talking," Peter says. "You were all set to take on a whole Russian caravan." He pulls two tins off the shelf, rummages through the utensil drawer until he finds the tea balls, then spoons some Earl Grey into one, the Russian Caravan into the other. "We'll just have to go our separate ways." Sheepishly, he fetches another mug from the shelf. Alan notices immediately.

"You selfish pig! You were only making tea for yourself?"

Sometimes tea 'n' tease backfires. From past experience, Peter knows the best way out of this one.

"No, actually Lance and I were going to share a cup." He picks up the steaming kettle and pours the water into their mugs.

"Lance" is their fantasy boyfriend. Blond and boyish, with a terrific body and winsome smile, he has developed over the years into a combination of the neighborhood greasemonkey, a Harvard swimteam captain, the kid next-door, one of several fashion models, Peter's long-lost fifth-grade buddy, Alan's sophomore-year roommate. Every now and then, Lance's name comes up at tea. They trade off stories of his latest escapades, how one week he's coming on to Alan, the next week to Peter. In the stories, Lance often shows up at their door whenever the other is out of the house for several hours. They never bed him. Exquisitely, he is always just out of reach. At the moment of truth, when the wine and Ella Fitzgerald (Alan's scenario) or the irresistible magnetism between them (Peter's) is taking effect, the other shows up and Lance must be whisked away, out the bedroom window or stuffed in a closet.

"Well," Alan drawls.

It's worked. Peter has headed off a scene. Back to tea 'n' tease, they sit down at the round oak table.

"Yes," he begins, casually. "I bumped into Lance in the Square. He asked if he could come over for a cup of tea and . . . well, how could I refuse? Besides, you said this morning that you weren't coming home until late. But when I heard you upstairs, I had to send him away. Pity. So what's up? Why are you home so early?"

"The presentation we were gearing up for got post-poned a month," Alan explains, "so there was no need to stay late. We've got some breathing room now." He dips the tea ball in and out of his cup. The way Alan steeps his tea, this careful monitoring until it's just right, Peter finds it fascinating, and annoying. "And how *is* Lance?" Alan asks, finally pulling out the tea ball, holding it above the mug to catch the drips.

"Terrific," Peter says, pushing a saucer between the mug and the dripping. "Let go," he says, and Alan releases the tea ball onto the saucer.

Peter is ready to drop the Lance thing. He leafs through the mail, which his lover has stacked, as he always does if he gets home first, next to the toaster. All bills: Filene's, Exxon, the health club. This thing with the mail, it's an-other one of those domestic rituals, and today it releases in Peter a little flurry of gratitude and affection, makes him want to banish Lance forever.

But Alan wants to press on. "What a shame I was home. If he's so terrific, maybe you should call him back. Better yet, wait till tomorrow. The company's sending me out of town: Indianapolis. I'll be back Saturday afternoon."

"Yuck! Indianapolis in February. You poor dear." Peter is relieved to get the conversation back to domestic affairs.

"Boynton says I'm the only one who has a chance of snagging this account."

"That's because you're so sexy," Peter says, giving Alan a big, warm grin. It's nice to salvage some of that lust for Lance and drop it into his affection for Alan.

"Don't worry. The guy in Indianapolis is a real nerd."

Peter is not reassured. Where there are nerds, there are also not-nerds, Lances, flesh-and-blood Lances. He wonders. And then there's the two of them: *PeterandAlan* they've become to their friends, even their parents. Where do they fall? Somewhere in the vast middle, he suspects. Poised, intelligent, handsome enough, but, at thirty-one and thirty-three respectively, on a fast train to Nerddom. Sometimes Peter gets the nagging suspicion that he is already there. His reassurance: that nerds aren't susceptible to sex appeal, and he, Peter, is *so* susceptible. "I fall in love at least once a day," he gleefully confesses to their friends, even in front of Alan.

But this week he hasn't had time to fall in love. It's that score, a woodwind quintet he has been trying to finish. When he's not rehearsing the players, he's hard at work trying to get the last movement right. The copyist wants the final movement by early next week. So the pressure is on, and there is no time to fall in love. Which is why he is in no mood to be teased about Lance. Were Lance to materialize, Peter would have to send him away.

They make supper together, pasta primavera tonight, and eat on the living room sofa watching the evening news. It's a cozy ritual, one it seems they've always kept. Peter is sometimes embarrassed by how cozy it is. He drinks only one glass of chianti and refuses a second helping of pasta. Tonight he is itchy to get back to his composition.

It's Alan's turn to sense something.

"Go on," he tells Peter. "I'll do the dishes." He pours the rest of the bottle into his glass and drinks it off. It's his way, Peter knows, of announcing that it's back to work for both of them.

"Are you sure?" Peter says.

"Stop feeling guilty. Go!"

Peter wants to stop feeling guilty, but the truth is Lance is hiding in the living room. In the manuscript under his jacket on the piano. He's in that last movement that Peter is so anxious about. The quintet was supposed to be a cerebral piece, and that's what the three finished movements are all about: an intellectual allegro, a meditative andante, an ironic scherzo. When it came time to tackle the finale, Peter found he had nothing more to say in this vein. It was worn out. For a week he tinkered with one preliminary sketch after another. They all felt wrong, too fleshy, too sensuous and full of weight. Then at the conservatory this morning, toying with another opening, he got the idea that he should give in to these rejected sketches. He was fighting them when, in fact, they were providing just what he needed, a counterpoise to the imperturbability of the first three movements.

That's when Lance got himself into it. The clarinet starts out with an agile, athletic theme that is all Lance. It's rakish and romantic, and Peter loves it. He can hardly wait to get back to it. It's for Lance that Peter is leaving the dirty dishes to his lover.

But at the piano, within earshot of Alan, he feels self-conscious, exposed. He stalls: lays out, side by side, the three new pages of manuscript he got down this morning; plays some warm-up scales. With the damper pedal down, Peter starts to pick out the opening theme, but stops before he's finished the first phrase. It's too romantic. There's too much here that he doesn't often show to Alan. He can't go through with it, won't. He pounds on the keys.

There was a little boy on the subway this afternoon. He must have been about five. He was wailing hysterically, screaming something about "I want, I want" to "Mommy," gagging on his own tears. Peter had watched the mother try to comfort him, but everytime it seemed the boy was calming down, the tears would come again, like one of those sparkle guns Peter remembers from his own childhood—as it expired, you pumped the trigger real fast, making it whir and flare out once more. The kid refused to wind down. He wouldn't be consoled. Mucus and saliva and tears smeared his face, his mouth. Peter remembers pulling these tantrums when he was that age, inconsolable, but secretly fascinated by his own cussedness.

"What's the matter?" Alan asks, coming into the living room.

"I can't concentrate," Peter lies. "Let's watch TV."

They cozy up on the sofa. Alan is the first to fall asleep.

■　■　■

When Peter opens his eyes, there is light in the bedroom, gray light. Because they keep the alarm clock on Alan's side of the bed, Peter has to twist over to see it. Six-fifteen. So Alan must be nearly ready to leave for the airport. Peter can hear him puttering in the bathroom. Behind a closed door, the medicine cabinet snaps shut; the toilet flushes.

Peter senses that Alan might let him sleep. It would be like him to do that. And when Alan returns to the bedroom, Peter doesn't say anything. He's always wondered if Alan kisses him good-bye when he's sleeping. Peter stays very still, trying to regulate his breathing. It excites him to think that he may finally find out what Alan does when he's asleep.

It is so quiet, Peter can hear Alan winding his watch; can hear the change on the dresser being brushed up and dropped into a pocket; the keys jangling. He can smell Alan's cologne. He lets all this waft over him. It's a kind of domestic music. He wonders what it would be like to give up making new music for this, for accepting the music that's already there.

He hears Alan descending the stairs.

"Good-bye," Peter calls out in a mock forlorn voice.

"I thought you were asleep." Alan has returned to the threshold. "I didn't want to wake you."

"I know," says Peter. "Have a good trip."

"Thanks. Happy composing." Alan gives him a kiss on the forehead.

When he hears the door close, Peter jumps up. He throws on the shirt, jeans, and sweater he was wearing yesterday, as if their sweaty grime contains the essence of yesterday's inspiration. He bounds down the stairs, two at a time. In the kitchen he pours a tall glass of orange juice and takes it to the living room, where he sits down at the piano.

This time, he plays the clarinet melody straight through and follows this with what little of the development he has drafted: yearning caresses from the oboe, whispers from the horn, a bit of the bassoon's robust good nature.

When the manuscript breaks off, Peter closes his eyes and listens. The music, that gorgeous music, keeps bubbling up. He can't stop it. He plays. Listens. Jots down what he likes, almost all of it. Goes back, plays through from the beginning. That theme, that theme.

In this way, Peter works all morning. Sunlight, the crisp, clean light of a cloudless February day, streams through the window. The movement becomes expansive, and wilder. The instruments weave and tumble about in lines of sinuous counterpoint. The middle section builds—writhes, leaps, dances. In the wake of the previous movements, will the audience think this is a joke? *No joke*, Peter shouts, and writes the spondee into the score: two loud chords for the five instruments. Something big is at stake.

He keeps going. The music becomes more frenzied. Each instrument is working on its own theme now. The idea is that, at the last possible moment, they'll fall together, collapse, like the spent shell of a firework. Peter doesn't know if he's up to pulling this off. It's a technical feat he's never tried before. He's scared. But he's afraid to stop. If he stops he's afraid he'll lose it.

But by the middle of the afternoon, he is lost. The piece has been driving toward that end, but he can't hear it, can't quite get it right. He knows what it will feel like: a mad burst of energy, then silence. A fist hitting a glove. Peter tosses his pencil onto the music rack and punches a fist into his left hand. That's what it will feel like—that cadence—one, huge, satisfying thud.

He picks up his pencil again, poised to write something, but before he can get a note down on paper he knows that it's wrong. He throws his pencil onto the keyboard. He needs to get away from this thing for a while. His muscles feel cramped from sitting so long. Jumping up from the piano, Peter races upstairs. In the bedroom, he strips off his clothes. His armpits smell. He rubs his right hand over the stubble on his cheeks. His scalp itches.

The sky has been clouding over all afternoon. He flicks on the bathroom light, turns up the faucet in the shower stall, lets it run a long time before getting in. He wants the bathroom hot and steamy.

The shower feels good. He lathers his chest, his arms, his crotch. He remembers he hasn't eaten all day. There is plenty of food in the refrigerator, but Peter figures it's no fun eating alone. He'll hit the Square.

It's snowing by the time he leaves their apartment. There are few people on the street. When he gets to the College Yard, it's dark and the snow is coming down hard. A few undergraduates are throwing snowballs in the silent, frozen landscape. He breaks into a jog, through the Yard and into the Square.

He decides on a small basement coffeehouse, a place where he can linger and look. But tonight it's deserted. Peter hesitates. He feels foolish and conspicuous occupying a table. He's about to leave when a handsome waiter with severe Iberian features motions for him to sit down. Peter indulges him. The waiter hands him the menu. Peter smiles. The waiter does not smile back.

Despite his hunger, Peter only orders a cup of soup. He feels lightheaded and he doesn't want to spoil that sensation. It's then that he decides to go dancing. He hasn't, *they* haven't, been in two years. Alan hates the disco bars, the smoke, the incessant pounding. "How can *you*, a composer, tolerate that mindless music?" Alan asks him whenever Peter brings up the idea of going. "And the cruising," he adds, a final fillip to his catalogue of objections. "Can't we go just for the electricity, the camaraderie?" Peter remembers once asking. Alan had just smiled.

He eats in a hurry and leaves a 10-percent tip.

The wind is picking up. Waiting for the bus, he starts shivering. The snow falls faster. At last the bus pulls up and Peter gets on. He is one of three passengers. He can't believe it is ten o'clock on a Friday night. He starts to wonder if he has lost the only Friday in two years he's had without Alan.

∎   ∎   ∎

The club is packed. It's young and alive, the kind of place Lance would go to. When Peter steps from the coat-check area into the dance bar, the music attacks him. It's painfully loud, and the beat punches his stomach. Even with the snow outside, the air conditioning is on full blast, but a haze of smoke, blue, then red, then green, hovers above the dancers.

Peter buys a beer, settles himself against a post to watch the dancers on the floor. There are several Lances here tonight. Their bodies move perfectly, right on the edge between seduction and innocence. The energy of these guys is astounding. What have they been doing all week that they've got so much left on a Friday night? He sees the electricity all around, but doesn't feel it. All he feels is the weight of that bill on the kitchen table, the one from the gym: two hundred and a quarter for another six months. Winter is a bad time to keep in shape.

Halfway through his first beer, the exhaustion hits. Peter has to admit it: the fatigue of composing and his last hour fighting the weather have left him drained. If it weren't for the fact that this is his first time in two years and that it will take him another hour to get home, he might leave right now. He'd love to curl up and go to sleep. If Alan could see him now, he'd be giving him that I-told-you-so smile. Peter decides to hold off through one more beer.

With a deft use of fade-outs and fade-ins, the d.j. changes the record. Guys leave the floor, others enter it, jostling Peter. He begins to feel like the post he is leaning on.

"Wanna dance?" someone asks.

Peter looks up. Standing in front of him is Lance: a kid in his mid-twenties, blond and slightly scruffy. He's wearing the baggy clothing of guys who know they have great bodies. And his overly padded high tops, sloppily laced—Peter finds this, well, fetching. With blue eyes and a blond mustache, the kid seems perfect. Peter looks around to see who the kid is talking to. No one else. It's really *him*. Peter smiles. If there's a flaw, the germ of a turnoff, it's the sultry look in the kid's face. Peter forgets this, tells him he'd love to dance.

The kid turns around and walks toward the dance floor. Peter follows, watching the kid slowly rolling his shoulders to the music, like a cat settling into a chair. On the dance floor, at first, Peter takes his cues from the kid, whose body moves in slow, dreamy undulations. The music modulates to another number. The beat gets louder, more throbbing. Guys shuffle on and off the floor. Peter and Lance stay where they are. Peter can't keep his eyes off him. He's suddenly full of energy, full of what he needs to finish his piece. His body wants to break out, fly off the handle, fall to pieces. He's gyrating now, grinding, gesticulating with his shoulders, his arms, his hips and chest and ass. He's hot. Yet the more abandoned his dancing becomes, the more he senses an awkward contrast with the kid's dancing. Lance remains cool, detached, his mind on some other music. Peter tries smiling, but the kid just stares through him.

Finally, at the end of the fourth number, Lance jerks his head toward the bar, his signal for them to leave the floor. It is the first direct communication he has made with Peter since they started dancing.

"How 'bout a drink?" Lance says when they are far enough away from the speakers to hear each other.

"Sure," Peter says. "By the way, my name's Peter." The kid pushes his way through the crowd.

When they approach the bar, the bartender looks at Peter. Peter asks for a draft; the kid orders a double Dewar's on the rocks. While they wait for their drinks, Peter tries another smile, but the kid's mind is elsewhere. He's mouthing the lyrics to the number they're playing. The bartender hands them their drinks. Lance takes his double and starts making his way back toward the dance floor.

"Eight bucks," the bartender tells Peter.

They watch the dancing for a while. Peter starts to feel the warm effect of the beer. It doesn't bother him anymore that Lance doesn't say anything. The kid's attitude is beginning to excite him. It's that staying just out of reach that does it. After a while, he just turns to Peter, his signal for them to move back onto the dance floor. There's an edge to this that Peter thinks is dynamite.

The singer keeps asking "What's love got to do with it?" Peter wonders what a second round of dancing's got to do with it. He has never been unfaithful to Alan. But all those years of teasing about Lance must mean something. (The guy's terrific!) Besides, a fling could provide "material" for his quintet. The beat goes on. Hey, he'll be careful.

This guy is just too terrific to pass up, Peter thinks.

After they dance another twenty minutes, Peter needs to urinate, but he is afraid he'll lose Lance if he goes off to the men's room.

"How about another drink?" he asks.

They head back to the bar. Peter orders another double Dewar's and a draft. He hands his beer to the kid.

"Would you hold this for me? I'm just going to pee."

He hustles off to the restrooms. At the urinal, he has a hard time pulling out his cock. It's sweaty and tumescent. He's back to the bar in less than a minute. The kid hasn't moved.

They dance again. Then Peter isn't sure what to do. He doesn't want to feed the kid any more booze, but he is too inexperienced to know when to put the move on.

Then it just becomes clear that they will go home together.

"Just one more and we'll get outta here," the kid says. Peter hangs on that *we'll*. The attention in that phrase—the first the kid has given him all evening—is sizzling. It's almost better than the prospect of getting him into bed.

Peter pays for the coat checks. He can't tell whether the coat-check boy who keeps staring at Lance is also taken by his looks or is only showing prurient interest in the kid's zombielike swaying. As for Peter, he tries to focus on the kid's beauty, on the events ahead.

Outside it's a blizzard. Peter hunkers down into his jacket, pulls a knit cap down over his ears, arranges the scarf more tightly around his neck. In the frigid air, his mind clears enough to feel a twinge of uncertainty. As his head becomes accustomed to the new environment of sounds—the faraway thump-thump of the disco, the metallic flapping of street signs in the wind, the silent piling up of tons of snow—the euphoric logic of what he is about to do starts to fade. He looks at the kid standing a few feet off, bouncing his head up and down as if in acknowledgment of something that never fades.

"How 'bout another drink, man?" he says when he notices Peter. He is shivering now, stamping his feet, blowing into his cupped hands.

Peter can't believe the kid went out on a night like this without gloves or a hat. He takes off his scarf, Alan's scarf, and wraps it around Lance's neck. The kid pushes it up like a kerchief and ties it under his chin.

"It's too fuckin' cold out here. Let's go back inside." He turns to go back to the bar.

Peter grabs his arm. The kid doesn't put up any resistance. Under Peter's tugging, he staggers backward a few steps and leans into Peter.

"Come on, man." The kid's eyes focus momentarily on Peter. Peter sees him staggering home, imagines him passing out in a hallway, or worse, mugged and tossed onto a snowbank. He could be dead before morning.

"I think we should get you home, my friend," Peter says. He tightens his grip on the kid's arm, digging his fingers into the down parka, trying to make contact with his muscle. He is surprised at how easily the kid suffers all this. It would be a cinch for anyone to rape this guy. They start walking.

At the first dark alley they come to, Peter fishes out the kid's wallet and looks for an address. He rummages through the credit cards. His name is not Lance; it's Ronald. He finds a driver's license. Twenty-two. An address. An easy eight-block walk into the South End. Peter eases the wallet again into Ronald's back pocket. The kid's got great buns.

"Come on, Ronnie. You're almost home."

Two blocks from his apartment, Ronnie stops short, retches, pukes all over the sidewalk. Peter wants to help, but there is nothing to do but let the kid empty his stomach. Bent over, coughing and gagging, the kid exposes those fabulous buns again. But the stench of the vomit—it throws Peter off. He's temporarily embarrassed by his lust. Not breathing through his nose, Peter takes in great gulps of cold air through his mouth.

When the kid has finished, he straightens up and turns around. The fringes on the scarf, where it was tied under his chin, are smeared with puke. Peter scoops up some snow and tries to clean the wool. Ronnie is so unsteady that Peter has to support him, with his left hand on the kid's shoulder blades, while his right hand rubs snow into the ends of the scarf against his sternum. The kid's breath is disgusting. When he is through cleaning the scarf, Peter pulls off his gloves, scoops up some more snow, and washes Ronnie's mouth. As the snow melts, his fingers brush the kid's lips.

"You'll feel better soon," Peter says. He'd like to cradle the kid in his arms.

Again, when they get to the address—it's a mangy townhouse on a mangy tree-lined square—Peter has to fish through the kid's jeans for the keys. He reaches deep down into his left pocket and feels an inhaler. The right pocket produces the keys. The kid just stands there letting this all happen. By now Peter has an erection. Someone could have raped him, he thinks. After several tries, and still holding on to Ronnie, who is shivering violently, he puts the right key into the front door lock.

The vestibule is overheated. Peter is roasting. It's been hard work holding the kid up, fighting the wind and the snow, keeping the Lance fantasy going. He figures he'll make them both a cup of tea; it will sweeten the kid's mouth, clear his head a bit.

But upstairs, the kid wants to talk. He plops down on the edge of a turned-out convertible sofa that fills almost half his studio apartment and just starts talking. The bed looks as if it hasn't been made for days: the sheets are coming untucked, bunched up under what Peter assumes have been nights of hot sex. Opposite the sofa bed is an overstuffed chair, frayed and pocked with several cigarette burns. Partially out of revulsion for this chair, and partially to get closer to the kid, Peter opts to join Ronnie on the bed, buddy-buddy style. With his hands folded between his legs, the kid bends his head to the floor, confessing his troubles.

It's his boyfriend, a guy named Scott. Ronnie says that Scott took off for Key West three weeks ago, saying he needed a winter vacation. Hasn't called or written since. The first week, the kid figured the mail was slow or he'd been out when the telephone rang, but now . . . he should have known. It's Scott this and Scott that. How he met Scott at a bar in the Combat Zone; how much he loves Scott; how they used to do it three times a day; how he'd been planning to move in with Scott in April when his lease was up.

Peter puts his arm around the kid, works his fingers into Ronnie's shoulder, massaging, soothing. The kid doesn't react. He just keeps talking about Scott, about what a bastard he is, about how much he loves him. With his other hand, Peter starts kneading one of the kid's thighs. He wishes he would stop bringing up Scott. It makes Peter feel like a bastard himself. The windows rattle against the gusting wind. Peter tries to imagine himself in warm, tropical Key West, with Lance, with Ronnie, with Scott. It's when he thinks of Scott that he gets really excited. Scott, faceless, almost nameless, Scott, with his power to make the kid so fragile, so hurting. There's something magnificent about Scott. Peter wonders if he could ever compete with Scott. Right now Scott might be caressing some trick's thigh just like this. Peter imagines Scott's thumb describing little circles on someone else's kneecap, just as he is doing now. Imagines Scott's lips nibbling someone else's earlobe. Imagines the other guy's breath quickening.

But Ronnie's breath does not quicken. He's too preoccupied to respond to Peter's come on. It would be so easy for Peter to pull him down onto these crumpled sheets, these sheets of God knows how many similar nights, to smother him with torrid and gentle kissing, to let his tongue pierce Ronnie's acidic mouth, his ears, his nostrils, his eye pits, to suck on his Adam's apple, drool all over his cheeks and chin, lap up the spit, to make Ronnie writhe with pleasure. But Peter can't. He draws the line at rape.

Instead, he just holds Ronnie very tightly, very gently, and rocks him back and forth, waiting for the tears to come. They don't, and after a few minutes the kid wiggles out of Peter's hold. "I gotta get some sleep, man," he says.

Without saying anything, Peter gets up, and the kid immediately lets his body flop onto the mattress. Peter finds his scarf and jacket, puts them on. There's an eerie familiarity to these movements—they're like stalling, waiting for the kid to change his mind. (He's so beautiful, even in this state, Peter thinks.) But the kid is out of it.

Moving one last time toward the sofabed, Peter asks, "Do you want me to tuck you in?"

"Yeh, yeh," the kid mumbles, in a way that sounds like he'd agree to anything just to get a little sleep.

Peter pulls the sheets and the blanket over Ronnie's body. They're filthy, like they haven't been changed in weeks. This kid needs someone to take care of him, Peter thinks. He considers undressing him, and starts to pull back the blanket. The kid's on his stomach now. Peter can imagine reaching under to undo the belt, can see himself slipping the jeans down, pulling them off, can see the white cotton of the jockey shorts over those buns. He wonders what fathers feel when they undress their children. The window rattles again. It feels as if the heat's been turned off for the night, but the kid is dead to the world. Peter replaces the blanket, watches the kid sleeping, then bends down and kisses the back of his hair. It smells like sweat and smoke.

On his way out, Peter flicks off the lights, then pulls the door shut with the faintest of clicks.

No matter when Alan returns home from a business trip, it always feels too early to Peter, as if there are still things that need tidying up. This time—the afternoon following the storm, a brilliant blue afternoon—he is at the piano, trying to finish the quintet. When he hears Alan's key in the lock, he begins playing over the one sketch he's managed to get down so far. He knows that Alan will leave him alone if he finds him composing, but there's no more music in his head. The sketch is ten seconds long. It takes three replayings for Alan to get himself and his luggage into the house and the door closed.

"Stuck?" he asks Peter.

"Fuck you," Peter says. He pounds the keyboard with his fists.

"That bad?" Alan says. He pauses; Peter keeps glaring into the keyboard. "Okay, so what's wrong? Didn't you finish your quintet?"

Alan moves behind the piano bench. Peter senses he is about to give him a hug. He gets up and walks to the kitchen.

"I still can't get the ending right."

Alan follows him into the kitchen. He is trying to give him a hug.

"Alan, please. I'm drained." Peter looks up at Alan as if for reassurance. Alan pouts, little boy style.

"Oh, I get it. You and Lance were partying." He winks at Peter.

"Wrong, smarty pants. I was not partying with Lance." Peter feels himself blushing. He's too close to telling the truth. He sidles past Alan again and makes for the cupboard. "Tea?" he asks.

"So why are you so *drained*?"

"You choose," Peter says, laying down three tins of tea.

"I want whatever you want, darling."

Peter grabs a tin and throws it at Alan, who catches it with one hand.

They go about making tea together. While Peter fills the kettle from the tap, Alan spoons out leaves into the pot, gets down cups and saucers, pours milk into a smaller pitcher. Peter keeps alert to his movements, wondering what Alan can see in his moodiness. As he returns the tins to the shelf, one slips from his hands, popping its lid as it hits the floor. Tea leaves are strewn all over.

"Scott has completely undone me," he says with casual weariness.

"And who, pray tell, is Scott?" Alan says. He is putting out spoons, the sugar bowl.

"He's Lance's older brother," Peter improvises. "While you were away, Lance introduced us. In fact, Scott and I had quite a time. If you must know, that's the reason I'm drained. Friday morning, the hunk showed up all by himself. Borrowed Lance's key and let himself in. Crept right upstairs."

Alan sits down at the kitchen table, his chin cupped in his right hand, staring at Peter across the room. Peter catches a glimpse of what looks like amusement and goes on improvising.

"I opened my eyes and there he was," Peter says with a kind of presto-chango lilt in his voice. "Standing over me, slowly unbuttoning his flannel shirt, real seductivelike."

"Sounds lovely," Alan says.

The water is boiling now. Peter pours it into the teapot.

"It was. It was. Scott's different, Alan. The dark, beefy type. Bushy mustache, bushy eyebrows. Deep olive complexion. Even in February, he manages to have a gorgeous tan. Said he'd just returned from a month in Key West. You know the type: nothing subtle or sensitive, all animal. A chest to die for, Alan! When he took off his shirt . . ."

Peter doesn't know where this is headed. It just starts pouring out, stuff about Scott, Scott taking off his shirt, Scott taking off his sneakers.

"With his right toe on his left heel," Peter explains. He can see it all so clearly. "He kept his arms out slightly to balance himself like a tightrope walker."

Now Peter is going on the intoxication of it. He'd love to drag this story out so long Alan would get up and leave. He's a little scared, but he can't stop either. He keeps talking even when he pours their tea, keeping his concentration on the amber liquid falling through the tea strainer. In that way, he doesn't have to look at Alan, especially when he gets to the part about sunlight streaming through the curtains, cutting a yellow stripe across Scott's hairy pecs. How Scott is wearing tight jeans. How he isn't wearing a belt and the top snap on his jeans is open.

"He unbuttons his fly real slow—it's driving me crazy, Alan—bends down to tug at the cuffs. Then he's just in his jockey shorts and moving toward the bed. Everything is very quiet, very soft. He pulls down the comforter and crawls in with me. I pull him even closer, digging my fingers into the soft cotton of the briefs covering those buns. Those buns, Alan. And then . . . and then . . ."

Peter feels himself clutching. If he looks at Alan, he will lose it. Out of the corner of an eye, he sees Alan rising from the table.

"And then, very slowly, I'm slipping the jockeys off. I'm kneading those buns, those thighs . . ."

He is desperate to deliver this story finished. He can't wind down yet, even when Alan starts coming toward him, like someone out of a crowd, someone full of comfort.

". . . that blond hair, I'm running my fingers all over that gorgeous head of blond hair, those lips that won't quit . . . and he's holding me, Alan, he's holding on to me real tight . . . he's telling me . . . he's telling me . . . Alan, this time I almost had it . . . I almost . . ."

The pain, from holding back so much, in his throat, in his face, is excruciating. If he looks at Alan . . . but then he doesn't have to. He is in his arms now, nuzzled into his neck, sobbing like a child, trying to hear another voice, another's longing.

"Petey, Petey, Petey," is all his lover has to say.

SALON

ARLY ON, WHEN
he'd been going there only a few months, Duncan committed the outrageous faux pas of referring to Robertino
OTG as a shop.

"*Shop!*" Robertino shrieked. "Debbie's Beauty Parlor
in East Boston is a shop. My place is a *salon.*"

Robertino's real name is Anthony, but everyone calls
him Robertino because that's the professional name he goes
by. The OTG stands for On The Garden. Actually, the
salon faces Newbury Street so that the only way it's "on"
the Public Garden is in Robertino's imagination, of which
he has plenty.

The place is a "statement"—in turquoise, peach, and
gray. Clutter is kept to a minimum. No jars of scissors and
combs, no piles of curlers, no papers and pins and clips like
the mess Duncan remembers seeing at the beauty parlor
his mother still goes to (not Debbie's, but Anita's) in
Chelmsford. At Robertino OTG everything is tidy, stream-

lined, chic. Even the music Robertino plays over the stereo system seems state-of-the-art. And the gladiolas, arranged in huge black glass bowls, are always fresh.

Robertino's boys are a statement, too. There's Virgil, tall and svelte, with platinum blond hair that's cut in a modified punk style, one side Dutchboy, the other close-cropped. Every winter Virgil spends his vacation in Rio, bringing back snapshots of himself lying at Ipanema with some bronzed Brazilian number. Erroll, black and built like a football player, specializes in manicures. He wears his hair in a crew cut and paints pictures of movie stars, which Robertino displays on the salon's walls. Last, there's Ricky, pudgy and sweet-faced. Ricky's still got his Boston boy's accent and goes home on Sundays for his mother's lasagna, but he dresses like it's always time for disco and wiggles his fanny that way too.

Every month when Duncan shows up for his haircut, he feels like a '65 Valiant trying to enter the L.A. freeway at rush hour. He can never quite keep up with that—what's the word for it?—style? flair? vitality? Whatever it is, it's the hallmark of Robertino OTG.

It's like this: Once, while cutting his hair, Robertino found out that Duncan had missed the Black and White Ball. "What!" he shrieked. "You didn't go to the social event of the season! What kind of a fairy are you anyway?" That's what going to Robertino's makes Duncan feel like, a fairy out of Fairyland.

"You're absolutely right," Eli tells him the morning of Duncan's January appointment. "It's not our kind of place anymore. All that superficial, silly nonsense!"

They are in the kitchen, each chowing down a bowl of oatmeal before heading off to work. Duncan's not sure how a casual, joking remark about preparing himself "to go on" at Robertino's has launched this diatribe from Eli, but there it is.

"Superficial and silly," Eli repeats.

Duncan listens to these words. Eli's very good at

words, but somehow "superficial and silly" don't exactly capture what Duncan was trying to say. All he meant was that going to Robertino OTG made him feel out of it. He wasn't criticizing the place. If anything he was criticizing himself. But there's no time to explain this now. He's got an eight-thirty meeting at the computer store where he's head of customer service; Eli is racing, too, to teach his morning class at the community college.

"I'm ready to find myself a new barber," Eli announces.

"*Stylist*," Duncan teases. He flicks on the TV, a twelve-inch black-and-white that's sitting on top of a pile of newspapers on the kitchen counter. There are two days' worth of dishes in the sink, the kitty litter needs changing, and it's his turn to take out the trash tonight.

"Right," Eli says, digging an English muffin out of the toaster with his knife. "What does Robertino do that a barber doesn't?"

"Pull out the plug, you'll electrocute yourself," Duncan tells him.

He looks out the window. Mrs. Nguyen, their tenant downstairs, is scattering breadcrumbs onto the crust of snow. Pigeons and sparrows have already flocked about her, pecking at the food. Mrs. Nguyen is an immaculate housekeeper—she puts her landlords to shame—and her children, Sam and Joe, whom Duncan and Eli occasionally tutor on Sunday afternoons, are model new Americans. The Nguyens moved to Dorchester last year after Mr. Nguyen was beaten up for the third time in their previous neighborhood.

On the TV, Jane Pauley is asking someone Duncan has never heard of what it's like to make a movie with someone else Duncan has never heard of.

"Maybe he does the same job as a barber," Duncan says. "But," he adds quickly, "I'm not saying what you think I'm saying." He chooses his words carefully because, after seven years with Eli, he knows his lover can sometimes miss the point he's trying to make. "Just because I feel out of it there doesn't mean I want to drop him." *Out of it* is a phrase Duncan reminds himself to teach the Nguyen boys next time they have a lesson. "I'm actually kind of fascinated by the whole scene."

"Oh, Dunk." The way Eli says this—half amused, half disgusted—makes Duncan feel like Robertino has been selling him a bill of goods.

Duncan sometimes wishes he'd had a liberal arts education like Eli's. All he's got is a B.S. in computer science from Salem State, which Eli, once during their worst fight, said limited Duncan's understanding of human nature. Now he watches as Eli scrapes some butter over that English muffin. Duncan can tell by the sound of the knife that the muffin is dry and cold. Eli's skin is dry and cold, too. And so is his own skin. He's almost embarrassed to present this body at Robertino's this afternoon. He and Eli could use a vacation, someplace warm, but this is the winter they're paying for two new furnaces.

It was Eli who had originally suggested they go to Robertino OTG—seven years ago, when they were both still in their twenties and feeling gay, in all the senses of the word, but mostly in the sense of bright and lively and on top of it all. That's what being new lovers meant then, and Robertino had seemed a natural adjunct to all that.

Sometimes Duncan reminds Eli of this, but from the way Eli is scraping at his muffin this morning, Duncan gauges that the time isn't right for teasing. Besides, he already knows Eli's response: "I've grown out of that phase," he will say. Or, when he's especially testy: "Please accord me the dignity of acknowledging that I've changed." Eli can get pretty adamant about how he's changed. About how he's no longer the kind of person who wants a stylist On The Garden.

"Can't you see," Eli continues, "that we've grown and Robertino hasn't?"

Duncan tries to see this, but what catches his attention is Eli rushing his plate and cereal bowl over to the sink, dumping them onto the growing pile.

"Isn't grown-up life glamorous," he tells Eli.

"Oh, Dunk," Eli says and gives him what they both call a reassurance hug.

Robertino isn't seeing many clients anymore. He's too busy with plans to open a salon-cum-gallery-cum-mineral water bar on Dartmouth Street. (ACS, he's going to call it: At Copley Square). So he's in and out of the shop a lot, meeting with the architects and contractors. Robertino, of course, will act as his own decorator. Today Ricky, the cute pudgy one, will cut Duncan's hair.

When Duncan arrives, the place is alive with disco. It's loud and throbbing and Duncan immediately feels energized. The eight-thirty meeting had lasted until one, and that was followed by a long afternoon returning phone calls. A haircut at Robertino will be a pleasure after a day like this.

Ricky's at the receptionist's desk talking on the phone. He looks up and blows Duncan a kiss. Virgil and Erroll are snipping away, grooving on the disco and chatting with their clients. Everyone who comes to Robertino OTG is a "client."

Robertino calls out to him from his private styling room.

"Hi, Duncan," he says. Robertino looks a little sheepish, and he should since he told Duncan he was going to be busy with construction people at the new shop today. But the guy in the chair is a real cutie, which explains a lot. Robertino is always on the lookout for what he calls "a new husband."

Duncan sits down, picks up a magazine, one of those oversized trade glossies. He leafs through it, trying to look casual, stopping now and then to study the latest cuts. The issue seems to be featuring the electric shock look: spikey, firey-orange dos from London. "What are they trying to accomplish!" Duncan's mother says whenever she sees something like this. "Tell me!"

The cutie and Robertino are trading stories about this

year's Black and White Ball. They can't quite agree on the best costume. Robertino thinks it was the Marlene Dietrich; the cutie says that one was fabulous but that the two men dressed like Zeus and Ganymede were even better.

Duncan isn't sure he knows who Ganymede was, but when the cutie says that going to the Black and White Ball always convinces him that being gay is a superior form of being, Duncan figures Ganymede was a guy, and probably another cutie, too.

Ricky hangs up the phone with a "Bye, hon!" and turns to Duncan. "Girlfriends," he says. "They're the best! I love my girlfriends. I can always count on them to listen." He sounds like he's being interviewed for *Teen Screen* magazine.

"Boy trouble?" Duncan asks. Along with his mother's lasagna, Ricky is always telling someone about his boyfriend problems.

"What else?" Ricky says.

And this, Duncan suddenly understands, is one of the reasons he likes coming to Robertino OTG. Whether it's Ricky or Virgil or Erroll or Robertino, someone is always telling him the latest, taking him into their confidence, making him feel like he really is part of their bright, glamorous, romance-hungry world.

"So what'll it be today?" Ricky asks.

"The usual," Duncan says. "I guess."

The cut always begins with a shampoo. At Robertino OTG they use a shampoo that smells like orange blossoms. It's called Totally Fabu and Just For You. Ricky puts a cape around Duncan, swivels the chair, and leans him way back so that Duncan's head is in the sink. Duncan loves these three minutes. He can close his eyes and inhale the fragrance of orange: slightly sweet like teeny-bopper candy, but with a hint, too, of the chic, the up-to-the-minute, the scientifically formulated. It's essence of Southern California, liquefied, gelled, put in a tube.

Ricky turns on the water and tests the temperature by running the nozzle over his hands and adjusting the faucets, not too hot, not too cold. When he finally moves the spray over Duncan's head, it's just right, a tepid baby's bath.

"*Mmm*," Duncan sighs.

"You like that?" Ricky asks, and the way he says it sounds like he's talking about something else. Whenever he cuts Duncan's hair, Ricky flirts. It's not serious, but still there's that suggestion, that acknowledgment: it's fun being sexy. He moves the nozzle around, over his ears, along his forehead. Trickles of water slip down Duncan's temples, into his eyes, and Ricky sops them up with a towel.

Then the water is gone and Duncan can hear Ricky squirting a big dollop of Totally Fabu into his palm. Ricky begins to lather Duncan's hair, vigorously working the suds in, his fingertips scurrying along Duncan's scalp. Soon he slows down, caressing, sculpting, massaging, low down at the base of Duncan's skull.

Duncan knows this is just part of the service you pay for at Robertino OTG; he knows that all Robertino's boys provide this shampoo massage. He knows that, as Eli says, he's being manipulated, made to feel that the twenty-five dollars he'll pay is worth it, especially when you get this— even only three minutes of it.

"What would I have to pay to get an hour's worth of this?"

Ricky slows down the massaging. "For you, Duncan, nothing." This doesn't sound exactly like flirtation, and it makes Duncan feel terrific. It's a kind of verbal reassurance hug.

And then, lickety-split, Ricky rinses off the suds, tilts up the chair, and Duncan's being towelled off.

"Your hair's got winter dryness," Ricky tells Duncan in that only-your-hairdresser-would-tell-you voice.

Duncan opens his eyes and looks at himself in the mirror. He hates his hair, especially the way it looks when it's just been shampooed. All those magazine ads with men coming out of the shower or rising out of a blue-green Caribbean Sea. Windblown, wet, disheveled—their hair always looks terrifically sexy.

"Oo, nasty gray hairs," Ricky announces. "We'll take care of those, won't we?"

"Take care of it all," Duncan teases.

Ricky goes right to work, combing, snipping, pulling strands through his fingers and then lopping off the ends. Duncan watches the clipped, wet ends of bangs fall to his lap; he watches his sideburns rise, the tips of his ears emerge from his shaggy mop. Ricky cuts, then looks, cuts and pats, cuts and combs. It's kind of magical, Duncan thinks, this transformation. He understands why his mother goes to Anita's once a week.

The disco tape they've been playing runs out, and one of Robertino's boys hurries off to the back room to find more music. In the moment of silence Duncan can hear Robertino and the cutie still talking about costumes. Then over the speakers two women are talking. Duncan recognizes those voices. Wait, it will come to him: yes, Dorothy and Aunty Em! And in the next minute Judy Garland breaks into "Somewhere Over the Rainbow."

"This is so pretty," Ricky says, snipping away at Duncan's hair and softly singing along with Judy. "I've seen this picture seventeen times. How many times have you seen it?"

Duncan has seen it exactly twice, once when he was eleven, and once the year he and Eli were dating.

"Five times," he tells Ricky.

"It's the best, isn't it?" Ricky says.

The Munchkins are next, singing in those voices that sound like 33 r.p.m. played at 78. With his comb and scissors, Ricky conducts them, little-toy-orchestra style.

"I love the next part," he tells Duncan.

Sure enough, the voice of Glinda, the Good Witch of the North, comforting, schoolmarmy, comes on. She tells Dorothy that the house has just landed on the Wicked Witch of the East and killed her. Everyone can be happy now. She presents Dorothy with the Ruby Slippers. Ricky is mouthing and pantomiming the whole scene, even curtseying just where Glinda does in the movie.

"So tell me about your boyfriend problems," Duncan says. This seems a little personal, but he knows from experience that Ricky doesn't mind. Besides, Duncan wants to get off the subject of movies.

"Two weeks ago," Ricky begins, right on cue, as if this is part of the soundtrack too, "he brings me roses, right? Then last night I call him to set up a date for Saturday. He goes, 'Well, I'm sorry but I have other plans.' 'No problem,' I say, 'we'll make it Friday this week.' You know what he says? He goes, 'Uh, I don't think so. Look, I'm sort of busy. I'll call you.' *I'll call you!* From roses to I'll call you? Tell me! What's that supposed to mean?"

Duncan has no idea what that's supposed to mean, but he wishes he did. He wishes he could put it all together for Ricky, explain to him what attraction and flirtation and boredom are all about. *Tell me*, Ricky wants to know. *Tell me*, Duncan's mother wants to know. And he wishes he could. Wishes he had explanations as to why some styles turn you on and some styles don't. Wishes he had the right words—beautiful and coordinated like a Hollywood story or a haircut On the Garden—to tell Ricky the one thing they both already know, that it's not always going to be glamorous or exciting or new.

Tell me. Duncan wishes, too, that he had the right words to tell Eli why he's still going to keep coming here anyway, even if he does feel out of it, even if he doesn't believe that stuff about gay being a superior form of existence, even if he'll never look like the cutie or dress up like Marlene Dietrich or ever again have the kind of boyfriend problems Ricky is talking about.

INITIATING HIM

A LOT OF PEOPLE have said a lot of ridiculous things about men like me. The night I took Robbie Doyle to his first bar I remembered one of them. The old "recruiting" theory. Which goes like this: that we deliberately lure hapless young men into this life of ours, catching their fancy with God knows what enticements. (Since we've been depicted as sick, pathetic, depraved, it's hard to see the logic here. I guess the theory is that, like drugs, it's supposed to be addictive: one hit and you're hooked.)

Our own histories say otherwise. Despite all our fears, all our resistance, each of us in his own time and in his own way eventually claims himself. Eventually.

The night I took Robbie Doyle to his first bar, I remembered something else, too. It occurred to me that our ages—he twenty-two; I thirty-nine—were almost identical to the ages that Philip Bursey and I were some twenty years before when Philip, under similar circumstances, introduced me to my first bar. I mean the first bar of any real consequence to me. In fact, there are a lot of parallels between these two events, separated though they are now by almost a generation's distance and time. And these parallels—the ongoingness of these rites of initiation, an older man showing a younger man the ropes—are part of my story. They're not, however, the whole story.

I practice medicine. A "science" they call it. But one of the least precise sciences I know. A lot's left up to intuition, to the feel of the thing. In the eleven years I've been a doctor, I've come to trust my intuition about a lot of matters. That means letting the voice beneath the voice speak to you. If there's anything I could "recruit" for, it's that.

Philip Bursey was the alumni advisor to my college glee club, one of those all-male, white tie and tails clubs that are, incredibly enough, still popular among the ivy and near-ivy schools in the East. In Philip's advisory capacity, an official one mandated by the club's constitution, he would periodically appear at our Tuesday night rehearsals to check up on things. He usually arrived toward the end of practice, slipping unobtrusively into the second tenor section, where I sang, to join us in a final chorus or two. (We always ended rehearsals by belting out a few football songs, hand-me-down classics that generations of glee clubbers knew by heart.) Then, when the singing was over and it was time for announcements, our conductor, "Doc" Dewey, would extend a hand toward Philip—"Gentlemen, I give you our old friend and alumni advisor, Philip Bursey!"—and a chorus of Gounod's *Domine, Salvum Fac*, our standard rousing greeting, would burst forth. Applause, huzzahs, and reciprocal adulation: Philip would compliment us on how good we were sounding. More cheers. Afterward, he and the club's officers and managers would retire to a local tavern where, over beer and hamburgers, they'd discuss business until the wee hours.

Philip must have been in his late thirties—as I said,

about the same age as I am today—but his manner with us was young and lively, even flirtatious. Still boyishly handsome despite his thinning blond hair and tortoiseshell glasses, he embodied, for me, answers to questions I had only vaguely begun to ask. There was something wonderful, romantic even, about his interest in us. And I now see that my volunteering, during junior year, to become one of the club's managers was a way to come even more fully under his wing, this adult-boy from the far off Class of 1954.

It's hard to recall what words I used to explain Philip to myself. If I was ignorant about how to rent a piano or how to get a program printed, I was equally naive about the exact nature of his attentions. For though I had started sleeping with men—by which I mean that I was in the midst of a secret, mushy, and ultimately painful affair with another boy in the glee club—it was difficult to imagine that there were other guys like me, or, if there were, that they would have had the least interest in someone so hurt and confused and awkward in the ways of love. In the ways of life. I must have decided that Philip was just being kind, that he was doing what college alums everywhere do: initiating callow young men into the world of professional and social competence.

And so, through the next year, through all of those friendly, beery managerial meetings, Philip and I gradually became acquainted. There were times when he was very tough on me, especially when it came to the budget, which I had a tendency to overspend. And when I tried making excuses—"For the sake of art," I'd plead—he'd stare deeply into my eyes, a broad smile slowly emerging on his face, and laugh.

Which did I feel more intensely, his mockery or his attention? He wanted me to run a tight ship, to learn fiscal accountability and the virtues of disciplining my enthusiasms for fancy four-color posters and guest soloists imported from New York. At the same time, I suspected that Philip's laughter was also an expression of his delight in my delight, of his letting it all be okay: my youth, my innocence, my not being ready yet to take up full responsibility. Despite his occasional displeasure with the way I handled the financial affairs of the club, I knew he liked me. Eventually I realized I could tell him everything.

It was in the late winter of my senior year. We were going out to dinner, just the two of us, to go over final figures for the spring tour, another extravagance on my part, a trip up and down the coast of California. As a child I'd always wanted to visit Disneyland, and, when the time came for me to select a tour route, I'd decided immediately, selfishly, on the West Coast, a place farther away—by some twenty-five hundred miles—than I'd ever been before. By February, the itinerary had been mapped out and all the contracts signed: ten concerts in eight days, with a morning and afternoon off to play in Disney's Magic Kingdom.

Philip picked me up at my dorm. He drove a fancy foreign car—I can't remember what, though I know it wasn't a Volkswagen, the only foreign car I'd ever ridden in before then. What I do recall is that he leaned over to push open the passenger's door and that, as I got in, settling myself into the leather interior, I saw that this evening, this "date," presented the perfect opportunity to broach *the* subject.

We drove across one of the graceful Georgian bridges that spanned the river, leaving behind the precincts of the college, a world of cupolaed buildings and elm-arched paths, straight as vectors. I must have been mulling over how to do it—when during the evening to open up to him— because after a few minutes of silence he turned to me and asked, "Why so quiet, Marty?" Even in the intermittent light of the street lamps along the river drive, I could see his friendly, boyish face.

"Tommy," I said. I had never before spoken my boyfriend's name—already now my ex-boyfriend's name—to anyone in quite the way I spoke it that moment to Philip.

I knew he would know who Tommy was and what, exactly, I was telling him.

We did not discuss the spring tour that night. Instead, over filet mignon and French wine—an expensive dinner, but one Philip insisted on, "given the occasion," as he put it—over this long, quiet dinner whose intimacy both excited and terrified me, I told him all about Tom. How, over a year ago, under the balminess of an October evening, we had casually struck up a conversation on the way back from rehearsal; and how, after a few weeks' acquaintance, we started meeting before rehearsals for supper or afterward for a cup of coffee; how we used to study together in the library; and how, one night, when his roommate was away on a hockey tour, Tom had invited me up to his room. And then I quoted to Philip the line from Dante, from the Paolo and Francesca canto—"That day we read no farther"— which I'd memorized as a token of my first night with Tommy.

"Do you like poetry?" Philip asked. It felt like a more personal question than any of the others he'd asked me during the course of our dinner. I tried steering the conversation back to my lost romance with Tom.

"This year Tom and I were going to room together." I began to swirl my wine in the boozy-contemplative way I'd seen in old romance movies. "But then we had a huge fight last spring . . ." My voice trailed off. I kept my eyes on the glass, watching the red wine coat its sides.

"That was eight, nine months ago," he said. He was speaking in that no-nonsense voice he often took with me when I was being fiscally irresponsible. But I could hear something else, too—like the urgency of an impatient wooer.

I looked up.

"What?" I said, as if coming out of a stupor.

"Martin"—Philip always called me Martin when he was trying to hammer home a point—"it's over."

"But I don't want it to be over." It was the first unguarded thing I'd said to him all evening. I waited for him to respond, and when the silence grew uncomfortable I told him an even deeper truth. "I don't know what I want."

He took off his glasses. "That's not a bad place to begin."

I want to switch now to the part about Robbie. Not because I'm trying to be coy—Philip and I never slept together, if that's what you want to know—but because I want to set down the parallel details. Everything I've told you so far is preliminary to the story, and is the story. And I'll bring Philip back before the end.

The evening I met Robbie Doyle, I'd put in a long day at the clinic. In addition to my rounds at the hospital, I work one night a week at the gay health center in town, not far away from the restaurant where Philip Bursey had taken me, seventeen years before, in that Year of Relative Innocence, 1971.

It was well past supper time, nine-thirty, and my lover, Douglas, I knew, would be asleep by the time the subway got me home. Doug and I have been together eight years. He works for the state's Department of Transportation. His job, as he puts it, is to make sure people get to where they're going. He's up very early in the morning. Bedtime for him is ten, at the latest.

Even at nine-thirty, the station was crowded: late-workers, evening college students, and the usual assortment of people who enjoy being out—even on an autumn evening as chilly as this one was—drifting in and out of record stores, bookshops, pizza joints. There's a wakefulness, a restlessness, that mid-autumn brings out in people, especially in this city that gets so gray and cold and shut-in for so many months during the winter. I wanted to be out in that activity.

When I left the clinic, I thought about poking into a bookstore. There are some good late-night bookstores not too far from the clinic, where, if you linger long enough in certain aisles, you'll soon come to identify other restless, wakeful people.

But on that particular night, I did not go looking for poetry or promiscuity. Instead, I just pulled on my beret (as Philip's was, my hair is now thinning too) and walked to the station to catch the subway. When I got to the platform, a train was just pulling in. It was crowded, and I had to squeeze to get on.

I carry a backpack—a lot of the younger doctors in this city do—which I now began to unzip in order to take out my subway reading: the local gay weekly. The headlines invariably contain all those words—the G word, the A word—which many people prefer not to see. And which is precisely why I choose to read the paper in public.

Across from me stood a guy in his early twenties. He had the blondest hair, flaxen really, the kind that in this part of the country you only see on preppies and bleached-out punks, though in the Midwest, where I went to medical school, towheads are a dime a dozen. And blue eyes: pale blue, Midwest blue. His skin radiated the healthy, wholesome look of the Midwest, too. *Beautiful and straight* is what registered in my head. Future Farmers of America type. I opened my newspaper.

At the next stop, when more people got on, I moved farther back into the car. The blond kid did too. As I was bringing my paper up again, he spoke to me.

"That's a great beret you're wearing." A couple of the other passengers looked absentmindedly in my direction, then went back to their own late-evening thoughts.

Compliments, even from naive straight boys, are nice to get. I thanked him and said that I'd picked it up in France two summers ago. Doug and I had spent two weeks in Paris and the Loire, a trip we've come to speak of as our Seven-Year-Itch Trip because he and I each ended up having brief affairs with guys we met over there: Doug with an American and I with a German. Needless to say, I didn't tell the kid any of this.

"I was in France two summers ago, too," he said. He seemed delighted by the coincidence. It was this fact, his having travelled in Europe, probably on a Eurail pass, that helped to explain why he might be in the habit of striking up a conversation with a perfect stranger.

"I know it's corny," he apologized, "but I loved the Eiffel Tower."

In the three short sentences he'd uttered, his voice had modulated twice—from low and masculine to high and boyish, then back to a middle range, somewhere between the two.

"Are you a student?" I asked. It seemed obvious he was.

"I graduated last year."

Through three more stops we traded information: by day he worked in an office downtown; at night he was taking a course to help him prepare for the law boards. Robbie— we had introduced ourselves by this point—was aiming to become a criminal lawyer. It was hard to imagine anyone of such youthful charm doing that kind of work. I wondered, then, what his thoughts might be on the criminal trespass charges currently being brought against a group of AIDS activists who had demonstrated against a pharmaceutical company. It was all in the paper that I'd let fall to my side.

About three weeks after our initial encounter, Robbie came out to me. We had been meeting every Thursday: both his course and my stint at the clinic let out at nine-thirty, and so, because the trains don't run that frequently after rush hour, every week we found ourselves waiting together on the subway platform, riding the four stops to the station where we parted company, he to switch to a southbound train, I to go north. But I had not picked up anything that would have told me he loved men. He was just, I told myself, a friendly kid, someone who had spent four years at an upcountry college and was now tackling the big city.

Or maybe he was grooming himself to be a politician or a D.A., someone who needed to make a lot of savvy contacts in the outside world.

Then one Thursday evening, I saw him sitting in his usual place on one of the station's benches. But instead of the hopeful, eager face he usually wore, he looked dejected. One leg was up on the bench. He was clasping it with his arms, resting his chin on his knee.

"What's up?" I asked.

"Hi." He gave me a forced little smile.

"Well, give me a hint," I teased. "Is it job-related, law boards-related or love-related?"

"Love-related."

I hadn't expected that answer. I hold stereotypes, too: with regard to straight boys it's that they are not in the habit of public displays of love-mopeyness, especially in subway stations. So, as soon as Robbie said that, the story I was telling myself about him changed.

"Can I take you out for a drink and we'll talk about it?" This was a risk, but my curiosity was winning me over.

"It's getting late," he said.

"I know."

There was a pause. I could hear the rumbling of the train as it approached the station. The other people on the platform began to rouse themselves, but Robbie stayed put.

"Sure," he said, "why not." He got up. "But I need to tell you something first."

"Let's take a walk," I said.

He told me everything. About his four-year crush on his college roommate, about the one brief liaison he'd had the summer he was in Paris (what is it about Paris?), about seeing me the first time with my gay newspaper and wanting to make contact. "Just to have another gay man to talk to," he quickly added. And about the past week, when he'd slept with a fellow from work who was not the least bit interested in pursuing things further. It all came out a jumble. At one point he even pulled his wallet from his back pocket to show me photographs of his college roommate, his friends, his family. There was one snapshot of himself, which he flipped over very quickly.

"Go back," I said. We'd paused under a street lamp.

He handed me the wallet. The photo, one of those photo booth shots, showed him in a tanktop shirt, head cocked to one side and tilted back, hair ruffled. "That's me looking not quite so angelic," he said sheepishly. But I could tell he liked it. I took a closer look, then handed back the wallet.

"I just want it settled, Marty," he said as we rounded a corner. "There's so much else happening in my life: work, the law boards, my sister's getting married. I just want to *settle* this . . . this gay thing, this sex thing, once and for all."

"I know," I said.

"Where are we going?" Robbie asked. We'd been walking for about fifteen minutes.

"I'm taking you to a gay bar."

He stopped. "I don't think so, Marty."

"Come on," I said, "it's time you saw this life you want settled."

He gave me all the reasons why it was not the right time: the lateness of the hour, the fact that he had to get up early the next morning, and what if he saw somebody there he knew?

"Marty, I don't think I can get into that."

"Into what?" I said. "A lot of angelic guys, just like you?"

Philip Bursey took me to my first gay bar late in the spring of my senior year.

After our dinner together that night in February, I didn't see him for the rest of the semester—none of us in the Glee Club did—though there was nothing unusual about this. After all, the spring tour was firmly in place; there were fewer reasons for him to make checkup visits.

Then, in May, after the tour, after final exams, while I was waiting to graduate, he called me up.

"Congratulations, I hear the tour was superb."

"I loved Disneyland," I told him.

He chortled, as if he recognized a coverup in what I was saying. "But what did you think of those California boys?"

I laughed, too, but an embarrassed laugh, for the truth was I hadn't paid a bit of attention to the California boys; I'd been too busy pining away over Tom, who, I was sure, was having an affair with another boy in the Glee Club.

"What's the matter?" Philip asked. And when I told him about Tom, he chided me. "Are you still moping over him?"

I didn't know what to say.

"When was the last time you went out?" Philip pressed.

"What do you mean?"

"You know what I mean: to The Sport, to Frederick the Great's, to Our Side."

I told him I didn't know what those places were.

"Jesus, Marty. Now I know what I'm giving you for graduation. I'll pick you up tonight at eight."

I still remember the way I dressed—or rather, how quickly Philip saw through the way I had dressed: baggy corduroys, an old madras shirt, lace-up shoes.

"Do you think you could have put on something a bit sexier?" he asked when I got into his car.

It was the first time I'd ever seen him out of his business suit. He was wearing chinos, a Lacoste shirt, sneakers—an early version of what years later we learned to call the clone look.

"Can I have one of your cigarettes?" I asked, pushing in the lighter.

Philip tossed me the pack. "I thought you didn't smoke."

The lighter popped out. I grabbed it and tried to light up, but I couldn't get the tip of the cigarette, which was twitching between my lips, to meet the glowing coils. Philip looked over at me and grinned.

"Virgil leads Dante to the lowest circle in hell," he intoned.

I willed myself to laugh.

We drove on. I managed to get the cigarette lighted and took a few puffs, not inhaling. Still, the nicotine made my head reel.

"So, where are we going?" I asked.

"Right here."

"Where?" I squeaked.

"Here," Philip said, backing the car into a parking space.

I looked out the window. No sign, no lights, hardly even an entrance. Just shadows. And men.

"Come on," he said. The way he'd parked, the way he'd opened and closed his car door—so casually—for a second it reminded me of childhood trips to the grocery store with my mother, and I felt relieved. I followed him to the sidewalk, and then we went inside.

Could The Sport really have been darker than any of those collegiate taverns we used to frequent? Could it really have been more crowded, so much so that it was impossible not to brush against people, against guys? Could the throbbing of the music really have been that much more electric?

We made our way to the back, stopping first at the bar to pick up a couple of beers. I'd lived in an essentially all-male environment during my four years in college, but The Sport was of a different order altogether. The rules of behavior I'd been following for years didn't apply. The body—*men's* bodies—meant something else here. And in the air, along with the loitering clouds of cigarette smoke, was a silent, deliberate hunger. I began to hate the clothes I'd worn.

We had been there a half hour—thirty minutes during which, if this is possible, I didn't look at anyone and yet looked at everyone—when we bumped into Tommy. I had had no idea that Tom knew about places like The Sport, much less that he went to them. He seemed quite at home. He was slightly drunk and acting silly. Apparently, he and Philip were well acquainted, which was unusual since Tom was not an officer in the Glee Club. He gave Philip a big kiss, the first time I'd ever seen two men, outside of myself and Tom, kissing. I wanted to kiss him too, wanted to hold him in my arms again, but Tom's silliness, and his flirtatiousness with Philip, clearly indicated that he had no interest in resuming anything with me.

As we stood there talking—or rather as the two of them talked—Philip put his arm around Tom, massaging his shoulder, caressing his ear. And it suddenly hit me: they had been having an affair.

The Sport still exists, but the night I took Robbie Doyle to his first bar it was another, Club Metro, that I selected, about as clean-cut a place as he could want: bistro, bar, and nightclub all in one. Tasteful, chic, expensive—very eighties. Just the kind of place for an up-and-coming gay lawyer like Robbie. Nevertheless, his reactions were the same as mine had been. It was fun to relive, through him, the "first time" syndrome, fun to watch for that combination of not looking and looking, fun to watch all his preconceptions getting blown away. At one point, I left him alone for five minutes while I "went to the john," a strategy to force him to look at someone other than me. It was a strategy Philip had used on me seventeen years before.

"I can't believe it, Marty," Robbie said when I returned. "All these guys look just like the straight guys I've been attracted to for years."

"Just one difference," I replied.

I wanted to give him everything, all the information he would ever need: the names of the bars in town, the places where he could buy gay books and newspapers, the neighborhoods to live in, information about the gay health club, the gay lawyers league, safe sex. As we sat at our table, sipping imported beer, I wanted to dump the entire cornucopia of our history and culture onto his lap; I wanted to say, "Here it is, Robbie, take it, all of it: the splendor and the triviality, the joy and the heartache."

"My lover," I told him, and watched to see, sure enough, the little jolt his head made when he heard that word, "my lover works for the Department of Transportation. He says his job is to get people to where they're going. That's what I want to do for you now. Help you to get to where you're going." And lest he think I was offering to take him to bed—he wasn't hot enough for me—or to be his sugar daddy—a word he probably didn't even know—I added, "Culturewise, that is."

In the next few months Robbie learned the culture fast. It seems that all it took was that initial visit to Club Metro to bring him out of whatever despondent things he was thinking about himself. I never heard another word about the guy from work who had dropped him. Actually, I heard very few words at all from Robbie, because he was hardly ever home when I'd call him to find out how things were going. And because my shift at the clinic was changed to Wednesdays, our weekly rendezvous at the subway station fizzled out. So one night during the winter I arranged to meet him at the club for a light supper and a "progress report."

"So yes, Marty, things are going well," he told me when the maitre d' had seated us. He smiled broadly. "Very well. I mean, so much is happening to me: I read that book you recommended; I came out to my roommate Holly last week." He paused, fingering one of the menus we were both ignoring. "I even joined a health club."

"Which health club?" I asked. I was teasing.

"Well, there were two that I knew of," he began. "Health World; but that's pretty straight. And then there's The Health Club, you know, the Cosmopolis Health Club, which is for"—he stopped, trying to avoid the G word—"for guys like us." His eyes widened. "Marty, I can't believe how comfortable I feel there. It's so nice to be able to go do my workout and not have to worry about . . . you know."

I nodded. Yes, I knew.

"But then, let me tell you what happened last week." From his tone of voice, I could tell there was a story coming. "I was working out on the Nautilus equipment, and all of a sudden I noticed this guy?" He ended his sentence with a little up-turned question, as if he needed to make sure I was following the gist. I smiled. "He was sitting across from me, on one of the benches, with his legs spread apart, not doing anything, just staring at me. I mean it was so *obvious*." Again I nodded and smiled. Yes, yes, I was saying, this is how it happens.

"So I tried to ignore him," Robbie continued. "I mean, I just wanted to concentrate on my sets. But he kept looking at me. He must have been about thirty-five or so. Dark hair, mustache, sort of Italian looking." I watched Robbie trying to suppress a smile of pleasure. He went on: "So next thing I know, this guy comes up and asks me if I want to go out. Can you believe it? He doesn't even know me and he wants a date."

The waiter came to take our orders.

"So then what?" I asked. This was perverse of me— asking him to continue his story in front of the waiter—but I wanted to give Robbie the understanding that in a place like Club Metro our stories are for everyone.

He looked up at the waiter. "I'm not ready yet." The waiter acknowledged Robbie's request with a quick snap of his head and walked off.

"So go on," I said.

"Well, that's really it," Robbie told me. "That's the whole story." He sounded confused, as if I'd missed the point.

"But did you go out with him?"

"Of course not!"

"Why?"

"Because I didn't want to." He was quick with his responses. And when I just kept staring at him, Robbie came back with another. "I go there to get in shape, not to cruise."

It was good to hear him picking up the vocabulary. I told him so, and he blushed.

"So explain to me once more why you picked Cosmopolis over the straight gym."

He looked down at his menu. "Okay, okay," he said.

That's when I knew it was time to tell him the story of Philip Bursey and Tom.

"I was furious at them," I told Robbie as I began to wrap up the story. "Furious and humiliated."

During the course of the tale, we'd ordered drinks. Robbie now took a long gulp.

"Furious, humiliated, hateful," I repeated. "I didn't know who I hated more, Tommy or Philip Bursey. They'd been sleeping together all that winter and spring."

"I'd be angry and humiliated, too," Robbie said. I could see he was sincere.

"Yes," I said, "that's what I felt—anger, humiliation, betrayal. At least at first." I paused to make sure he heard this. "But underneath all those romance movie responses"—I paused again—"were other feelings, feelings I didn't want to own up to."

I looked at Robbie's face. It was the classic look of one of those "hapless young men" we're supposed to prey on: all confusion and curiosity.

"What kind of feelings?" he said.

I remembered the photograph he'd shown me, the photo booth pose in the tanktop.

"Robbie, the anger was a coverup." He blinked. "What I was really feeling was envy. Envy. Jealousy. Maybe even admiration. I wanted what they had. Even if I didn't quite have a name for it, deep down I knew it was better than all those lovesick, moony stories I'd been telling myself about the one, great lost love of my life."

At that moment, it would have been easy to reach across the table and take Robbie's hand, to touch him reassuringly. That's what Doug and I had done our last night in Paris: touched and cried and told each other we were sorry, even though we knew that our respective affairs had unlocked feelings we had never wanted to own up to.

"Kill that angel, Robbie."

"But . . ." he began to protest.

"Kill him," I whispered.

And then I just waited, waited for him to recognize those words. I guessed he'd been wanting to hear them for a long time. When he let out a little sigh, I continued.

"Now, what exactly are you going to say if that guy asks you again for a date?"

"I don't know," he said. He sounded exhausted.

"Good," I told him. "That's a good place to begin."

FATHERLY

Every Sunday afternoon, just when he's trying to catch a movie on the tube, Roger has to endure another story about Father Barry. Today, like most Sundays lately, the routine goes like this: Roger gets up around noon, fixes himself something to eat, tunes in a flick. By then Willy and Ted are back from church and they start up all over again, on and on about this Father Barry, his sermons and jokes, the hearty embraces he gives at the Peace, the way he winks at you as he passes the chalice.

"You should have heard him this morning," Willy says, barging into Roger's room. "The man is just wonderful."

"Right," Roger mumbles. He's slouched in his lounge chair, scraping a plastic spoon along the bottom of a carton of honey yogurt. The Sunday Afternoon Movie is a Grade B Civil War picture. Ted wanders in, loosening his tie. Willy puts his arm around Ted's shoulder. When Roger doesn't say anything else, they turn their attention to what's happening on the TV screen.

A doctor is making the rounds of the Confederate wounded. He pauses at one cot where a young lieutenant stares out blankly. "We'll have to cut, soldier," the doctor tells him. In the next scene you see the focused, weary face of the doctor bent over his patient, you see the scalpel touch the leg, the quivering of the soldier's lips as he gulps from a bottle of whiskey, and back to the doctor, sweating now. Then a single, horrific scream. The idea, Roger knows, is to make it sound like excruciating pain *and* a blessed relief. He's not sure the director pulled it off. He looks back at Willy and Ted. They're staring intently at the screen, their arms around each other's waists now.

The ad comes on. Roger heaves himself out of the recliner and punches the on/off switch. The picture sizzles and disappears.

"What I want to know," he says, collapsing back into the chair, "is why a Protestant minister calls himself Father." He picks a section of the Sunday paper off a disheveled heap next to the chair.

"Episcopal," Willy corrects. He uncoils from Ted and moves in front of Roger. "They say *Father* in the Episcopal church," he tells him and looks up at Ted for reassurance. (Willy isn't an Episcopalian, and wasn't much of a churchgoer until he met Ted, who sings in Father Barry's choir. It bugs Roger, the way Willy has given himself over to this new boyfriend, this church, this Father Barry.) "Really, Rog," Willy continues, "it feels natural calling him Father. I guess because he's so big and burly, and he makes you feel like he'll take care of you. He just acts like a Father, that's all."

Roger listens to the enthusiasm in Willy's voice. Willy, who is always being taken in by somebody. If it's not this one it's that one: a new partner at work, a new boyfriend, guys Willy would give the shirt off his back to after a day. No matter how many times he gets burned, Willy just keeps falling for people.

And now a priest. In Roger's book, priests are bad news. And have been ever since the one who seduced him eight years ago, his freshman year in college. It still gives him the creeps, all that loneliness pretending to be something else, pretending to offer you something.

"You can just tell," Willy continues, "that no matter who you are, he'll love you."

Roger smiles. "And no matter who you are," he says, throwing the paper down and pushing himself up from the chair, "no matter how many creeps you bring home"—he friendly-punches Ted in the stomach—"I'll still love you." He walks out of his room, into the living room.

Roger and Willy have been roommates for two years now, ever since the summer they met at DataControl and carried on a two-month office romance. The romance didn't go anywhere, though eventually they did decide to pool their resources and take the apartment together, a condo in a highrise on the Waterfront.

Though he doesn't let on, Roger is still in love with Willy. Most of the time he can keep it under control, but every once in a while, something that Willy will do—a story he tells, the way he washes the dishes, these rhapsodic descriptions of Father Barry—just hits Roger so sharply . . .

"We're making eggs Benedict," Willy says, tailing Roger. "You want some?"

Roger says he's got stuff to do. From the center of the living room, he shoots a basket with his empty yogurt cup into the plastic trash bin in the kitchen. Then he wanders to the picture window overlooking the Harbor. Boats are on the water, the first of the season, their sails taut or fluttering. The sun sparkles on the waves and it looks chilly outside. He turns back to the room. Next to the window there's a large terra cotta pot that holds one of his tropical plants. The soil is dry. He picks up the brass watering can and goes to the kitchen.

Willy's at the sink, washing lettuce for salad. He moves over to let Roger fill his can.

"I forgot to tell you, Father Barry's inviting us for dinner."

"Us?" Roger says. He shoves the can under the faucet.

"Sure. He's dying to meet you, and his wife's going out of town this week . . ."

Roger flips off the water. "Why's he inviting us when his wife is out of town?" He waits for the implications to sink in, but Willy just shrugs. "Jesus, Willy. You didn't tell me he's a closet case, too."

Ted comes to the rescue: "That's not exactly it," he says.

"Well, what exactly *is* it?" Roger gives him a vicious stare, the kind even Willy is sure to notice. He pauses, lets out an exasperated sigh. "I mean, wake up, you two. A priest who just happens to enjoy having a house full of homosexuals to dinner when his wife's away? I don't need it."

Willy pats him twice on the arm.

"Hey, Rog. Trust me, you'll like him." There's a confusion in Willy's voice that makes Roger feel guilty. "Barry's completely comfortable with who he is."

"That's the point: who *is* he?"

"Relax," Willy tells him. "He's not going to bite you." He drops an egg yolk into the blender.

"Jesus," Roger says. He pushes past them, into the living room again. He dumps the can of water onto the plant. " 'Dying to meet me'!" Roger calls out. "What the hell have you told him about me anyway?"

"That you're smart and attractive and are looking for someone," Willy yells above the whirring blender.

Roger saunters back to the kitchen. He looks at the toasted English muffins, the eggs poaching in a skillet, Ted, in an apron, slicing Canadian bacon. "So now this Father Barry is going to put the make on me?"

Willy laughs. "You're not his type, Rog."

They are standing on the granite steps of a Beacon Hill townhouse, waiting for Father Barry to answer the bell.

Then Roger hears a high, fluty voice—"Who is it?"—followed by a deep-chested laugh. The door flings open. Before he can look, Roger is enveloped in a bear hug, his face pressed between Willy's and Ted's, his body squeezed. An unfamiliar hand, fat, heavy, is massaging his back. He can hear muffled laughs, and catches a whiff of Willy's cologne, the same Willy was wearing on their first date, or maybe now it's Ted's. A jocular voice, bellowing somewhere above them, keeps saying, "Babies, you're beautiful!"

Someone lets out a cry of pain, and the hand that is tightening around Roger's side releases. Roger inhales again, a cool draught of this April evening, and looks up. Towering above them, Father Barry keeps laughing. So heartily, in fact, that Roger begins to feel laughed at. He moves one step up, now even with the priest, who nevertheless still looms above him, a good six-three to Roger's five-ten.

He is a bear of a man, with a frame that is somewhere between a Patriots tackle and Friar Tuck. A full, well-trimmed beard, the color of pigeons, outlines his deep red face. At first, because of the striking quality of the beard, Roger doesn't notice that he is bald. Father Barry could be a sport-fisherman, red and rugged from too much Caribbean sun. He's wearing a Hawaiian luau shirt and a pair of blue-green cotton drawstrings that Roger recognizes as hospital intern's pants.

"Alice dear!" Father Barry calls out in mock endearing tones, halfway between the fluty voice and the big bellow. "Our guests have arrived." He turns back to the men and adds, sotto voce, "Alice didn't go to New York, so behave yourselves." Then he laughs and looks directly at Roger.

"So this is Roger," he says and gives his upper left arm a squeeze, pulling him into the foyer. Instinctually, Roger tenses his muscle. He never lets men touch his body unless it's tight. Father Barry lets out another deep belly laugh.

Alice appears. She is wearing a tailored gray flannel skirt and a cashmere sweater, in a softer shade of gray, with a single strand of pearls. "Nice to see you all," she says. She shakes hands with Ted and Willy, deliberately pronouncing each name and making a little nod with her head. Like a church social, Roger thinks. Alice turns to him. "And I don't believe we've met."

"Of course you haven't met him," Father Barry snaps. "He doesn't come to Grace Church on Sunday mornings. But God, Alice, don't go embarrassing us all by asking where he does spend his Sundays. It's probably not a story for a respectable family to hear!" Surreptitiously, for only the men to see, he raises his eyes heavenward.

Alice gives Roger a well-schooled, hostessy look and starts fingering her pearls.

"Actually," Roger says, trying to lighten things up, "I spend my Sundays in solitude contemplating the ocean. And in the summer, I bike or sail." He figures someone of Alice's stripes would approve of sailing.

"Alice," Father Barry orders, "get these men a drink."

"Why doesn't everyone come into the parlor?" Alice suggests. She gestures toward a long, curved flight of stairs that leads from the foyer to the second floor. Roger begins to follow Willy and Ted up the steps.

"Not you," Father Barry says in an amused way that sounds slightly accusatory. "You're helping me in the kitchen."

Halfway up the stairs, Alice stops. She gives her husband an annoyed look. "Barry, he's our guest," she says. "We didn't invite him to work in the kitchen. He might just want to relax, you know."

"Alice, just cool it with the Brahmin airs. You're dragging two of them off; let me have one. I need some company too, you know." He chuckles and waves them off. "Enjoy your drinky-poos."

Alice continues up the stairs, Willy and Ted tagging behind, trying to mask their amusement. Roger can't tell if Alice is hurt or not. She looks more bewildered than hurt, as if life with Father Barry never quite settles down into anything predictable. Reluctantly, he follows Barry into the kitchen.

It's a long, narrow affair tucked into a space—originally

it must have been the serving pantry—on the left side of the foyer. Father Barry motions toward a small bar set up in one corner. "Help yourself," he says, hardly paying Roger any notice. He retrieves a pair of half-glasses from the counter and puts them on, bending over an open cookbook.

The liquor is all the best brands. Roger fixes a hefty Scotch on the rocks. All this happens in silence, and when Father Barry still doesn't say anything, Roger wonders if he needs to talk about the incident out in the foyer.

"Do you and your wife always fight over the guests?" he asks, putting a little joking lilt into his voice.

Father Barry cocks his head up from the cookbook and flashes him a smile.

"She's jealous. She thinks I'm after you."

"Are you?" Roger asks. Suddenly he feels like flirting.

"*You?*" Father Barry says. He laughs and gives Roger the once-over. "When there's my Patrick?"

"Who's Patrick?"

"My, my," Father Barry says, "so curious. Well, I'm curious, too. Let's start by your telling me about *your*self."

"Well," says Roger, "what do you want to know?" He pushes back, bracing his buttocks against a kitchen stool.

"For openers," Father Barry says, and he starts to pull cloves of garlic from a fat, white head, "tell me why you're so afraid of me."

"Am I?" Roger takes a casual sip of his drink.

"You are." Putting down the garlic, he turns back toward Roger and peers, almost sternly, over his half-glasses.

Roger holds his own. He's not the type to concede a point so easily. "I don't think *afraid* is the right word. It's just that I don't know you, so I guess I'm just naturally hesitant."

Father Barry roars. "Oh, baby!" The flower print over his belly heaves up and down, and the hospital pants flutter. "Hesitant! Baby, if you were any *more* hesitant," and he gestures toward the stool, "you'd be in the hallway by now. What do you think I'm going to do?"

Roger watches him turn back toward the lamb. He's got this little knife in his hand, which he uses to make tiny incisions in the roast. Into each cut, he wedges a sliver of garlic.

"What's the matter?" Father Barry asks, "don't I get good reviews from that former boyfriend of yours?" Then he looks directly at Roger. "Willy's told me all about the two of you, you know."

"What's to tell?" Roger says.

"Baby, it's okay, it's okay. We've all been in love." He gives Roger's shoulder a little massage. "He's still very fond of you, too."

Roger looks down at the drink he is holding. This pose—sitting on a stool, head bowed, with a drink cupped between his legs—it's weirdly familiar, even here in this priest's kitchen, with the priest kneading his fingers into Roger's shoulder. It feels good, and Roger realizes how much he could use a good massage right now.

"Mmm, nice," Father Barry murmurs. Then he chuckles again. "But not as nice as my Patrick. Patrick isn't afraid of me." He makes a deep, pleasurable gurgle, like a lion's purr, way down in his throat.

"So are you going to tell me?" Roger asks.

Suddenly Barry stops rubbing his shoulder and looks up, past Roger. "Roger wants to know who Patrick is," he says to someone in the foyer.

Roger turns around. Alice is standing there, a tasteful scowl on her face.

"Come on, you two," she says, and Roger feels implicated in something he knows nothing about. "We're getting lonely upstairs."

"Relax, Alice," Father Barry snaps. "Can't you see I'm working on a masterpiece?" When he turns back to the lamb, Roger can see an impish expression on his face.

"You were pretty quiet," Willy says on their way home. "Didn't you like him?"

"Well," Roger says, trying to decide, "he comes across awfully strong."

"It's obvious he likes you," Ted encourages.

They are on the subway, and the noise as it speeds through the tunnel is so loud that Roger rests the back of his head against the cold, vibrating window. It's late and he's a little drunk from too many cocktails and too much red wine. He closes his eyes, but the events of the dinner party won't leave him.

Willy and Ted had done most of the talking: about music at Grace Church, Ted's work in the M.I.T. physics lab, their upcoming summer vacation to Greece. Toward dessert, already a little tipsy, Roger had questioned the amount of money Grace paid out for the music program. "I know you're worth it," he said to Ted, "but, damn it, the church should put that money toward helping really needy people."

"And what kind of needy people do you have in mind?" Father Barry had asked. He was teasing.

The train screeches and stops with a jerk. It's not their station, but Roger half opens his eyes. He looks over at Ted and Willy. They seem to be dozing, leaning into each other. There are only a few other people on the train, none worth cruising.

The next stop is theirs. Upstairs, the breeze off the ocean is heavy and unrelenting, like the wind that pounds your face on a rollercoaster. That's what being with Father Barry is like, Roger thinks, a rollercoaster.

For a while, the three of them walk in silence. Then Roger hears himself ask, "Who's Patrick?" He sounds a little drunk to himself.

"Patrick," Ted says, "makes Barry's vestments."

"He's a costume designer for some theater company in town," Willy adds. "On the side, he makes ecclesiastical vestments."

"Church drag," Roger mutters.

"Anyway," Willy continues, "Barry commissioned him to make some stoles, and . . ."

"What I want to know," Roger interrupts, "is are they lovers?"

Willy puts his arm around Roger.

"No, they're not lovers, Rog. I don't think there's a word for it. It's fatherly, I guess. I used to think Barry was just infatuated with Patrick's body—Patrick has a dancer's body—but that's not really it either. Think of it like this: fatherly, but with erotic overtones."

"Jesus," Roger says.

They are in the lobby now, waiting for an elevator. The light is a pasty white fluorescent. It makes Roger realize how hung over he'll be in the morning.

"And what does Alice think of all this?" he asks.

A woman in a mink coat walks up to the elevator and punches the call button several times. Then she stands, waiting with her hands folded in front of her, tapping her foot and looking up at the floor indicator.

"I think she realizes she can't have all of him," Willy says, and Roger hears that characteristic enthusiasm winding up again. "Barry's just got too much love for any one person."

"Well, if you ask me," Roger says, and out of the corner of his eye he catches the woman giving him a quick glance, "if you *ask* me"—he blinks and looks directly at the woman—"she doesn't deserve any of him."

With the coming of the long afternoons of light, Roger puts himself on the regimen of a daily bicycle ride after work. He bikes over to Haymarket and down Cambridge Street toward the river, across the bridge over to the Cambridge side, then west along the embankment all the way to Harvard Square. Here he crosses back over to Boston and rides east with the setting sun at his back.

Saturdays and Sundays, if he's not sailing, he starts out early so that he can end up spending the afternoon sunning on the Esplanade, the grassy strip between the river and Storrow Drive.

Willy calls it the Yes-planade. In the spring and summer months it becomes a beach of hunky men, basking like cats after the long, gray Boston winter. Sweaty from these weekend rides, Roger strips off his sweatshirt, balls it up into a pillow, and stretches out on the grass, legs spread-eagled. Sometimes he brings a book, and, propped on one arm, he pretends to read while he surveys the passing scene.

On the first Sunday in June he scores. As soon as the guy sets down his bike next to Roger's, Roger knows they'll go home together. It's just a matter of the usual formalities: comments on the weather, chitchat about the books they're reading, other talk, maybe museums or flicks or computers. Roger keeps catching the guy checking out his face, his legs, his basket. They end the conversation by talking about AIDS and safe sex, enough for Roger to learn that the guy will be as cautious as he.

The guy's name is Marcus. It lasts three weeks.

The middle of July, Willy and Ted leave for Greece. Roger goes to see them off at Logan. Father Barry is there, too, wearing an embroidered Greek peasant shirt, white linen pants and sandals. He opens a bottle of Mavrodaphne and pours some into four wine glasses he's brought along in a picnic hamper. Roger notices people looking. Then the boarding announcement is made. Everyone hugs, and Father Barry gives Willy and Ted slurpy kisses on the mouth.

"Bring me something from Mykonos!" he shouts as they disappear down the boarding tunnel. Laughing, he turns to Roger. "Baby, I thought you'd dropped off the face of the earth. Why haven't you called me? Was there something wrong with the lamb?"

Roger tells him he's been busy.

"So I hear," Father Barry says. "But I hear you're not so busy now."

Roger looks at him hard. "You sure do make it your business to find out all about me."

Father Barry smiles. "What are you hiding?"

"Are you sure you have the right to ask that kind of question?" He's determined to win one against this guy.

"Right!" Father Barry bellows. "Oh, baby, that's choice."

Roger doesn't understand what's so funny. "Look," he says, "how about a drink?

"Now you're talking. But, baby, I'm famished. That godawful Greek wine has given me an appetite. Let's go out for dinner."

Roger hasn't eaten, and returning to an empty apartment suddenly seems lonely.

"Sure, why not," he says.

"Sure, why not," Father Barry teases. "I'll even let you pick the spot." He rubs Roger's shoulder. "And on the way, I'll hear your confession."

"Like hell you will."

Roger directs them to a health club-cum-restaurant in the South End. The waiters look like daytime TV actors, and the clientele is mainly gay men who've spent the afternoon working out.

When they walk in, Father Barry lets out an amused chuckle.

"What's this supposed to prove, baby?"

The maitre d' approaches, smiles in a way that seems too understanding, and escorts them to a table.

"I thought," Roger says, "that a nice intimate bistro like this would be just the place for you to hear confession."

"Baby, you're still afraid of me, aren't you?"

Another waiter comes by to fill their water glasses. Roger watches Father Barry lift his eyes to the man. The waiter smiles back flirtatiously.

"So let's have it," Father Barry says when the waiter has gone. He lights a cigarette and inhales deeply.

"It seems you already know all about my peccadilloes," Roger says. He watches the smoke issuing from Father Barry's nostrils, mixing in with the gray mustache and beard.

Father Barry coughs a couple times, and then he coughs heavily, almost retching.

"God bless this shambles of a body," he says after he's regained his composure.

"Why do you smoke that shit?" Roger asks, glad to get the subject off himself.

Father Barry takes another deep drag. The hairs around his lips are yellow, stained by the nicotine. Roger can't imagine anyone falling for this shambles of a body.

"Because I can't stop, baby." He gives Roger a hard, sober look.

"For a priest, that isn't much evidence of self-control," Roger says, teasingly.

"Oh, baby," and Father Barry starts laughing and hacking, a disgusting, phlegmy cough. "*Self-control!* Is that what you think it takes?"

"Look," Roger says, "you tell me I've been ignoring you, and then when I try to show a little concern for your health . . ."

"Then *show* me, baby. Show me that concern. Give me something, anything, but don't just sit there expecting the world to think you're so wonderful because you're so perfectly in control. Give, dammit. Give, and stop worrying about being in control all the time."

"And what the hell are *you* giving?" Roger challenges. In this restaurant, surrounded by handsome men his age, Roger feels he can stick it to this priest, this guy who's giving him a line about giving. "Tell me that, huh? Like, what are you giving that Patrick of yours?"

A look of recognition comes over Father Barry's face. "Patrick," he says, "Patrick." He's looking directly at Roger. "So that's it."

Roger hesitates. Then another smirk comes over his face.

"That's what I'm giving you," he says. "I'm giving you the pleasure of introducing me to Patrick."

"You got it, baby."

Two days later, in the late morning, Roger meets Father Barry at his office in Grace Church. It's the first time he's seen the priest in clericals. The temperature is in the nineties, and the Boston humidity makes it feel even worse. Father Barry's black shirt is wet with perspiration.

"Lord Almighty, you didn't wilt on the way over, did you?"

"I'm pretty tough," Roger says.

"So I've noticed. Well then, come on, tough guy. Patrick is serving lunch at the soup kitchen. We might as well grab some of it."

They take the elevated to the South End, to a section Roger doesn't recognize. It's not the neighborhood of gentrified townhouses and fashionable bistros he's familiar with. Rumpled drunks stand in the shadows of doorways, clasping rumpled paper bags from which the necks of open bottles protrude. The men congregate in twos or threes, speaking and mumbling, sometimes talking to themselves. Even though the day is a scorcher, many of them are wearing flannel shirts over their T-shirts, the sleeves partly rolled up. Their shoes, some old leather workboots, some sneakers, are dusty and torn. Roger does not look at the faces.

"Here we are," Father Barry says.

They are standing in front of a dilapidated building, a townhouse once, whose first floor has been boxed in with a cheap brick addition that juts onto the sidewalk and is pierced by a row of small windows too high to be peered into from street level. Except for the absence of a display window, it looks like a convenience store. At one end, there is a heavy, metal-sheathed door painted a bright blue. Father Barry tugs on the handle.

"After you, baby."

The place is crowded with men, brown, black, white, and for an instant Roger thinks it looks like some illicit bar. The men are like the ones on the street: grimy, disheveled, unshaven. Long wooden tables fill the central space. At these tables several of the men huddle over mugs of coffee. In a far corner others are crowded around a TV set. Nearby, in a small alcove equipped with an old porcelain sink and a mirror, a black man is dragging a razor across his soapy cheeks.

When Roger turns around to find Barry, he catches a glimpse of the rest of the place. There is a large, industrial-grade kitchen, set up behind a long counter that faces onto the hall itself. Several people, in better shape than the men, are busy behind the counter, chopping onions and other vegetables, stirring cast aluminum pots, washing dishes. Barry is already behind the counter talking to an older man with a sad, kind face. He sees Roger and motions him over.

Roger moves so quickly that he bumps into an old white-haired man carrying a mug of coffee back from the counter. The coffee sloshes all over the man's hands and onto the floor. Roger looks up into the man's face. The skin hangs on his cheeks and under his eyes like a discarded leather pocketbook, and his sparse hair is the color of watery tomato soup.

"Excuse me," Roger says.

The man stares past him, then shuffles on, steadying his cup in a palsied hand.

"Try to be a little more gentle," Father Barry teases.

The man Father Barry has been talking to gives Roger a calm, gentle gaze. He isn't particularly handsome, and is a lot older and in less good shape than Roger has imagined, but he has a kind face that Roger warms to at once.

"Patrick, I'm Roger," he says.

"Patrick!" Father Barry yells. "You think this ugly old fleabag is Patrick?" He laughs and the other man laughs, too.

"I'm Father O'Sullivan," the man says. "I run the soup kitchen. As you can see, Barry is one of my fondest admirers." He winks at Roger. "Patrick's over there."

Roger turns to see a tall, lean man in his late twenties walking toward them. Like most of the others in the kitchen, he is wearing jeans and a blue workshirt.

"Barry!" he exclaims in a voice that is both hearty and slightly feminine.

They throw their arms around each other and hug, holding tight for what seems like an excessively long time, rocking each other back and forth. Roger can hear Barry's voice, muffled in the cradle of Patrick's neck:

"Patrick, Patrick."

Then Barry pushes Patrick away. "Let me take a look at you."

Patrick is tall and lithe, with deep brown eyes set into an olive complexion. There are dark circles under his eyes, which makes him look like a Spanish mystic in a painting by El Greco.

Barry strokes Patrick's unshaven cheeks and rubs his thumb over the dark circles as if it is just a matter of wiping away some mascara. "Oh, my baby."

"Barry, it's so good to see you," Patrick says and hugs him again.

Roger looks around the kitchen. One of the volunteers, a good looking blond guy, turns around, and gives Roger an amused smile that looks to Roger as if it might be a cruise. Roger smiles back.

"So, tell me, it's going well?" Father Barry asks.

Patrick looks at Father O'Sullivan.

"Patrick is doing beautifully," Father O'Sullivan says. "He's a favorite with the guests."

Roger keeps waiting for Barry to introduce them, but Barry seems to have forgotten that he is there.

"Baby, we've got to get you outside for a while," Father Barry tells Patrick. "Into the beautiful sunshine. You'll suffocate cooped up with O'Sullivan here."

Roger wonders what's happened to the idea of lunch.

"The three of you get out before I have to fumigate the place," Father O'Sullivan jokes.

"*Three?*" Father Barry roars and looks down at Roger. "I thought we'd leave this one here to do some work. He's trying to learn what it means to give." He chuckles and digs his fingers into Roger's shoulder.

"Barry, stop teasing," Patrick scolds playfully. He smiles at Roger. "Hi, I'm Patrick."

Roger introduces himself. It doesn't seem as if Barry's ever mentioned him to Patrick. That figures, he thinks.

The three of them leave the soup kitchen. Even with the stove going, it is hotter still outside.

"Jesus, let's go have a drink," Barry says. "Isn't that fruity bistro you took me to around here somewhere?" he asks Roger.

Patrick says he doesn't want to drink, that he'd rather just have a quick cup of coffee, and motions to a luncheonette on the opposite corner.

They settle into a booth, and Patrick tells them about his work at the soup kitchen, his daily schedule, the other volunteers. Then he tells them about Dave.

"Dave's the blond guy who was making soup. He's a photographer, came over one day to do a series on the soup kitchen, and next thing you know he's coming regularly to help out."

As he's telling all this, Patrick turns his head back and forth from Father Barry to Roger, as if he doesn't want either of them to miss a thing. There's the same enthusiasm in his voice as when Willy tells a story.

"We've had some really good talks," he continues. "Dave's coming to the studio next Saturday to photograph me dancing. He wants to do another series of shots of me in my costume designs. Isn't that terrific?"

"Baby, that's great!" Barry says.

Roger feels the priest's hand dig into his thigh—squeezing, massaging—under the table.

"I owe a lot to you, Barry," Patrick says. He reaches across the table and touches Father Barry. "You were my first commission." He turns to Roger. "Barry's been encouraging me right along. If he hadn't asked me to design his stoles, I might never have developed any confidence in myself."

He glances at the clock on the wall and tells them that he needs to get back to help serve lunch.

"Would you like us to help?" Roger asks.

Father Barry lets out a belly laugh.

"You are such a phony, baby." He eases himself up from the bench.

Patrick gives him a curious look.

"He's just trying to get into your pants," Father Barry says.

Patrick blushes. "Barry."

"Big Daddy's been around," Father Barry tells him. He pulls out a wad of bills and throws a five on the table.

"Actually," Patrick says, turning to Roger as they step out of the luncheonette, "the rules are you have to go through a training session before you can volunteer. There're a lot of sensitive areas you need to be aware of."

"Hear that, baby?" Father Barry interrupts. "Sensitive areas." Overhead the rumble of an elevated train breaks the humid stillness. "Come on, baby. This is our train."

The noise grows louder, so that Patrick has to shout. "It was great to meet you, Rog." He shakes Roger's hand. "You take care of Barry now."

The train is coming into the station. Patrick turns to Barry smiling. "Well, Barr." They hug long and hard. Roger hears Barry say, "Oh, my beautiful Patrick." The train squeals to a halt. Roger sees Patrick trying to release himself from the bear grip, but Barry clings hard.

"Barry, let go!" Patrick yells.

Barry slaps him hard on the back, lets go, and starts running up the steps—so quickly that Roger is left alone for a second.

"See ya," says Patrick, and raises his hand.

Roger scampers up the old iron stairs. He doesn't catch up to Barry until they are both on the train, panting.

"You'll kill yourself, running that fast," Roger says and he collapses next to him on the seat. The train lurches forward. He looks over. There are tears in Barry's eyes.

Roger keeps quiet. Out of the corner of his eye he can see Father Barry's fat, sweaty, black-clothed body heaving. When Father Barry stops, Roger says, "For such a hard-boiled old coot, you sure do have a soft streak."

The priest drops his head and shakes it back and forth.

Roger pats him reassuringly on the leg. Father Barry grabs Roger's hand, squeezing tightly. Roger tries to pull his hand away, but the priest's grip tightens. He holds on, kneading Roger's fingers, his knuckles, his fingernails. Roger is aware of people staring. At their stop, Father Barry inhales loudly, a deep sniffle that signifies he's recovered his composure. He lets go of Roger's hand and the two of them walk back to the church in silence.

In his office, Father Barry snaps on the air conditioning. It comes up with a stodgy, reluctant murmur. Then he turns to Roger.

"Pulling your hand away: you couldn't even give me that much, could you?"

"Barry, it was embarrassing."

"What was embarrassing! Holding hands? You would have done it in a minute had it been Patrick's hand reaching out to you."

"Come on," Roger scoffs.

"Or what if it had been Willy's . . ."

"Barry . . ."

"Or Marcus—*ah*! Now there's the rub, eh? What if it had been that trick you picked up on the Esplanade?"

"Barry, stop it!"

"Stop what, baby? Stop what?"

There is a brief moment of silence. Roger listens to the air conditioner buzzing on as it tries to make some headway against the intense heat outside. Beads of sweat cover Father Barry's forehead and the top of his bald, scarlet head.

"Look, Barry, I don't need this humiliation," Roger says. "A lot of other guys may think you're terrific, but . . ."

"You jealous little shit!" Father Barry is shaking his head, trying to calm himself down.

"Jealous my ass! Jealous of what? A dirty old priest who goes after young hunks behind his wife's back?"

"You're alone, Roger."

"Admit it! You're a sad, frightened closet case . . ."

"You're alone, Roger."

". . . who can't stand the fact that the one guy who has ever paid you any attention . . ."

"Alone, Roger."

". . . is not going to let you sweep him off his feet. And stop saying that!" he screams, an ache coming into his throat. "Stop trying to make me in your own image. I am *not* alone."

Roger is gasping for air. He takes several deep breaths.

"Baby." Father Barry's voice is calmer now, soothing. "You're trying to carry too much. It's too much for you alone." He pauses, reaches out to stroke Roger's cheek. "Let Daddy take some of it."

"You're sick!" Roger screams, and thrusts Father Barry's hand away. His breath comes convulsively now.

"That's it," Barry encourages, soothingly, gentle. "Give it to Daddy. All of that anger."

Roger tightens his fists, raises them to smash the priest's chest, to push him away, anything to stop these words, these hideous, familiar words.

"That's it," Barry says, grabbing his wrists. "Come on, all of it. Give it . . . give it."

Roger tries to wrestle free. He can hardly breathe, he's gagging so much on mucus and saliva. He opens his mouth, but the *No*—the final, incontrovertible *No* he wants to deliver—won't come. What he hears instead is a noise, half-groan, half-scream, like the sound of someone under a scalpel. Then he's in Barry's arms.

"That's it, baby. That's it. Give it to him."

TOO MUCH

MAYBE IT WAS THE way Tim bounded out of his apartment building when I tooted the horn, that huge leather travel bag jouncing off his hip, or the way he took the stairs two at a time, like one of the dancers he accompanies at the ballet studio—he was waving at us, giving us goofy looks. He was so eager, and my heart sank.

It wasn't just Tim, either. Caleb, too: all glee and readiness, bouncing up and down on the car seat next to me, playing trampoline and singing one of his madeup songs, something about "We're on our way/This very day."

"Enough!" I snapped at him.

Caleb is six—"six and three-quarters," he'd say—and this was his first summer with me since Charlotte and I got divorced. Earlier in the season, wanting to do the right thing, I had started with guidebooks to the city: walking tours, adventure trails, a book called *A Kid's Boston*. Every

afternoon we would do something from one of them, until
one day, Caleb said, "Dad, just 'cause you're a teacher
doesn't mean you have to show me all this stuff. It's getting
to be like field trips." When I asked him what he wanted
to do instead, he said, "Just mess around."

"So here's the deal," I told him. "For the rest of the
summer we'll just mess around, but you're going to have
to teach me how to do that without making it like field
trips."

"Deal," he said.

That was in June. Now it was late August, our final
week together before Caleb had to return to the West Coast.
We were on our way to Vermont for an end-of-the-summer
non-field trip.

Caleb had been ready for days. Every evening after
supper, he had been up in his room, arranging little piles
of his favorite clothes, making up a box of toys, explaining
things to his teddy bear. "You can come, too, Teddy," I
heard him say one night. "As long as you behave." Apparently Teddy had behaved; he was propped up now
against the back seat of the car.

All this should have made me happy: a week in the
country, the five-day forecast calling for beautiful weather,
Caleb so tickled. And Tim coming along, too. I was happy
enough, but not like Caleb, not like Tim. Tim is twenty-
eight, six years younger than I. And when he came out of
his building like that, like a kid, it all seemed, as Tim often
says, but meaning something else, too much.

It's not that I was uncomfortable having my son and
my boyfriend along on vacation together. Even Charlotte
didn't mind. It's just that all this gladness: no one but me
seemed aware of the ways it can throw you.

I reached over and undid the lock to the left rear door.
Tim opened it, threw the bag across the back seat, and got
in.

"Hi, kiddo!" he said, tousling Caleb's hair. "Hi,
Teddy." I looked over my shoulder. He was patting Ted-

dy's little furry head. "Hi, Ned." He beamed at me, then rubbed his fingers in my hair, too. I turned back, popped the clutch, and we pulled away from the curb.

"Tim, are you going to stay with us the whole week?" Caleb asked. He had turned around and was kneeling, peeking through the space between the headrest and the top of the seat. He'd known Tim only six weeks and already adored him.

"The whole week!" Tim said. "Too much, eh, Caleb?"

"Too much!" Caleb shouted.

I turned to him. "Sit forward and put on your seat belt."

He obeyed. Caleb is the classic good kid. He has his cranky moments, and he's sometimes painfully honest with me, but basically—sometimes I think miraculously—he's a happy boy with a happy boy's disposition to please. At his age, he's been through the divorce of his parents, changed schools twice, traveled across the country four times in a plane, this last trip alone.

"Doesn't your mother make you put on your seat belt?" I asked him. I looked over again: he was having trouble getting the buckle into the catch.

"Daddy, I can't get this," he said pleadingly.

At this point, when I was Caleb's age, my father would have shrugged his shoulders and said, "And what do you want from me?" It was the expression Pop used whenever I tried to get away with acting helpless. He'd fling out that question, curt and clipped, as a way of letting me know that helplessness, the kind you can help, is your own mess to deal with.

Which explains why I turned to Caleb, still fiddling with the seat belt, and said, "And what do you want from me?"

Caleb didn't answer, just kept pulling at the strap, as if he'd already learned what Pop had tried to teach me years ago. Then came the reassuring click of the belt locking, holding Caleb's little body in place, so that in the event of an accident (you can be sure it'll be someone else's fault, not mine), he'll stand a good chance of being saved.

"So," I said, presenting him with the evidence, "you *can* do it yourself. Is it tight?"

"Yup," he said, giving a satisfied tug at the belt to show me how snug in he was.

"You back there, you buckle up, too," I told Tim.

"*Any-thing that you want*," Tim said, mimicking the rhythm and lyrics to a disco number I've heard him play at his place.

"And Teddy, Tim, don't forget Teddy," Caleb called out in his high, happy voice. He arched his head back as far as he could. "Teddy can't do it himself."

The trip from Boston took about three hours. During most of it Tim and Caleb chatted away: baseball, computer games, dinosaurs.

Tim amazes me. He never seems to tire of Caleb. In fact, he never seems to tire of the whole family. He'll play with Caleb for hours, put up with my moods, even talk to Charlotte on the phone if she calls and he happens to be over at my place. A few weeks ago, for instance, I called her to talk about Caleb's school. (On his final report card, he'd gotten an Excellent in everything, and I'd written Charlotte to suggest that maybe Seattle schools were too easy and that we should look for alternatives.) Tim dialed for me and when Charlotte answered the two of them settled into a half-hour conversation—dance world news!—after which he hung up. Just like that. Without even mentioning schools. I had to call Charlotte back.

That's Tim. Quite happy to drop into the family, to chat up a storm, but totally oblivious to the day-to-day responsibilities, to the care you have to take. (He lets his laundry pile up for weeks, covering his bedroom floor like seaweed cast up on a beach until you're wading through it.) We've been seeing each other for seven months now; he wants to exchange rings.

"Ned, let's stop for ice cream," Tim called out when we'd turned off the interstate and were traveling the local road toward Woodstock. "I'm dying for a big dish of double chocolate chocolate chip." It was eleven-thirty in the morning.

"Yeh, Ned!" Caleb sang out. "Let's stop."

"The name's *Dad*," I told him, "and what about lunch? I think we should hold off on ice cream until after lunch."

"What do you think, Caleb?" Tim asked, his voice still full of excitement. "Lunch first, then ice cream?" He was giving Caleb the opportunity to let us both be right.

"Yeh," Caleb pronounced again, this time with a drawn-out "Cool with me, man" attitude.

"So where are we going for lunch?" Tim asked. He'd unbuckled his belt and scooted forward, leaning into the space between my seat and Caleb's. I kept my eyes on the road.

"How about us getting there and unpacking first?" I said.

"How about that, Caleb?" Tim said, reaching down and giving him a little tickle.

Last week I told Charlotte that I wasn't sure about Tim anymore.

"Not sure about what?" she said.

"Not sure I can handle it."

"It?"

"A relationship with him," I told her, and when she didn't answer I tried again: "Who he is, the way he acts." She didn't respond. Charlotte has a way of waiting for me to hit the right word. "All that vitality," I said.

"Vitality!" she pounced.

"You know what I mean?" I said.

"That you're five years older than Tim?"

"Six," I said, "six years older." She went silent again. "Charlotte, he wants to marry me. He doesn't have a full-time job." She still wasn't saying anything. "Okay, okay," I conceded, "I enjoy him enormously, but there are times when he just doesn't seem to know any limits."

"You mean he walks through walls?"

"Why are you teasing me?" I said. There was silence on the other end. "You know, you're not being very helpful."

"Just like your father, right?"

"Charlotte," I said, "this is not a case of my acting helpless."

"Well, what is it then?" she asked.

And when I told her I didn't know, that's when she suggested I take Tim along on the Vermont trip with Caleb.

The place I'd rented was an old one-room schoolhouse that had been converted into a vacation getaway. It sat just off a dirt road, about two miles from the village where Charlotte and I once stayed on a ski weekend. The road ran between two large tracts of farmland, and the school building, brick with a rough-cut slate roof, was situated on a tiny plot nicked into the edge of one of these farms.

As we unloaded the car, I told Caleb about how, in the old days, kids from different grades used to go to school altogether in one room. "While the teacher was working with one grade," I explained, handing Caleb his box of toys from the trunk, "the others would be doing their lessons at their desks, and sometimes the older kids would teach the younger kids."

"Did the younger kids ever teach the older kids?" Caleb asked.

"Yeh, Ned," Tim piped up. "Did they?" With Teddy perched on his shoulder, he was returning from carrying a load into the house. I thrust a bag of groceries into Tim's stomach, and Teddy toppled forward.

"Oopsie," Tim said, as he caught Teddy in the grocery bag.

"Oopsie," said Caleb.

After we unloaded the car and I fixed us some lunch (with promises of a trip into town later on to get that ice cream), Tim and Caleb went off to explore the stream that ran beyond the field. I took to an aluminum chaise longue on the small patch of lawn, Teddy sitting next to me on the grass, because, as Caleb, who had put him there, told me, "He doesn't like adventures." I closed my eyes and thought about adventures.

I haven't had many, at least not the way most people count them. Marrying Charlotte, having Caleb, even coming out: those years of clandestine forays to the bars. Even the divorce. In retrospect none of these seem like "adventures." They were all just steps I was taking—important ones, sure, but steps nonetheless. You take one, you take another. Things happen, time passes. I teach high school science and math. My seniors do a unit on probability and predictability. That's what these steps were: predictable.

But an adventure—what's that? Something unpredictable? An interruption in the way things are supposed to go? A step you don't have to take? Tim wants to exchange rings.

These are the things I was thinking as Tim and Caleb were off exploring. Then I heard them racing across the field, running back to the house. I opened my eyes: they were in their bathing suits, droplets of water glistening all over their bodies. Tim is in good shape. He has a trim, toned body, half by virtue of regular workouts at the gym, half the gift of his youth. And Caleb is beyond the baby fat stage, so that, stripped to their bathing suits, they looked almost like father and son: lean figures and dirty blond hair, hairless chests, lanky arms and legs. Waving a large bath towel, Tim was chasing Caleb, who was gasping for breath. He dashed across the road and up to the chaise longue.

"Help, Dad!" he screamed, in that way that's both terrified and full of hilarity. It was nice to be "Dad" again.

Before I could say anything, he turned to face Tim, who suddenly threw the towel over Caleb's head. It was such a large towel that it completely draped his little body. Tim began to rub Caleb's hair vigorously. I could hear, mixed with sounds of glee, Caleb's muffled cries for help. Grabbing him around the waist, Tim flipped him upside down. Caleb began slicing his feet back and forth in the air. His voice sounded as if he had cotton in his mouth. For a moment, I thought Tim might be smothering him. I got up.

"Tim?" I wanted him to hear the uncertainty in my voice.

Tim let Caleb gently slide from his grasp, and Caleb collapsed onto the lawn, still under the terrycloth, his chest heaving. I thought he was suffocating. I sprang from the chaise and ripped the towel away. Caleb was laughing uncontrollably.

"Come on, you two," I said. "That's enough. Time to dry off."

They were laughing so hard, I thought they hadn't heard me, but then Tim said, "Okay, out of these wet trunks," and stripped off his bathing suit. Caleb jumped up from the grass, pulling off his trunks, too.

Tim quickly towelled off Caleb's body, then started to dry himself. Caleb grabbed hold of a little piece of the mammoth cloth and continued to wipe off his own arms and tummy, all the while giggling. When he was finished drying himself, he tried to help Tim, going for the thighs, the ass, those beautiful calves.

"Go get dressed, kiddo," Tim told Caleb and gave him a slap on the behind. Caleb dashed into the house.

Wiping off his back, Tim turned to me. He thrust out his pelvis seductively and winked. "I love you," he silently mouthed, respectful of Caleb's being within earshot, then wrapped the towel around himself.

"Tim," I said. I was relieved that he'd covered himself up. "I think I'd like some time with Caleb this afternoon."

"Good idea," Tim said.

"I mean alone," I explained.

"I know what you mean," Tim said.

Caleb and I set off on a hike, really a long stroll down the dirt road that passed in front of the house. There were fields on either side, and occasionally a dilapidated barn.

When we'd gone a little way, I asked him in my best dad-and-his-boy-shooting-the-breeze voice, "You like Tim, don't you?"

"Dad," Caleb said, "you ask me that every time we do something with Tim."

"Well," I tried to explain, "I just want to make sure that you're having a good time."

Caleb's attention was already elsewhere, on a clump of blue, daisylike weeds growing along the side of the road.

"So, what is it exactly you like about Tim?" He didn't answer. He was picking some of the wildflowers, pulling them up by the roots because the stems were tough. "Watch out for poison ivy," I called out.

Caleb ignored me. He was adding stalks of the blue wildflower to his bouquet.

"That's chicory," I told him. He turned and held out the clump for me to examine. "They're pretty aren't they?"

"Yeh." He pulled at another clump growing nearby.

"It's actually a member of the sunflower family," I told him. "It grows everywhere: fields, roadsides, even dumps. Some people eat the leaves, and you can grind up the roots and roast them for coffee." Then I caught myself. "Hey, Caleb?" He looked up at me. "Is this too much like a field trip?"

He smiled. "Sort of, Dad, but that's okay."

"No, really, Caleb"—I was sloughing off his good kid response—"do you know why it is I keep showing you stuff?"

" 'Cause you want me to be smart?"

"Well sure, but why do you think I want you to be smart?"

"So I'll keep getting all Excellents in school?"

"That too," I laughed. "But mainly because if you're smart, if you know a lot of things and understand how they work, you won't be afraid of them, you'll be able to use them."

This is the promise of science, I tell my students. That

knowledge of the world wipes away our terror, our help-lessness. Half of them don't know what I'm talking about.

Caleb was silent, the kind of silent I've learned means he doesn't quite get it.

"It's just that I want you to love all the wonderful things in the world," I tried again.

"I liked the Science Museum."

"The world is like a hundred Science Museums, Caleb. A thousand Science Museums. The more you know about the world, the more you realize just how wonderful it is."

He still didn't say anything, and in the quiet of that moment, the field alive with the sounds of rustling grass and crickets, I thought about just how ready I was to let the world be wonderful.

I took his hand, and we walked on for a few moments, each of us lazily holding our bunch of chicory and being quiet with our own thoughts.

"Dad?" Caleb asked after we'd gone on a little ways. "When I go back to Seattle, will you and Tim come visit me?"

"I can't speak for Tim," I said, "but if your mother will have it, yes, of course I'll come visit you. How about Christmastime?"

"Tim will come, too," Caleb said.

"What do you mean?"

"He said so."

"When did he say that?"

"When we were swimming."

"Caleb," I told him, "I don't want to disappoint you, but what if Tim and I aren't still friends at Christmas?"

"Come on, Dad. Be serious," Caleb said. He sounded annoyed, as if I were toying with him, deliberately ignoring the most obvious facts.

"I am serious, Caleb. Maybe I'll have a different friend by Christmas. Don't you make new friends all the time?" It was an analogy I thought would work. Caleb is pretty popular around the playground.

"But Tim said he was going to live with you."

"Caleb," I began. I could hear the teacherly quality starting up again in my voice.

But Caleb didn't wait to listen. He threw down his clump of chicory, pulled away from me, and ran back toward the house.

When I got back, Tim was still stretched out on the chaise, an arm over his eyes, Teddy on his chest. He appeared to be asleep, but as I made for the house, he peeked out from under his arm.

"How was your walk?"

"Where's Caleb?"

Tim pushed himself up from the chair, moving Teddy onto his lap. "Inside," he said cautiously.

I walked over to the chaise and stood over him. "Why did you tell Caleb you were going to move in with me?"

"What I told him," Tim said, fingering Teddy's ears, "was that I'd *like* to live with you."

"Well, what I'd *like*," I told him, "is for you to stop putting ideas in Caleb's head."

Tim was squinting into the late afternoon sun. He shaded his eyes. "What kind of ideas?"

"Ideas that get him all excited. Ideas that won't work."

"What won't work, Ned?"

"Us," I said.

We were staring each other down.

"The reason being?" he asked.

The sun was casting an orange glow all over his body. And for a second, I couldn't think of a reason.

"Tim, there are a million reasons why."

"Of course there are," Tim said, as if he were conceding a point, but a point that opened up, rather than closed, the argument.

"Look," I said, letting my voice get calmer, more rational, "we're very different, Tim. We're practically opposites. And that's okay," I quickly added. "There are a lot of things I love about you: your spontaneity, the way you throw yourself into things." I was trying to do what Tim does so well, give us both a chance to be right.

"But?" he said. He picked up Caleb's teddy bear and addressed him. "Listen carefully, Teddy."

"But it just feels like too much right now."

"Ned!" He scooted forward in the chaise. "I *want* it to feel like too much!"

That's when I told him he was being crazy, that he was young and naive and why didn't he find a responsible job instead of playing the piano thirty hours a week for a second-rate dance company. I told him that when he was as old as I and had a kid to consider, well then maybe he could teach me about his kind of too much, but until then I was not about to mess around with the life I'd just begun to reestablish for myself.

He just kept sitting there, grinning at me and toying with Caleb's teddy bear. When I went to grab it out of his hand, Tim pulled away. The chaise tipped and he fell to the ground. Just then Caleb came out of the house.

"Caleb, catch!" Tim shouted. He flung Teddy wildly into the air. Caleb dashed forward, head up, arms thrust out in front of him, squealing. This time I wasn't mistaken. It was a squeal of terror. Teddy flew over Caleb's head and landed about ten feet away on the grass.

Tim sprang up. "Get him! Toss him here!" he shouted. "Over here, Caleb!"

But Caleb was already crying, running hysterically toward his little friend. Teddy was face-down, a motionless bundle of fur and stuffing. He actually looked unconscious. Then Tim realized that Caleb was crying. He gave me a sheepish, helpless look. I fired back a searing glare and looked over at Caleb again. He had picked Teddy up and was hugging him close to his chest, whimpering now.

"It's all right, Caleb," I called out. "Teddy's going to be fine."

Still clutching Teddy, Caleb walked over to me and wrapped himself and Teddy around my waist. I reached down and held them close.

Of all the crazy things to think of at that moment, what went through my head is that there was no phone in the schoolhouse, no way to get in touch with Charlotte, three thousand miles away. "Bring Tim along," she'd said. "See what happens."

"You see, you *see*?" I wanted to say to her now. "This is what happens."

Caleb sniffled and disengaged himself from my embrace. He ran his free hand over his eyes and down his cheeks. Then he stroked Teddy's head. I patted Teddy, too.

"Teddy's going to be fine," I told Caleb.

Tim was standing a little ways off. I'd never seen him so quiet before. Pensive. That's what he looked like. And a little awestruck.

"I'm sorry, Caleb," he said.

Caleb looked up, sniffled again, and began to walk toward Tim. He seemed almost in a stupor, as if he didn't know who Tim was. Tim held out his arms and Caleb fell into his embrace.

"Howya doin'?" Tim said, gently patting Caleb on the back.

"Okay."

They held onto each other for a few more seconds. Then Caleb looked up at Tim.

"Are you and Daddy still gonna be friends when I go back to Seattle?"

Tim looked over at me.

I thought of Pop—three thousand times three thousand miles away. I wanted to say something to him, too: "Daddy," I wanted to whisper, "I can't do it." But even here, under circumstances he never would have dreamed of, I know he would have given me that same old reply. And he would have been right. It was up to me now—but not just me, *us*: Tim, Ned, Caleb, even Charlotte—it was up to all of us whether this life together was going to be too much or too much.

THE BOY BLISS

AGAIN THIS YEAR,
James and I were vegetable people.

It's the kind of party where everyone's invited to bring
something: hors d'oeuvres, a bottle of wine, a loaf of homemade bread. There are people for salads and people for
desserts and people in charge of soft drinks and paper cups.
(No styrofoam at this party.) Harry and Jonathan, our
hosts, provide the house and the turkeys and the organization. And every year—for six years now—they've asked
James and me to bring a vegetable.

You can never have too many vegetables at Harry and
Jonathan's Thanksgiving party. They have a lot of friends
who are vegetarians: an Oxfam worker, a former nun, a
guy who's been to Central America on a fact-finding mission, people who for one reason or another don't believe in
eating meat. They have a lot of friends who eat meat, too.
This year they had fifty-two guests, so many that they had
to cook four turkeys, which some wag—a Democrat, but

then practically all their friends are Democrats—christened George and Barbara, Dan and Marilyn.

James and I met Harry and Jonathan a little over six years ago, at a wedding reception in a Cambridge garden. There we were, four gay men adrift in a rampant sea of delphinium and nuptial bliss. Or rather, three of us were adrift. Harry, with his Irish Catholic good looks—blue-eyed and already sporting his summer tan—Harry was busy meeting people, introducing them to each other, organizing conga lines. If he weren't a college professor, he might easily have been a cruise director on a ship. In the first twenty minutes of our acquaintance, Harry had already invited James and me to their annual Thanksgiving celebration, five months away.

It's actually a *pre*-Thanksgiving Thanksgiving party, a chance for Harry and Jonathan to assemble all their friends (and quite a few of their acquaintances) before we all scatter for the official holiday. And while it's billed as a party given by both of them, the choreography is typically Harry's: an imbroglio of gay and straight, male and female, black and white, students, professors, artists, political types. And kids. Always five or six kids under the age of ten. Harry, who spent a couple of years studying for the priesthood and who now teaches theology at a small Catholic college, once told me that he thinks of his and Jonathan's pre-Thanksgiving party as a foretaste of the sacrum convivium. "The heavenly banquet, Dan," he explained to me. "The gathering together of all the blessed."

Over the years, Harry's convivium has grown so big that he and Jonathan have had to move it from their own apartment, one floor of a triple decker, to the house of friends in a gentrified but still politically correct neighborhood elsewhere in the city. It's a grand house: high-ceilinged entrance hall, wainscoted double parlors, bedrooms you could get lost in. With the fireplaces going and the aroma of hot mulled wine in the air, it makes a festive setting for their annual event.

When James and I arrived this year, potato casserole

in hand, the house was already abuzz with conviviality. Jonathan greeted us at the door, full of hostessy welcome. (In heaven, at the eternal sacrum convivium, while Harry is flitting about, introducing Saint Teresa to Lily Tomlin, Jonathan will be the one to make sure there are enough napkins to go around.) He took the pan out of James's hands, told us where to put our coats, then excused himself to attend to other details. James offered to take my coat up to the bedroom.

James is full of thoughtful gestures like that. We've been together over twelve years, settling into something that's as close to the long-term, stable marriages of our parents as gay men seem to have these days. There have been times, of course, when I've thought about "divorcing" him, moments of anger or boredom or sexual temptation when it was hard to see how the pleasures of being with James could ever outweigh the disappointments. Right now things are fine, but from time to time I still kick around that idea of leaving him. For what? For whom? All I know is that I keep watching other gay couples for clues.

With my coat safely in James's care, I made my way to the pantry to get a glass of wine, and there I bumped into a guy I see once a year at this party. There are always a lot of people I see only once a year at this party. It's not that I don't like all these folks. I do. And many of them I'd be happy to socialize with at other times, too. But, as James says, "At some point you've just got to hang up the phone."

When James says this, he's letting me know two things: one, that of course there are lots of interesting, attractive people out there; and, two, so what? It's a phrase he coined originally in reference to Harry—Harry who never ever hangs up the phone on anyone—but recently James has been using it on me as well. "Hang up the phone": it's a valid point. Blunt perhaps, but one I'm more inclined to concede now that I'm past thirty-five.

"So how's your year been?" I asked the once-a-year guy, trying to remember if he was the one who worked in the mayor's office or was Harry's colleague in the theology department. The only thing I definitely recalled from last year was that he was straight.

"Well, I've stayed in good health and I still didn't win Megabucks," he said.

"Yup, that's about how it's been with me, too."

This year, James and I both tested negative, which means we really were in good health, definitely something to be thankful for. I took another sip of my wine.

"What would you do if you won Megabucks?" I said.

"Ah, Megabucks," he chuckled, shaking his head. It was as if it were too painful, or too wonderful, or both, for him even to think about coming into so much good fortune.

I have a friend in New York who would point to this as an example of the way straight people don't even give themselves a chance to fantasize. "Hets," Carlos says—that's what he calls them, Hets—"They can't even *imagine* alternatives."

And it was at precisely that moment, trying myself to imagine what I, a bank teller with a master's degree in German Romanticism, would do with such a windfall, that I caught sight of this other guy making his way into the pantry.

He was about my height, just under six feet, with a beautifully ruddy face, dark hair, and one of those well-groomed mustaches that, in these clean-shaven days, have suddenly become a distinguishing feature again. But it was the green eyes that really got me. Blue-green, like those postcards you get of the water in the Caribbean. I'd never believed that color really existed in nature. And suddenly here it was, in these eyes that were looking directly at me.

"Hi," I said. (I mean, if the phone's ringing you've at least got to pick it up, right?)

We shook hands and introduced ourselves. His name was Kyle Bennett.

"Dan Thibodeau," Kyle said and gave me a warm, friendly smile. "How many Dan Thibodeaus could there be? You know, we've already met. Many years ago."

"We *did?*" I took another look at his eyes, but nothing came back to me.

"I'm afraid I don't recall meeting you," I told him, and Kyle tried to refresh my memory: it was at a party in the Back Bay, summer, twelve years ago. I considered faking it, giving him a sudden big knowing *ah-ha, of course.* Instead, looking first at Mr. Megabucks, who didn't seem to be catching on, and then at Kyle—oh, those eyes! the Germans say *die Augen!*—I said, "I'm terribly flattered that you've remembered me all these years."

"How could I forget?" Kyle laughed. "I just took one look at those cute Clark Gable ears and knew it was you." He gave my left ear a little affectionate tug. "I remember," Kyle continued, "that you were dating someone pretty seriously at the time."

That would have been James. Next spring he and I will celebrate thirteen years together, and the summer I met Kyle—at whose party *was* it?—James and I were very much in love.

"Yes," I said. "James and I are still together."

"Is he here?" Kyle asked.

I looked out, through the pantry door and into the dining room, and immediately spotted him. After twelve and a half years together, one develops a second sense for where one's lover will be at any given moment.

"Over there," I said, nodding my head in James's direction. "The guy in the navy blue sweater."

"I'd like to say hello again."

"Sure," I said, though I didn't make any moves to call James over. Instead, I kept the conversation going.

Kyle and I rehearsed the past twelve years of personal history. He told me that he was, at the time we'd met, doing graduate work at the Design School, in landscape architecture (maybe I didn't like guys who planted trees); that after he got his degree he moved out of state, first to Rhode Island, then to New Jersey; and that he'd been back in the area a couple years. "So that Derek and I could be together," he said, looking over and smiling at a man who had joined us.

I greeted Derek. He was almost as good-looking as Kyle (minus the green eyes), but he definitely was less enthusiastic about being at the party. He returned my greeting with a quick handshake and an expressionless face. I guessed he was either shy, bored, or the only Republican in the house.

"So, how do you guys come to know Jonathan and Harry?" I forced myself to look at Derek, to somehow include him in this tête-à-tête. Mr. Megabucks interrupted to excuse himself and wandered off into the crowd.

"Have a good year," I called out to him.

"We met on the boat to Provincetown this summer," Kyle said.

I could picture the whole thing: a sparkling July morning, horizon of clear blue, gulls cawing as they kept pace with the plying ship, Harry and Jonathan all aglow and summery in their seaside togs, lots of men sunning themselves on deck chairs. Harry, trying to read Kierkegaard, puts down his book, turns to Jonathan, says he's going for a stroll. At the snack bar he meets Kyle, opens the conversation. Bingo. I'll bet you the Megabucks jackpot that by the time they had docked in P-town, Harry had already invited them to Thanksgiving, too.

Then James joined us. He looked as if he knew I was charmed. There was a half-amused, half-disapproving smile on his face. James was a lieutenant in Vietnam. He still has a lieutenant's sense of command: he walks stiff and tall. He shaves close. He wears "manly" colognes. I thought he was about to deliver his Hang Up the Phone orders.

"*Hel-lo,*" he said, slow and drawn out. Lovers speak this way to each other when they're waiting for information.

"Oh, James," I said, "I want you to meet these guys." "These guys" was the information he wanted. It said: Here is a *couple*. It said: There is no danger here. It said: You can disregard whatever it is you see on my face. "This is Kyle-and-Derek," I said.

More handshakes. Derek actually warmed to James. Maybe he'd been in the army, too. Maybe former lieutenants can spot each other the way gay men can spot each other. I filled James in about our past connection with Kyle, and James apologized that he, too, couldn't remember the meeting. (Twelve years ago we were *very* much in love.)

Then Jonathan, ever the good hostess, rang a little bell and over the noise of the assembled fifty-two announced that dinner was ready. In contrast to Harry's hunky Hibernian looks, Jonathan is soft and pudgy, a state he hadn't yet fallen into when he met Harry eight years ago. This last piece of information I'd gotten directly from Harry, at last year's Thanksgiving party, after he'd had too much to drink.

"For those of you who are new this year," Jonathan began, "it's become our custom to join hands, form a circle around the table, and observe a few moments of silence, which, as Harry puts it"—and here Jonathan chuckled nervously, just as he does every year—"is a reflection of my Quaker tradition, and afterward to sing a verse of 'Now Thank We All Our God' "—and out came the little slips of paper with computer printouts of the hymn, just as they do every year—"which," Jonathan continued, "is part of Harry's more liturgical tradition."

As we positioned ourselves around the table, I thought about Jonathan's nervous references to "traditions." He has never been able to understand why the Church and all its ceremony—the smells and bells, the prayers and pomp, the singing of hymns before Thanksgiving dinner—why it's so important to Harry. Jonathan's a little intimidated by it. And resentful, too. The Church is Harry's bride, every bit as much as Jonathan is.

In the shuffling to make a circle, I found myself between James and Kyle. This was happenstance, but a happenstance I had done nothing to avoid. During the minute we kept silence—James holding my left hand, Kyle my right—I tried to think appropriate thankful thoughts. What came up, though, was just a lot of theological-type questions, which I filed away to ask Harry later on. Questions like: Why are there so many different "traditions"? And how many "brides" can someone have? And why does God allow temptation?

Harry finally broke the silence by piping up with the opening words to "Now Thank We All Our God." He pitched it low, too low for most of us, but it gave him a chance to sound butch. When we finished the verse—"With countless gifts of love/And still is ours today"—I gave Kyle's hand a little squeeze. He squeezed back.

And then commenced the foretaste of the sacrum convivium. Besides the four turkeys, there were the traditional Thanksgiving accompaniments: squash, creamed onions, cranberry sauce. And a lot of not-so-traditional dishes that were the vegetable peoples' contributions: sweet and sour eggplant, mushrooms and artichoke hearts, curried carrots, and a potato, onion, and cream dish called Janssen's Temptation that is James's and my annual offering.

The kids went first, parents following close behind, bending toward them with words of restraint: "You can't eat a *whole* drumstick, can you, Willie?" The kids didn't seem much interested in restraint.

It was all new to Kyle and Derek. Heads tilted toward each other, waiting their turn to join the food line, they whispered commentary on the passing show. Kyle seemed charmed; Derek a bit tentative. I picked up a plate and started serving myself. James was right behind me.

"Do you have any recollection of this Kyle guy?" I asked him. "This Kyle guy" was my way of telling him I was trying to hang up the phone.

"Not at all," James said, and then he smiled. "I don't remember anything about that year except you, Danny."

"They met Harry and Jonathan on the boat to P-town this summer."

James raised his eyes. When I gave him a blank stare in return, not wanting him to have the satisfaction, he kicked me under the table.

"Hey," I said, but he kicked me again and fixed me

with a look that said, Stop thinking you know what I'm thinking and *look*, soldier. His eyes directed mine over to the entrance hall.

There, just arriving, handing his yellow quilted jacket over to Harry, was this cute blond guy in his early twenties, yet another newcomer to the annual feast. He was one of those pretty, preppy types that swarm all over the campus where Harry teaches. CLIBs Harry calls them: Cute Little Irish Boys. The CLIB's favorite color must have been yellow, because underneath the yellow jacket he was wearing an expensive yellow sweater. And tight jeans. Harry seemed as pleased as curried carrots to see him. I looked back at James. He raised his eyes again.

"Hey, what do you want?" I said. "It's Thanksgiving." Meanwhile, across the table, Jonathan was helping a little girl spoon some stuffing onto her plate.

Harry and the CLIB disappeared into the pantry, then reemerged in the dining room, glasses of wine in hand. James and I went over to greet them. In Massachusetts the drinking age is twenty-one. As I took a closer look at the kid, I realized that there was a distinct possibility that Harry was breaking the law here.

"Dan and James," Harry called out to us, "I want you to meet Bry Bliss."

"Excuse me?" James said.

"Bry Bliss," Harry repeated, more slowly.

We all said hello and shook hands.

"Bry is taking my course on the Spiritual Journey," Harry informed us. "Last week, he wrote a really interesting paper on . . ." He hesitated, looking at the kid for permission to go on. "On the coming-out process as a spiritual journey."

"*Awright*," I said, raising my glass.

The kid blushed, then nervously pushed up the sleeves of his yellow sweater, first one arm and then the other. He was wearing a thin gold bracelet on one wrist.

"Bry grew up in Washington, D.C.," Harry said. He was gushing.

"Oh, really?" James said.

The kid pushed up his sleeves even higher.

I filed away another question to ask Harry: What do the blessed saints talk about at their sacrum convivium?

"Are you a vegetable person, Bry?" James asked.

The kid looked momentarily confused until Harry came to the rescue.

"Bry lives in a dorm, so I didn't bother to ask . . ." He interrupted himself and friendly-punched the kid in the shoulder. "I guess we'll just have to put him to work in some other way, right?"

We all chuckled. I turned to the table. Jonathan, still oblivious to the latest arrival, had finished filling the little girl's plate and was following her to the far parlor.

"Bry, help yourself," I said, motioning toward the table.

"Thanks," he said. He had a high, youthful voice. He and Harry picked up plates and started making their way down the table.

"*Bry?*" James whispered to me. "Bry Bliss?"

I watched as the two of them helped themselves to food. Harry kept pointing out dishes and casseroles. He was beaming with pleasure. Bry would lean over to serve himself something, then straighten up, each time giving his head a quick toss to throw his blond bangs back above his eyes.

"The *Boy* Bliss, if you ask me," James said.

"He seems like a nice kid," I said.

"God," James continued, "Harry can be so transparent sometimes."

We made our way to one of the parlors, where everyone—in chairs, on sofas, cozied into windowseats, sitting on the floor—was contentedly noshing.

"Who's your little friend, Jonathan?" I asked, walking over toward him and the little girl.

"This is Alison," Jonathan pronounced, with grammar school enunciation. He was looking at the girl, as if to remind her of what we say when we've been introduced to someone. When Jonathan is around kids, he takes on the mannerisms of a Mr. Rogers, or, for those of us over thirty-five, a Miss Frances on Ding Dong School. "Alison, this is my friend Dan. Can you say hi?"

Alison looked at me, silent and doubtful.

"And who's Harry's little friend?" James said, casting his eyes back into the dining room. Jonathan looked up. Harry was feeding The Boy a slice of turkey.

"Oh," Jonathan said. "That's just one of Harry's students." He shook his head and let out another one of his nervous little chuckles. "You know Harry." He got up and made his way to the dining room, leaving me with Alison. Apparently Ding Dong School was over.

I tried to make chitchat with Alison, but she was still skeptical and wouldn't respond except to let out a perfunctory yes or no to each question I handed her. (She and Derek would have gotten along famously.) She kept glancing into the dining room, at Harry and Jonathan and The Boy. I looked, too. They were chatting away, happy, it seemed, to be together. At least at the heavenly banquet that's what they'd be. But here on earth, in this fallible, frustrated flesh, who knows what they were.

I dropped the small talk with Alison and started to work on my plate of food, occasionally casting a glance into the other parlor, where Kyle and Derek were eating. At one point Kyle looked over at me, winked and smiled. Then he put his hand on Derek's knee and gave it a little rub. In the dining room Jonathan and Harry continued to talk to The Boy. I ate, and watched.

(A woman came into the bank last week, wanting to withdraw all her savings. Over six thousand dollars. She wanted cash. In such circumstances, we're supposed to get the bank manager's approval, but something reckless in me just said, Do it. It *was* reckless, and it might have cost me my job. But sometimes it's fun to break the rules. The influence of all those years studying German Romanticism, I guess. James said that in the army that kind of behavior is called insubordination and it gets you court martialed. I said, that's why I never joined the army.)

By four o'clock, when it was apparent that all the guests had eaten as much as they wanted, and it was beginning to grow dark, the buffet was cleared away and the dessert people set out their contributions. This year's offerings included English trifle, poppyseed cake, toffee cake, frosted brownies called chocolate orgasms, and pies in the three traditional flavors: pumpkin, mince, and apple.

The kids, who had been hovering around the table ever since the desserts started appearing, went first again, and again—Ah, youth!—they threw restraint to the winds. When it came my turn, I took a slice of pumpkin, a slice of mince, and a chocolate orgasm. I started to reach for an oatmeal cookie, but James, who was next to me in line, pulled back my arm.

"Danny . . ." he said.

I broke the cookie in half and put one piece on his dessert plate. "How's that?" I asked. Kyle and Derek were right behind us. I turned to Kyle and said, "Sometimes it's hard to hang up the phone."

He gave me an accommodating but uncomprehending smile. I began to explain. "It's an expression James and I . . ." but James poked his finger into my back.

"Why don't we all sit down?" James suggested.

With our dessert plates, the four of us made our way to the quieter of the double parlors. (Guests had begun to leave.) We took seats, James and I on the sofa, Derek in an easy chair, Kyle on the floor next to the coffee table. I tried to read the body language in this arrangement.

We talked about the desserts. Common opinion: yum. We talked about our jobs. Common opinion: we like our jobs. We talked about Jonathan and Harry. Common opinion: they are nice guys. We talked about our relationships. We did not offer opinions about our relationships; we stuck to facts: how we met, where we live, that sort of thing.

"Twelve and a half years," Kyle said. "You guys should be congratulated."

"Thank you," James said.

"I still can't believe you remembered me," I said. "I really hope we can stay in touch this time." I tried to catch Derek's reaction, but he remained unreadable.

"I do, too," Kyle said. He reached for his wallet and pulled out a business card. "Here, this has both my work number and our home number on it." He placed the card on the coffee table.

Just then Harry came into the parlor proffering a tray of champagne flutes. "Champagne, guys?" he asked. Directly behind him was The Boy Bliss holding aloft, one in each hand, two bottles of Asti, which he clutched by the neck.

"Who's that?" Kyle whispered, bending toward me.

"One of Harry's . . ." But I didn't quite know how to finish the sentence. "A student at Harry's college," I said.

Harry put the tray down on the coffee table. The bottles were still corked, but now The Boy, handing one to Harry, grasped the other tightly between his legs and eased out the cork, which suddenly shot with a pop, releasing—*Ach, die Jugend!*—a foamy outpouring of Asti Spumante.

Kyle and I took up our champagne flutes and held them out over the coffee table for The Boy to fill. The glasses touched; our fingers brushed. Asti was spilling over everything: the carpet, the table, our hands.

Then Jonathan scurried in, a pompom of paper towels in his hand. "Harry," he scolded, "be careful. This isn't our house you know." He daubed at the carpet.

"Hand me some," said James, and he, too, began to wipe up the mess on the table. I watched him take up Kyle's card, fold it in two, and stick it into his pants pocket. Meanwhile, The Boy continued to pour.

Kyle and I clinked glasses. The scene was beginning to feel like the climax in a French farce when all the players—in this case Harry and Jonathan, Kyle and Derek, James and I, and the femme fatale—are brought together for the final, frothy confrontation scene.

My friend Carlos, the one in New York, would have

been proud of me right then, because I was imagining lots of terrific alternatives to the one that was actually unfolding before us.

My favorite: Harry and Jonathan suddenly explode in a nasty scene, a real bitch-fest, over The Boy Bliss. "Enough!" Jonathan announces, abandoning his long-suffering, hostessy ways. In the midst of the ensuing hubbub—words flying, tears flowing, guests scurrying—Kyle and I are jostled onto the sofa, where we . . .

In fact, what actually happened was this:

Derek, casually looking over at Kyle (a gesture I recognized), suggested that it was time for them to go. And next thing I knew, we were all standing, saying our good-byes, repeating our intentions of getting together.

"I'm so glad you guys all got a chance to meet," Harry told me, taking the opportunity to put his arm around The Boy, a move that was, apparently, supposed to look like part of the general bonhomie of the moment. "We thought you'd like each other."

The Boy stood there, virtually encased in Harry's grasp, holding the empty bottle of Asti.

"It was nice to meet you, Dan," he said, shaking my hand. It was the first time all afternoon he had spoken more than two words to me. Then he turned to the others and, one by one, shook hands with them, too, saying each person's name in turn. "James. Kyle. Derek."

I saw how anxious he was to please—not just Harry, but all of us, the adults in his midst.

"It was nice to meet you, Bry," I said, catching his eye and smiling. Suddenly I wanted to please him, too, wanted to tell him he was doing fine, that it was all going to be fine. I don't know how I knew that—wouldn't it be nice if you could be that certain about winning Mega-bucks?—but that's how I felt, seeing him so awkward and eager, in his tight jeans and his beautiful yellow sweater, this kid from Washington, D.C., with a freshman paper on the spiritual journey and a forlorn bottle of Asti in his hand.

Coats were fetched (James sent me upstairs this time). More good-byes were said. Bry started collecting the champagne flutes and brought them into the kitchen. I watched Kyle shaking hands with my lover and tried to recall what it had felt like to be so in love once, that hanging up the phone on all others had been easy. Everything was going to be fine, that's what it had felt like.

"I'll call you," I assured Kyle.

When Harry opened the door—it's a grand paneled oak door—I saw that the evening had already lowered and that it had started to rain. Kyle pulled up the collar of his coat, and he and Derek dashed out into the wet night. I saw him put his arm around Derek's waist. With his back still toward us, he waved good-bye.

The four of us who remained at the door turned away, each at his own pace: Jonathan first, exclaiming, "It's feeling like winter"; then James, with that efficient military precision of his; and finally, together, Harry and me. I put my arm around his shoulder.

Kyle's card has been tucked away in a file box of address cards that James and I keep by the telephone. My guess is that James will let it be forgotten, that I'll be the one to pull it out—at Christmastime when I set us to the task of addressing greeting cards. (I always send out three times as many as James.)

"James," I'll say, "why don't we get together with Kyle and Derek?" Then James will give me that look, something between amusement and suspicion, and he'll dredge out the old refrain: Hang up the phone, Dan.

"But . . ." I'll say. In German the word is *aber*, which somehow has always seemed gentler to me, less importunate.

As Harry and I walked back into the dining room, my arm still around his shoulder, I pulled him in a little closer.

"*Aber weisst du wie Liebe tut?*"

"But . . . do you know . . ." He was trying to come up with a translation. "Sorry, Dan, I did just enough German to pass my comprehensives."

"But do you know," I said, helping him out, "*wie Liebe tut*—what love does, what love's about?"

"Ah, *wie Liebe tut*," he said.

"Harry," I told him, "I've got lots of questions for you."

"You've started with a good one," he said. He put his arm around my waist.

We had reached the dining room table. A few of the remaining guests were cleaning up. A mess of pie plates and cookie platters lay spread before us, crumbs and jelly stains and chocolate smears dotting the table cloth. From one of the dessert dishes, Harry picked up an abandoned brownie, broke it in half and fed me part.

"So what's another question?" he said.

I took the other half of the brownie and fed him, too. The Asti was beginning to get to me.

"This sacrum convivium," I said, the sweet, dark taste of chocolate still in my mouth. "This banquet of bliss you keep telling me about."

We tipped our heads toward each other.

"What about it, Dan?"

"Who'll be there?" I said.

Even amidst the bustle of the table clearers, we had created a quiet, intimate space for ourselves.

"All of us," Harry said.

"Kyle?" I asked.

Harry looked at me, his eyes suddenly wide with understanding. If it's possible to smirk and look affectionately at the same time, that's what he gave me right then.

"Oh, assuredly." He paused, then added, "And Derek and James, too."

"Spoilsport," I said, disengaging myself from his hold.

Harry laughed. "*All* of us, Dan."

"Well, how about The Boy Bliss?" I asked.

"Who?"

"The Boy Bliss," I said, returning the smirky-affectionate look he'd given me.

"Bry?" Harry chuckled. "Yup, I guess he'll be there,

too, won't he?" He laughed again. "Right there with Jonathan."

I glanced back at the table. Tucked under the flower arrangement was one of the slips of paper with the words to "Now Thank We All Our God." I picked it up.

"Harry," I said, folding the paper in half and slipping it into my pocket, "next year pitch it a little higher, will you?"

He clasped me on the shoulder again. "Sure, Dan."

"And one more thing, Harry. Next year? Can James and I be something besides vegetable people?"

ACCEPTABLE

JANICE AND I HAD
been friends since senior year in college when we met in
feminist lit. I remember deliberately sitting down next to
her the first day of class, my way of saying that whoever
she was—with those arms bangled in bracelets, the oversized earrings, that chaos of frizzled orange hair—whoever
she was, it was fine with me. I wasn't the kind of guy, I
wanted her to know, who'd be threatened by all that visual
turbulence.

She was vocal, too: the first one to ask a question—
two minutes into the course—the first one to challenge the
professor, the first to use the word *lesbian* in one of the class
discussions. She wasn't a lesbian, as I came to find out, but
she argued vehemently, in fact brilliantly, on their behalf.
Janice always spoke her mind. And even though I was
sometimes the recipient of her feminist critiques, I grew to
respect her integrity, the way she put herself out there,

never letting up until she'd convinced you with her wise and strident passion.

Later, when we found out that both of our post-graduation plans included fleeing smalltown Pennsylvania and moving to Boston—she to pursue a master's degree in chemistry, I to work at a gallery on Newbury Street—we decided to share an apartment together. It was a sunny, and cheap, two-bedroom in the North End, reputedly the safest neighborhood in the city because of all the Italian mamas who would sit by their windows, keeping an eye on the streets below. Janice still rents there, but by that first winter it became pretty clear to me that I was going to need my own space. I had started dating guys (a fact I thought Janice didn't know), and so I figured she would want me to clear out.

"Brian, you asshole, what are you trying to prove?" she said the morning we sat down and had our talk.

I couldn't believe how hard she took it. It wasn't that she felt slighted—we'd never been lovers. And it certainly wasn't that I'd finally admitted to her I was gay. She said she'd known since that first day in class. So the anger in her voice: well, it surprised me, and I told her so.

"The point, Brian," she said, "is that you're trying to tell me what I need. You're saying I need space from you." I remember her waving her arms as if to describe a huge volume, the sleeves of her orange kimono flapping, a clove cigarette between her fingers. "Don't you realize I was giving *you* space—and all the time you needed—to get comfortable with yourself? You jerk!" Her voice was punctuated with frustration. And then she said it: "Real women—real *people*, Brian—you're still not ready for them, are you?"

Rather feebly I told her, "It's just that I need to be alone." And by the end of that week I'd found another apartment.

In the eight months between my moving out and Laura's coming into our lives, Janice was accepted into a Ph.D.

program and I switched from gallery tending to a typing job at the university library. Janice thought it was very advanced of me to take work as a secretary, until I told her that I was actually the overseer of an all-female typing pool.

Despite this, and our going separate ways, we continued to be friends. Better ones, in fact, since the gay stuff was now on the table. Mainly I'd see Janice on the Saturdays when we went to the clubs together. Because we're attracted to different types—for me the rebellious angel look; for Janice swarthy mustachioed Middle Eastern guys (many of whom seemed to find her hair and clothing irresistible)— we sometimes made a game of scouting for each other. There was one club in particular, Leporello's near Fenway Park, where we went a lot.

Then one Monday night, late in August, Janice called up to say she'd gotten a new roommate, a woman this time.

"After eight months of happy solitude, you're going to try to live with someone again?"

"There you go again, Brian," she said. "Assuming things for me. I've always wanted to have a roommate. It's just that most people find me too intense." She paused. "Too *real*, Brian."

"Go easy, Janice," I said. "I've had a bad weekend."

She explained how she'd placed a ROOMMATE WANTED ad in the paper. Laura—that was the new roommate's name—called up, arranged for them to meet, agreed to move in.

"What's she like?" I asked rather perfunctorily. I was still preoccupied with thoughts of my own: the guy I'd been seeing for three weeks had given me the brushoff. When Janice began the story, I thought she was teasing again.

Imagine it, then. Janice was trying out new makeup when the door buzzer sounded: orange lipstick, kohl around the eyes, red eye shadow. She went down to answer, and there was Laura, wearing granny glasses and a pretty skirt-and-blouse combination. "Some little midwestern frock," Janice told me with a giggle. "I liked her immediately." She gave Laura a tour of the apartment, after which the two of them sat down and got to talking, splitting a can of cola. (Janice had offered Scotch, but Laura declined.)

"She comes from Davenport. Iowa, Brian. She has a degree in biblical studies from some Lutheran college, and a master's in library science. And guess where she's taken a job? At the university. She's going to be working with you!" Janice giggled again, a gleeful, impish laugh.

"What are you setting me up for?" I said.

"She moved in yesterday," Janice continued, ignoring my question. "I thought she was coming in the morning, and when she didn't show up I figured she'd gotten cold feet. But no, it was just that she'd gone to church. It was Sunday, you see. I tried calling you up to see if you could help us unload . . ."

"I was on a date, Janice."

"I tried calling you Saturday night, Brian."

"It was a long date."

"I thought you said it was a bad weekend."

"Janice."

"So when can you come over to meet her?"

"I'll meet her at the library," I said.

Two days later, Laura started work. I spotted her immediately. She looked like what we used to call in that lit class a prime candidate for a major feminist overhaul. In short, the demure librarian type: the granny glasses, a pageboy haircut, a perky jumper. I tried to avoid her but, after lunch, she came by the typing division to introduce herself.

"I guess we'll be seeing a lot of each other," she said. There was a deep resonance in her voice that I hadn't expected. It didn't seem to fit her, and I suspected she was covering up for shyness.

"Yes, here at the library, our paths are bound to cross," I told her. I tried to look busy and inconvenienced.

"Well, maybe at the apartment, too," she offered. "I mean, Janice tells me you come over a lot."

She was ruffling a stack of cataloging cards with her thumb.

"I wouldn't say a lot. We're just friends, you know."
Laura blushed, so I added, "I'm pretty busy most evenings."
That seemed the end of it. I mean most women I know
would have picked up the signals, but Laura kept staring
at me, getting redder and redder in the face. "I'm gay," I
said.

"Oh, I know that," she said, the deep resonance coming
back into her voice. "Janice already told me."

"You two seem to be getting along pretty well," I said.

"We are."

"Well, you'll soon find out that Janice can be pretty
weird at times."

Laura laughed. "That's what she says about you."

"What have you done?" I asked Janice on the phone that
night. "I mean, you two are like night and day."

"You know, you and I are like night and day, too,
Brian. And that's never stopped us."

"What do you mean?" I said. "We're not that different."
It annoyed me, the way she was trying to put us into different camps.

"Brian, honey, it's okay, you know, that we're
different."

"Look, Janice," I said, "I know you. You'll go out of
your mind."

"My God," she said, "that's so sweet. You're trying to
protect me, aren't you?"

Throughout that fall I tried to keep my interactions with
Laura strictly on the professional level. She was pleasant
enough, but somehow she put me on guard.

Twice a day, Laura would bring over a batch of cards
to be typed. The university library had impossible stan-
dards. Even the preprinted Library of Congress cards
weren't deemed good enough. The head catalogers were
always making fussy modifications, so most of the LC cards
that accompanied the books had to be altered or completely

retyped. Cards to be changed came first to me, to be distributed among the three women in the typing pool.

Despite my businesslike manner with Laura, the typists—May, Steph, and Phyllis, all in their mid to late fifties—soon decided something was up. Whenever Laura brought me a pack of cards, I noticed that we were being watched. As Laura and I went over the changes, one or another of them would stop their own work, as if to double-check something. But I could tell they were keeping an eye on the two of us.

May was the least discreet. Everytime Laura passed by her desk, May would slowly remove her glasses, which were attached to a black cord, and let them fall onto her bosom—I think this was meant to be taken as her resting her eyes—and then she'd tip her head slowly toward the aisle, enough to watch me accepting the cards from Laura. She was looking for a smile, some sign that things were "happening" between us. And when I did smile at Laura, May would make poker-faced eye contact with Phyllis or Steph, as if to say, See, I told you so.

It surprised me, but Laura soon picked up on May's interest, too. One day, as she handed over a stack of cards, she rapped her fingers on the top one. I looked down. There, in perfect Library of Congress format, it read:

McLaughlin, May.
   My secret life as an office matchmaker.
Boston, Love Publishing Co., 1986.
   xxii, 175 p. 24 cm.
   1. Courtship—Rituals and mores—U.S.
I. McLaughlin, May. II. Title.

I looked back at Laura. She was biting her lip to keep from laughing. Then I started chuckling, too, and that set Laura off. She couldn't stop, which, of course, was just what May wanted to see, and that made Laura laugh all the harder.

∎   ∎   ∎

"It's a wonder they're interested in seeing us together," I told Laura at lunch that day. She had joined me in the library cafeteria and was unpacking her brown paper bag. It was soft and wrinkled as if she had reused it several days in a row.

"How so?" she asked, taking out an apple, carrot strips, and a sandwich wrapped in wax paper.

"They're all Catholics, those three, and that makes me acceptable, and you not. It doesn't matter that I haven't been to church in years. That's the way Catholics are. Always ready to see some sort of secret bond. They assume you're one of them forever. Apparently, they're willing to make an exception with you. Maybe it's because you've got that degree in biblical studies. Big of them, isn't it?"

Laura started laughing skeptically. I cut her off:

"You don't think May made it her business to find out all about you? Ever since I started working here she's been looking out for my welfare, especially my amatory welfare." I looked hard at Laura. "But I've been doing just fine without her, thank you very much."

Laura looked down at her carrot sticks.

"With me," I continued, "May acts like a cross between Sister Superior and a Match Game emcee. Somehow she's gotten it into her mind that I need taking care of. She's so fond of me she can't even see what's really going on. I mean, here I am, her supervisor for Christ sake . . ." (I threw in the swear for shock value. It was easy to feel that Laura needed shaking up.) "I can't even type, and yet I've been hired to tell *her* what to do. Why? Because I'm male? Because I've got a college degree? Because I know how to come across during a job interview? I've capitalized on every prerogative of my sex and class, Laura." She looked up at me. "Don't you see?" I asked her. "By rights, May should hate my guts, but here she is treating me like a good little altar boy."

"You're a nice person, Brian," Laura said, encouragingly.

I scoffed. "Does Janice tell you *that*, too?"

"It's what I tell Janice," she said.

On the Saturday nights when Janice and I went to the clubs, our evenings always began the same way: no matter what time I showed up, I'd have to wait for Janice while she finished getting ready. I'd sit on her bed and watch while she ironed a blouse at her desk, changed her makeup three times, rummaged through her boxes of bracelets. Janice was always at her worst in the hours before a night at the clubs. It was hard to believe she was such a brilliant and meticulous chemist.

After Laura moved in, the waiting ritual changed. Now Laura would "entertain" me in the living room while we waited for Janice to get ready. I'd sit in the easychair, Laura on the sofa, and we'd make polite conversation, trying to ignore the noise coming from Janice's bedroom. We could hear her crashing about, slamming drawers, running the sink, swearing. I felt like a junior high kid talking to his date's mom. As far as I knew, Laura never went out on weekends.

"So, how do you like it here in the big, bad city?" I asked Laura one Saturday night.

Before she had a chance to answer, Janice yelled from the bedroom, "Brian, can it. We already know how tough you are!"

Laura laughed.

"There are so many opportunities here," she said, sounding like the Chamber of Commerce.

"Like what?"

She told me she had signed up to teach a poetry workshop to some prisoners at the Charles Street Jail. "It's an outreach program my church is sponsoring."

The idea of Laura working in a prison seemed ludicrous.

"I don't know, Laura," I said, trying to sound as if I were weighing the pros and cons. Secretly I thought she was crazy. "A prison is kind of a dangerous place, don't you think? Teaching poetry to hardened criminals . . . I mean, most of these guys have one thing on their mind, and it's not Shakespeare."

Janice came out of her bedroom, fastening a huge brass earring.

"And what's that, Brian?" she said. "What is it that most of these guys have on their mind?"

Laura laughed again, a heartier laugh this time. She seemed to take great delight in the way Janice would try to bait me.

"Look, she's a nice kid and all," I told Janice on our way to Leporello's, "but she makes me nervous. At work, she gives me these looks." I looked at Janice to see if she understood. "I mean, she knows what gay means, right?"

"Of course she does."

It was early December, tinsel time. May, Phyllis, and Steph had already decorated the typing room with glittery metallic garlands that they stored, wrapped in plastic shopping bags, in their desk drawers during the rest of the year. Soon they'd bring out more seasonal paraphernalia: a little desktop tree (the kind you can plug in to make the candles glow and bubble), then daily baked goods from home, and finally presents. Last year they collectively gave me a scarf from Lord and Taylor. As Janice and I left the subway and made our way through Kenmore Square, I tucked that scarf tight into my leather jacket.

"Janice, you aren't in love with her or anything, are you? I mean, you two haven't become lovers, right?"

"Brian." She was using that combination of annoyance and incredulity she had so often mustered in fem. lit. "Sometimes I wonder if you're just a big fake."

"And what's *that* supposed to mean? 'Big fake'?" Janice's attacks never failed to irk me, they were so on the mark. But this time, she'd frightened me as well.

"It means that you try to come across like some big

feminist-identified liberal homosexual, but you can't even fathom the idea that Laura and I might be friends."

We were crossing a street. Janice grabbed my arm and stopped us halfway across. "She wants to be your friend, too, Brian. Do you hear that? You don't need to pull away."

A car honked at us. Janice pulled me across the street. We walked another block before she spoke again.

"You're afraid of her, aren't you?" she said.

"Come on, Janice."

"It's the same old shit, Brian. You're always running away from real women."

"Not that again. Come on, Janice. Have I ever run away from you?" She gave me that what-do-you-think look. "Listen," I told her, "when I moved out, I was *not* running away!"

We had reached the line outside Leporello's. People were huddled together, stomping their feet, trying to keep warm. A group of men, a couple of whom looked familiar, was singing Christmas carols rather boisterously. We added ourselves to the back of the line.

"She's seeing a guy, Brian," Janice told me.

"Good for her," I said. I pretended to be distracted by the cold and the singing. The line moved up. It was clear Janice wasn't going to volunteer any more information. "So what's he like?" I asked, just to satisfy her.

"If you want to know the truth, he's a lot like you," Janice said. "Mid twenties, cleancut, over-educated, and scared shitless."

The guy in front of us turned around, as if to verify Janice's description. He was blond, early twenties, and very good looking.

"Well, maybe I should seduce him away from her," I said, looking straight at the blond. He smiled at me.

The following Monday, Laura didn't show up for work. All day I felt May's eyes on me, trying to read my mood. She wanted me to give her a sad lovelorn look, but I refused. I wasn't even going to accept any of the homemade fruitcake she'd brought, but then I realized that this would make me seem sad. So at coffeebreak I helped myself to a big slice and chatted it up with the three typists. The more May tried to read my looks, the more I affected the festive holiday mood.

When I got home, I called Janice. She told me that when she had returned from our date Saturday night Laura was not in the apartment and had not shown up until very late Sunday.

"So things are perking with the boyfriend," I said.

"Things are definitely *not* perking with the boyfriend," Janice said. "They broke up. And where the hell were you yesterday? I've been trying to call you since yesterday morning."

"Janice, I'm an adult. A cleancut, over-educated one, remember? Apparently a lot of guys find this appealing. Remember the blond in front of us in line?"

"She wants to talk to you, Brian."

"Why me?" I said.

"I'm beginning to wonder that myself," Janice said.

I ignored her sarcasm.

"Getting hurt is good for her," I said.

"So sympathetic, Brian."

"Look, I'm sympathetic," I said, "but they were obviously wrong for each other. When Laura comes up with as many wrong numbers as I have . . ."

Janice interrupted me. "Yeah, then what, Brian?"

I'd never been in Laura's room before. I'd never wanted to see it. It turned out worse than I'd expected: all Aunty Em calico. Flounces on the curtains and bedspread, braided rugs, a teddy bear on her pillow, a small bookcase with neatly arranged volumes of poetry and theology. On her desk—it was painted a cheery, enamelled yellow—was a photograph in a silver frame of a homey-looking couple standing hand in hand. The man was paunchy and wore a baseball cap; the woman was in a beige pant suit of the

J. C. Penney variety. Her parents. Above the desk she had neatly pinned a poster, a Raggedy Ann-like waif with big eyes and a blueberry-stained face, standing amidst a clutter of pots and pans. The caption read: HAVE PATIENCE, THE LORD ISN'T FINISHED WITH ME YET. Laura was sitting in her rocking chair wrapped in a down comforter.

"Season's greeting," I said.

She looked up and gave me a brave little smile. There were traces of Janice's red eyeshadow on her eyelids—under those granny glasses, no less—leftover makeup, I gathered, from her date with the erstwhile boyfriend.

"You were really hooked, weren't you?" I said. "I mean, Jesus, Laura, that eyeshadow."

A blush of embarrassment came over her face. She brought a hand up to her eyes, smoothed her fingers over an eyelid, then brought them down again, to see for herself.

"That bad, huh?" She was chuckling, but I could tell it was just more of that bravery she kept wanting to show me.

"Here, let me," I said. I squatted down in front of the rocker and removed her glasses. Then, cupping her chin in my left hand, I wiped off the hideous color with a tissue I pulled from a box at her feet.

The perfume from her hair surprised me, too. It wasn't the sugary artificial aroma of cheap shampoo, the kind that goes with calico curtains. It was an expensive fragrance, again one of Janice's.

"Take it easy," I told her. "No one is worth all this."

"I'm sorry," she said.

"Whatever for? Laura, you haven't done anything you need to be sorry for."

"It's just that . . ." She bit her lip, but the tears started coming anyway. I stood up.

"Look, Laura," I said, "maybe it's time to reassess what you're doing here. I mean, you've tried everything, and it hasn't worked, has it? Not this city, not the guy . . ." I hesitated, then added, "Not me."

She looked up, wiping the tears from her cheeks. I met her eyes with a hard, unflinching stare.

"Maybe you're looking in the wrong places," I suggested.

"No more so than you, Brian." She had already regained her composure.

"What's that supposed to mean?" It was like a litany, my always asking these women what they meant. "Laura, you've got to get this: I'm gay. You're not going to convert me."

She chuckled again: her way of telling me she'd gotten that long ago. Then she added, "Brian, you're trying so hard to prove something."

"Laura," I said.

"Janice thinks you're trying to hide how scared you are . . ."

"Oh sure, of women, right? Of *real* women. Is that what she's been telling you?" But before Laura had a chance to answer, I cut her off. "Look, don't you go pulling that stuff on me, too. Just because I like sleeping with guys doesn't mean I'm afraid of women. I like women, Laura. I respect them, I want to see them liberated from all the crap that men have . . ."

"But what about me?"

"What about you?"

"Do you like *me?*"

I hesitated. What would this commit me to?

"Of course I like you, Laura. You're a very good person. I mean, if anything"—I snickered—"it should be me asking you that question. I mean, sometimes I'm not a very likable guy, you know."

She didn't say anything, just kept to her rocker. But a smile now came to her face. I handed her back her granny glasses.

"Look, Laura, I don't need what you're offering."

"And what's that, Brian? What exactly is it I'm offering you that you don't need?" That deep resonance was back in her voice, mixed with a little playfulness. She didn't put on her glasses.

"Laura, just don't go falling in love with me, okay?"

"But what if I have already?" she said. She looked to be enjoying this now, just as Janice always looked to enjoy her teasing bouts with me.

I might have left right then and there, removed myself from her room and not come back. But wouldn't Janice have loved that, I thought. Running away again, Brian, she'd tell me later.

"Laura, you can't," I insisted.

"Why not?"

I shook my head. "You just cannot fall in love with a guy like me."

She got up from the rocker. The comforter fell away to the floor. She was wearing a nightie.

"Is there some law against it?" she said. She was chuckling harder now.

"Look, why are you doing this?" I asked, more out of exasperation than anger. The situation was absurd—as absurd as anything I'd ever been in—which is probably what set me off chuckling, too. It began as an involuntary fluttering in my stomach. "Laura, this is ridiculous." We were standing, facing each other, about two feet apart.

"It's not *that* ridiculous," she said. And that set us both to laughing even more: the way she said "*that* ridiculous."

"We can't love each other," I told her. "It's absurd."

"Oh, Brian." There was the most happy amusement in her voice.

"Where the heck is Janice?" I said. I was trying to sound annoyed, but I kept getting tripped up on my own nervous giggling.

"Heck if I know." Laura barely managed to get the words out she was laughing so hard now.

"Hey, quit it," I said, not so much to her as to my own unruly stomach.

"I can't," she blurted out. As she laughed, her nightie

shook. There we were in this faceoff: she in that flouncy cream-colored nightgown with little blue roses; I in black jeans and my leather jacket. "I can't, Brian. I think you're so . . ." Her face was flushed. "You're so . . . sexy."

And then we had our heads on each other's shoulders, laughing uncontrollably in each other's arms. I didn't want to hold her too close, her body was that delicate, that foreign—her fine hair in my eyes and lips, the surprise of her shoulder blades through that nightgown—but I did, closer even than I'd ever held Janice, and we laughed and squeezed each other tight, not being able to do anything else.

"And I think you, Laura, are so . . ." There were tears running down my face I was laughing so hard. "So . . ."

Quickly, she disengaged herself from me, put on her granny glasses, crossed her eyes, and stuck out her tongue.

"So *this?*" she said. Then we burst into laughter again.

"Oh God," I said. "Oh God." My stomach was in pain.

"Brian," she called out to me. It was as if we were both drowning in an ocean of splendid silliness.

At last I calmed down enough to catch my breath. "Okay, okay," I said. I held her out at arm's length, trying to steady both of us. We were flushed and panting. I took a few deep breaths—Laura did, too—then rearranged her glasses, which had fallen askew on her nose. I was looking directly into her eyes.

"Well then, dear Laura, Merry Christmas, whoever you are."

I had never noticed the color before. They were hazel.

ENROLLMENT

Everyone says
that my second cousin Monica's was the first mixed marriage
in the family. Technically, this isn't true. Not if you count
all the cousins in the previous generation—my first cousins—who married non-Italians. There was Angela, who
married a Greek, and Denise, who married an Irishman,
and Robert, who married a girl of indeterminate extraction.
(My grandmother always referred to her as *l'inglese*, "the
Englishwoman," a phrase that delivered more disdain than
you might imagine.) In the late fifties, my oldest cousin,
Johnny, even became engaged to a Protestant, though apparently that doesn't count either, because she converted
some months before the wedding. So what the family
means, then, by mixed marriage is this: that Monica
Scarpetto—the daughter of two nice Italian parents—married a Jew.

This was two years ago, and when Monica and David
announced their engagement, though there were raised eye-

brows and whispers about how they would raise the children, everyone was essentially happy for them. "Hey, Nicky, times change," my mother declared, as if I were the one who still needed convincing. And then she proceeded to tell me, for the umpteenth time, about the "antique days," when all a girl had to do was smoke to become persona non grata with the family.

We'd all come to expect this marriage. Monica and David had been dating since college, and, by the time they graduated and were out in the work world—David as a financial analyst, Monica as a buyer for a large department store in Boston—he was showing up at all the major family gatherings. It didn't matter where we got together: at Monica's parents' or Aunt Carmella's or my mother's. Whatever the occasion—Fourth of July, Thanksgiving, Christmas even—David would be there, well-dressed, well-mannered, and charming. He praised everyone's cooking, told appreciative stories of the summer he traveled in Europe—Italy was his favorite country, he said—and, but only when asked, gave sound, conservative advice about financial investment.

You could tell, Aunt Carmella said, summing up all the evidence, that David came from a good family, which, as she later explained in one of those tête-à-têtes that aunts in my family are always having with me, was as important to Jews as to Christians.

For our part, we learned to wish David "Happy Hanukkah" at Christmas time and "Happy Passover" at Easter. And when they announced their engagement, my father even congratulated them with a "Mazel tov," chuckling at himself afterward the way one often does after using someone else's language for the first time.

If David's good upbringing—his *educazione*—made him eminently acceptable to the women in our family, what made him acceptable to the men was the fact that he was also a "regular guy." After dinner, he would join my uncles around the TV to watch football or basketball. And when the dining room table was finally cleared—dessert and coffee, nuts and fruit and *confetti* being an hourlong affair after the games—he would sit with the men for several rounds of cards and Sambuccas.

I was always the first to leave these parties. Even if it was Christmas. Even if it was my parents who were hosting. There we'd be, maybe fifteen or twenty of us—aunts, uncles, cousins—a kind of Italian Bob Cratchit and family, full of holiday *festevolezza*. I'd stay through the sweets and coffee and then, just before the card-playing got going, make my excuses: tests to correct (I taught school then) or other friends, perhaps old acquaintances from college, to whom I'd promised a drop-in call. After all, it was the holidays. None of this was a lie, though there were stronger, less explainable reasons why I wasn't staying.

"Eh, Mr. Russo," my mother would call out to me, throwing up a hand, like a jilted soprano. In our family's personal mythology, Mr. Russo was another person from the antique days, a family acquaintance—a *cumpare*—who was forever having to be somewhere else. According to my mother, you could be enjoying a cup of coffee and a nice conversation with Mr. Russo when all of a sudden he'd put down his cup and announce that he had an appointment elsewhere. "He never stayed in one place for more than ten minutes," Aunt Carmella added.

Everyone who remembered Mr. Russo called him a "curious" man. He might as well not have been Italian, I was led to believe, for all the regard he gave to the social customs of his own people. And now they were telling me—but jokingly, of course—that I was the new Mr. Russo. Aunt Carmella once even explained to David who Mr. Russo was and why it was such an apt name for me. She wanted him to understand everything about being a part of our family.

Mr. Russo was long dead and buried before I came on the scene in the mid-fifties. But in time I came to have my own speculations about his odd behavior. Speculations I shared only with my "roommate" Josh, the other—but un-acknowledged—Jew in the family.

For Monica and David's wedding, my parents offered to buy me a new suit. "So that you make 'na bella figura," my mother told me over the phone one night. "You know bella figura—a good impression?"

This had been one of my grandmother's expressions. Since Nonna's death a few years back, my mother was more and more echoing her own mother's Old World idioms.

I told Mom that I knew bella figura. And that I hardly needed their money. At thirty-three, a math teacher turned computer programmer, I was doing fine.

"We just want to make sure you look great," Mom said. "We're proud of our son." She paused, then added, "And this time don't you dare do like Mr. Russo. You stay for the whole reception. I want several dances with you."

As it turned out, everyone—Jews and Christians alike—dressed to cut a good figure. And while I've never been the kind of guy who makes free with words like stunning and ravishing, that's exactly how the women, especially the women in my family, looked. It was hard not to feel proud. A lot of my cousins and aunts, even the ones in their sixties and seventies, have aged well: "because of all the olive oil," my grandmother used to claim. And, though we're not a wealthy family—florists, dry cleaners, chefs being the family professions—still the women know how to dress. At Monica's wedding I felt caught up in all the enthusiasm they had for making 'na bella figura. I wouldn't have pulled a Mr. Russo for anything. Not that day.

The ceremony took place, not in a church or temple, but in the ballroom of a swanky new hotel in Boston. Despite the little canopied pavillion under which Monica and David exchanged vows—Josh later taught me the name, hupah—the ceremony was an ecumenical affair. Monica and David had both a rabbi and a priest officiate. Apparently, it took quite a lot of doing before they were able to find two clergymen who would agree to such a service. The priest, Father Joe, was a silver-haired man in his middle fifties, the kind who had probably entered the seminary right out of college and who—I was guessing all this, trying to figure out what had brought him to this wedding—had probably, maybe during the Vietnam War, had an affair or a bout with alcoholism, or some crisis of faith, and came out of it a lot more relaxed about all the rules. In short, a guy who had come to see that love could make everything— rules, tradition, even family—irrelevant. The rabbi, too, it was reported, was sympathetic. He came from a liberal synagogue in one of the suburbs west of Boston. They were my heroes that day, even more so than Monica and David, who, I felt, didn't really know (not as well as I) what they were getting themselves into.

"Did they smash the wine glass? Did you dance the Hava Nagilah?" Josh asked me late that night when I crawled into bed. He'd had his back to me, but now he rolled over, letting me hold him in my arms.

"All of that," I told him, cuddling up close. "I wish you could've been there."

"Me too," he said.

"Eventually they'll figure out who you are," I told him. "I give them another six months. Wait till next year."

"Next year," he said, then chuckled. "Next year in Jerusalem."

It was a warm evening. We were both naked. I buried my nose in Josh's shoulder and breathed in deeply. We'd been together about a year, but I was feeling—all over again—something like that first rush of falling in love with him, the thrill of another's body, at once so alien and so familiar, being offered to me.

Last month, Monica and David had a baby, a little girl whom they named Danielle Louise (part David's family, Daniel being his grandfather; part Monica's, Louis— "Louie"—being her father's name).

"Save the twenty-fourth," my mother told me over the phone one evening in early October. "Monica's going to throw a party for the naming of the baby. She's sending you an invitation next week." In the family network, my mother is the clearinghouse for invitations. "I don't think they're going to have her baptized," she went on. "Monica's calling it a Naming Party. It's like what the Jews do for baby boys, you know, a *bar mitzvah*, except it's for a girl."

"Well, not quite," I said. "A bar mitzvah is for when the boy turns of age, like Confirmation. Josh's nephew just got bar mitzvahed."

In the two years since David and Monica's wedding, I had taken every opportunity possible of keeping Josh focused in my family's mind. I hadn't actually spelled it out for them, what kind of a relationship we had, but I knew he had come together for them—in much the same way that objects begin to come together for an infant—as a distinguishable and significant "object" in their field of vision, as the person I was sharing more than just an apartment with, as the man, in fact, who had foreshadowed David and Monica's mixed marriage by almost a year. About six months after the wedding, we had taken a big step and invited my parents over for dinner. And when Uncle Rudolph died and Josh voluntarily attended the funeral, I think that clinched it.

"Well, whatever it's called, that's what they're doing," my mother said. "I think they're inviting Josh, too." In my mother's way of talking, "I think" means "I know." I tried to imagine what kinds of conversations had occurred to bring this invitation to pass. "I guess the rabbi will be there," my mother continued. "Remember the one who married them?"

"Sure," I said.

"But no Father Joe," she told me.

"Okay," I said, trying to sound as copacetic as a pear on a plate.

"What do you think?" she asked.

"About what?"

We were each waiting for the other to go first.

"I don't know . . ." She sounded discouraged by my not taking up the ball, and I suddenly felt guilty, as if she'd asked for something and I'd refused. "I guess it would have been nice if the baby could have been baptized too, that's all."

"What about times changing?" I asked. "Isn't that what you said when they got married?"

"Oh, but you understand, don't you?" There was confusion and annoyance, and a tinge of panic, in her voice.

"Let them do what they want," I told her.

"Nicky, it's not a question of letting them do what they want." Now she sounded just plain frustrated. "It's just that it looks like Monica's giving everything to David's family and nothing to ours."

"She's inviting all of us, isn't she?"

"Sometimes," my mother said—she was laughing, but I could tell she felt exasperated with me—"sometimes I just wish I'd had a daughter. She'd understand what I'm trying to say."

The Sunday of the naming, Josh and I took the turnpike out to Monica and David's. The directions they sent us— a computer-generated map that David had printed up at work—were written as if the only places from which guests might come were the towns around route 128 or interstate 495, the circumferential highways that ringed the city. On this map, Boston existed only as an alternative directional marker—"To Boston"—somewhere off in the east, an undisclosed bull's-eye at the end of the sure, true arrow that was the Massachusetts Turnpike.

"Where *is* this place?" Josh joked as we passed the exit for Framingham.

"One of those M towns," I said. "Millis, Medfield, Middleborough, Marlborough. I don't know, they all sound alike to me."

The suburbs were not our thing. Josh and I had been renting in the South End, the gay ghetto, for three years now. We had begun to ask realtors to show us property for sale, townhouse condominiums as close to downtown as we could afford. Even Cambridge felt too rustic.

We got off at the next exit. The sky was overcast: gray and sooty white like pigeons' feathers. And although it was just after noon, the sun, a dull glowing behind the cloud cover, sat low on the horizon. Sunday afternoons in late autumn we usually spent in one of three ways: curled up on the sofa reading the paper, giving or attending a brunch, or at the gym working out.

The directions took us through an old manufacturing town and then out beyond a sprawling high school. The road became country-ish, stone walls and large old maples flanking both sides. Maybe as recently as fifteen years ago this had all been farmland. On the hill to our right and through the leafless branches of the trees, we could see the new development where Monica and David lived: one- and two-acre lots planted with large contemporary colonials.

"The next turn is ours," I told Josh. "Apple Creek Road."

He looked at me. "This isn't going to be one of those developments with names like Wisteria Way, is it?"

"Two hours," I reassured him. "I promise we'll stay just two hours."

"And then make like Mr. Russo, right?" he added, grinning.

David greeted us at the door, and we stepped into the warm, tinkly, humming world of the party. Handsomely dressed people, none of whom I recognized, were coming and going through the tiled entrance foyer, itself almost a room, decorated with furniture one might call "sharp"—all chrome, glass, and marble. Descending the staircase from the second floor, where presumably they'd gone to leave coats and freshen up, were still other guests. Everyone seemed headed for the back of the house, from which I could hear the noise of the party in progress.

ENROLLMENT

As we were unloading onto David our coats and gifts and congratulations, the doorbell rang again.

"Go on in," David told us. "I'll catch up with you guys later." He was beaming. I wondered if having a son could have made him any happier than he was at that moment.

The living room, a large, cathedral-ceilinged space with a white brick fireplace at one end, was packed. I didn't see anyone I recognized. What I had thought was to be a small family affair had turned into an enormous party. There were lots of young couples and lots of children. It was the kind of party a couple of gay men would try to be anonymous in.

"I'm going to get a drink," Josh told me and headed off to the far end of the living room where a bar, complete with hired bartender—a young man in a crisp-fitting red vest—had been set up.

As if she'd tracked me on radar, my mother now appeared.

"You're here!" she said and gave me a kiss on the cheek.

"Mom, you look terrific," I told her before she could start in on the never-seeing-me bit. She did look great. Her hair, a strawberry blond that in the last few years has emerged as her color, was done up in soft, sweeping waves. She was wearing a new cocktail dress, a bold flowered print on silk, and gold jewelry. Though I knew she'd be sixty-eight in February, she could easily have passed for fifty. I hate the pretty boys at the gym, but when Mom dresses up she makes me realize that looking great often has more to do with generosity than vanity.

"Isn't this wonderful?" she gushed, as she absent-mindedly fingered my sport coat. "Do you believe how much space they have?" She kept firing questions at me: had I been given a tour of the house? had I seen the new baby? "Look, over there." She pointed to the sofa where Aunt Carmella was cradling Danielle in her arms. "Isn't she adorable?"

In her exuberance, Mom seemed to have forgotten her dismay that this wasn't a baptism.

"Let me go over and say hello," I said, pulling her fingers off my jacket.

"Did Josh come?" she asked.

"Sure," I said. "He's here somewhere." I looked about casually, as if his whereabouts weren't that big a deal: the same casualness I tried to affect whenever I pulled a Mr. Russo.

I gave Mom a so-long-for-now kiss and made my way over to Aunt Carmella, greeting people I knew, nodding and smiling at the others. Josh, I noticed, was chatting with the bartender.

"Eh, Nicky!" said Aunt Carmella when she saw me. She's my mother's sister, but the differences between them are amazing. Aunt Carmella's eighty-one, the oldest of my grandmother's eight children. She's got the heavy, doughy figure that Mom would have if she didn't watch her weight; and the bulbous Renzulli nose, a nose my mother had re-shaped back in the fifties. "I haven't seen you in ages," Aunt Carmella scolded. "Where have you been?"

I never have a good answer to this question, not one that can do justice to both of us. As if she understood this, Aunt Carmella shifted her attention to the baby. "Look," she said.

I squatted down. Danielle's tiny face, smooth and pink, was folded up in sleep. "Isn't she adorable," I told her. It seemed ridiculous to be echoing my mother's very words, but I wanted to say the right thing. I wanted to do the right thing. I couldn't tell if I—but *who* was I to this new one? the second cousin once removed?—if I was allowed to touch Danielle, take her in my arms. Maybe that would have been too feminine, the kind of thing only men who say "stunning" and "ravishing" can get away with.

"You make a beautiful great-grandmother, Aunt Carmella." This time I used my own words.

In the past, such a statement would have been an occasion for Aunt Carmella to suggest that it was time I got married and started having a family too. I had handed her the perfect opening. Instead she just blushed. "Three times a great-grandmother," she said.

Apparently, we were all learning to say our own words. Then Josh came over, a tall drink in his hand, looking like the Cheshire cat.

"Eh," said Aunt Carmella when she saw him.

I could tell that she recognized his face but couldn't quite come up with a name. That was okay; she had just done one wonderful thing. That was good enough for now.

"*Josh*," I said, loud and clear as a shofar, "I'll leave you and Aunt Carmella to visit a while."

"Go get yourself a drink," he suggested and gave me the Cheshire look again.

The young man in the red vest was standing, hands behind his back, waiting for business. When he saw me approaching, he immediately took a more formal stance. Then, just as quickly, his whole bearing relaxed. He smiled, and in an instant I knew what Josh's grin was all about.

"Hi," I said. He looked to be about twenty-six, twenty-seven—handsome, cleancut, friendly looking—the kind of guy I see all the time at the gym, except without the attitude. "A brandy and soda."

"Sure," he said, giving me another friendly smile, and set about mixing my drink. He had brilliant blue eyes, the kind I've heard guys say are "to die for," except I'm a brown-eye man myself.

"It's quite a party, isn't it?" I asked. An innocuous enough question, but under the circumstances it had the ring of openers I used to use in the bars.

"Yes, it's a beautiful party," he said. He might have been agreeing with me out of a sense of professional duty—the-customer-is-always-right syndrome—though the way he said "beautiful" sounded too genuine for that.

When he finished making the drink, he held it out to me but didn't release it into my grasp until I'd looked up at him. Then he kept watching me as I took my first sip.

"Perfect," I said. There was an awkward pause. Our business now over, I was free to wander off. Instead, I took another sip. I was the only person standing at the bar: nobody else was looking for a drink. "I'm Nick," I said.

"Dennis." We shook hands. It felt daring—and thrilling—to be making this contact under the eyes of all my relatives.

"The baby's mother is my cousin," I told him, though as soon as I said this, I realized I was babbling, just as in the old, pre-Josh days, when I would try to keep alive whatever ember of a conversation I had managed to kindle at the bars.

But Dennis seemed happy to talk. And so we did, occasionally interrupted by other guests wanting drinks, which he mixed with a bartender's quick efficiency.

He told me he came from a large Irish-Catholic family on the South Shore. Eight brothers and sisters.

"Nine kids," I acknowledged. "That beats anyone in my family, and we're Italian."

After we'd both chuckled over that one, he told me, "Usually on Sundays I'm at my mom's, unless of course I have to work a job like this. She does a big dinner for all of us who can come." He looked so happy telling me this.

"Every Sunday?" I asked. "Brother, would my mother love to have you for a son."

Someone came up to order a drink. While Dennis was mixing it, I tried to imagine spending every Sunday at my parents'. It was a tempting idea, all that family togetherness. And though I didn't think it could ever be more than a tempting idea, it made me want to know Dennis even more.

"So where do you live now?" I asked when he'd finished making the drink.

"Out this way," he said. "We moved out here from the South End last year." He was handing me all the rest of the clues I needed.

"Funny we never ran into you," I said, handing him all the remaining clues he needed. "We've been in the South End for three years now."

ENROLLMENT

Josh wandered over, taking casual mouthfuls of ice from his otherwise empty glass. From the way Dennis smiled at him, I could tell a couple of things: that they'd already introduced themselves, and that Dennis had already linked us.

"So," I said, "this is turning out to be quite an occasion." We all laughed. And then, according to an announcement the rabbi was making, it was time for the ceremony to begin. "We'll catch you later," I told Dennis. He nodded, and I winked.

Josh and I moved away from the bar, positioning ourselves with the other guests—there must have been sixty by now—to face the corner of the living room where the rabbi was standing. Monica and David had joined him, along with Monica's parents, David's parents, and a couple whom I did not recognize.

Because we were toward the back, and therefore inconspicuous, Josh took the opportunity to whisper to me.

"Isn't Dennis cute?"

"Adorable," I mouthed, then whispered, "but I still go for dark-eyed Jews."

I looked out over the gathering. It was clear that most of the people here were not Jewish. Of David's family, only his parents and his brothers and their wives had come. Most of us were goyim—friends, neighbors, relatives of Monica. And yet, in the midst of this party, this innocent enough Sunday afternoon gathering, we were all about to stand witness to a religious ceremony with origins that went back five thousand years.

I brushed my hand against Josh's.

"In the traditional Jewish family," the rabbi began, "the birth of a male child is a cause for high celebration. In accordance with the covenant God made with Abraham, the ritual of circumcision—we call it the *berit milah*—is performed eight days after the baby is born to mark his enrollment as one of the Jewish nation."

It seemed strange to be holding a drink, like holding

a drink in church. I glanced to my right where a large potted houseplant, a rubber tree of some sort, stood. On the Spanish moss that covered the base, I set my drink down.

"Good boy," Josh whispered to me.

"We in the Reform tradition," the rabbi went on, "think that the arrival of a girl should be attended with as much joy and celebration." A few people laughed.

He explained that, in addition to the baby, there were four people present who were most important in the ceremony: the godfather and godmother—he nodded to the couple I hadn't recognized—himself, the rabbi—again a few people laughed—and the prophet Elijah. "The empty chair here," and he gestured to a large easy chair, "is for Elijah."

Josh leaned over to me. "It's in case the baby is the Messiah. Elijah's present to announce the arrival of the Messiah."

"But this is a girl," I whispered back. "Girls don't get to be Messiah."

Josh is not against religion, and neither am I—I go to Mass a few times a year; he does the High Holy Days—but right then I couldn't control the urge to enjoy with him that little irreverent conspiracy. I needed it against all the family stuff. Against this family-embraced couple who, a generation ago, would have represented a greater blasphemy even than the sin—of Sodom! of Gomorrah!—which Josh and I performed weekly.

"Pay attention," Josh whispered.

Now David was reading from a book:

" 'In accordance with Jewish tradition we present our daughter to enter into the Covenant of Abraham and to be part of the Jewish people. We praise You, O Lord our God, King of the Universe, who has permitted us to reach toward holiness through observance of Mitzvot and commanded us to bring our children into the Covenant of Abraham our father.' "

There was something both foreign and familiar about this prayer. There were phrases—"King of the Universe," for example—that seemed lifted right out of the words I

remembered of the Mass; and others—"Covenant of Abraham," "Mitzvot"—that gave off an exotic perfume.

" 'We are mindful that we have come through a time
of uncertainty into strength and joy.' "

Monica was holding the baby, bouncing it slightly in
her arms. I recognized it as a nervous gesture, a way of
trying to calm herself. One hand went up to her eyes; she
was wiping away tears.

A time of uncertainty, I thought. What was that for
them, for her? Lots of possibilities occurred to me. Maybe
my mother knew, or at least guessed, though I knew I would
never dare ask.

Josh whispered, "At a bris we pray that the boy will
one day get married, too."

"Typical Mediterranean fertility anxiety," I whispered
back.

David was finishing with a prayer in Hebrew: ". . .
she-heh-chi-yanu v'ki-y'manu v'higi-anu lazman hazeh."

The rabbi then took up a crystal goblet into which had
been poured ceremonial wine, blessed it, dipped his finger
in the wine, and touched Danielle's lips. She cried out, and
everyone laughed. The ceremony ended with the passing
of the cup to Monica and David, their parents, and the
godparents.

"Don't we get to drink, too?" I asked Josh.

"What do you think this is," he said, "communion?"

What's left to tell is this:

After the ceremony everyone seemed more relaxed.
The party got louder and friendlier, the caterers laid out
quite a spread on the dining room table, Dennis was doing
a brisk business at the bar.

I made myself a hefty sandwich and wandered about,
happy to do some catching up with people, just as happy
to blend in with the crowd. Once, out of the corner of my
eye, I saw Josh checking out the prints and paintings Monica
and David had hung on the walls; later I saw him talking
to Dennis at the bar. I wanted to join them, but felt that

where three were gathered eyebrows might be raised. And then Mom found me again, and our conversation turned to when I was coming home for a visit.

"Isn't this a visit?" I said.

"Nicky, we never see enough of you."

"How about Thanksgiving then?" I asked her. "It's only a month away."

"Well of course Thanksgiving." She sounded annoyed. Apparently, Thanksgiving didn't count. Visiting at Thanksgiving was a commandment.

"Who's doing Thanksgiving this year anyway?" I asked. "You, or Aunt Carmella?" I knew that the plans would already be underway.

"We're going to Aunt Carmella's." Then she added, cautiously, "Monica and David won't be there this year."

"Aha!" I said, jumping at the opportunity to tease her. "So I'm not the only Mr. Russo in the family!"

My father joined us. He, too, looks younger than his years: ruddy face and a head of thick, silvery hair that Mom loves to tousle. Whenever I think of Josh and me being together forty years, I think of my parents and how they still get a kick out of each other. I want that, too.

"Where've you been?" my father asked me.

"Dad, do you know how many people have asked me that today?" I said, laughing. I was enjoying all these opportunities to tease them.

"Well, just don't be such a stranger," he said. He was trying to be brave and feisty, like Mom, but I could tell he had really missed me.

"Do you think Josh would like to be invited?" Mom asked. She glanced quickly at my father.

I could still see Josh chatting it up with Dennis. The two of them looked like they were having a good time.

"Gee, maybe," I said. "I'll find out."

"And call once in a while," my father added.

"*Oy vey*," I said, raising my eyes heavenward. We all laughed.

Josh and I have friends who every year throw a big

gay Thanksgiving party in the South End: fifteen, eighteen guys. We've been invited the last two years, and doubtless will be invited again this year, but again we'll decline. Josh will either come to Aunt Carmella's, a first, or he'll go to his folks' in New Jersey. We've often fantasized what it would be like to be with our "gay family" for just one of the holidays, and now, as my parents kissed me good-bye— the first time ever that they'd left a party before me!—I thought about this again. I knew that even at that moment Dennis was being enrolled into our—Josh's and my—other family, and that one day we would invite him and his other half to dinner. And that that would lead to their meeting other friends of ours, and our meeting other friends of theirs. And so it would go, on and on, *in secula seculorum*, as some of us used to say. At the same time, I couldn't wait to tell Josh that Aunt Carmella was inviting him for Thanksgiving.

I started making my way over to the two of them, then noticed, on a coffee table in the middle of the living room, the crystal goblet from which the rabbi and all the parents had tasted of the wine. It was still half full—a rich ruby color—and seemed, for that richness, sadly abandoned. I picked it up, drank, then carried the rest to Josh and Dennis at the bar.

THE SUMMER OF THE DAIQUIRI

No ONE IN OUR group ever drank daiquiris before three weeks ago, when Todd returned from a visit to Topeka full of enthusiasm for "this fabulous drink of my mother's." He'd been consuming them in happy quantities with her and her friends at one homecoming gathering after another. And so, when he returned to Boston, he decided to throw a daiquiri party for all of us, to introduce us, he said, to their "sharp, certain pleasures." (Todd is one of those people who use "sharp" to mean "handsome.")

We began by treating it like a joke, a bit of midwestern hokum, but by the end of the evening, the sweetness, the alcohol, the colors—like a decorator's palette: peach, lime, strawberry—had won us over. Through my lightheadedness, I could hear Todd going on and on about his mother, about how she would serve daiquiris at her Thursday afternoon Browning Club meetings, sitting in her white wicker furniture on the front porch, trying to stir up a little breeze with a fan she had bought on a trip to Havana with her girlfriends in the thirties. We got high on the booze and the campiness of the whole scene that Todd was painting. Topeka! Could there really be such a place, we marveled. And banana daiquiris! It was as if American Gothic had merged with Art Deco. "Grant Wood marries Erté," Chris Sabatini said, almost choking on his next sip.

Now I can see that this could well turn out to be The Summer of the Daiquiri. You see, with us it's become a tradition to come up with a name that's supposed to capture the style or preoccupation of each particular summer. Last year, for example, was The Summer Todd Hit Mid-Life (thirty-five). And the year before that was The Province-town Summer, when all of us acted as if we'd never reach that age.

Our group—three couples, now that Todd and Jimmy are a thing—has been together ten years. That's eleven summers, counting this one, since the core—Todd, Chris, Russell, and I—met toward the end of our first year in grad school. (We've come to laugh about it: how long it took us to recognize each other, but in those days we just burrowed into our study carrels and worked like crazy.) *Gli studenti della camera*, closet scholars, Chris dubbed us. But what would you expect from an opera queen doing a degree in romance philology? Well, the name stuck. At least long enough to become the inspiration for an on-going "closet drama" that we ad-libbed, in bastardized Italian no less, all through that first summer together.

We even gave ourselves *buffo* names. Chris, always the quickest to relax into a new scenario, called himself Lucrezia dello Sport, in homage to the North End cafe where he hung out, ostensibly eavesdropping on Southern Italian dialects for his thesis. To Todd, the oldest among us, he gave Old Gobbo. Russell, the quiet, bookish type, who became my lover two summers later, was Beatrice Biblioteca; and I, at that time still horrified at the idea of a female nickname, inherited Carlo Masculino-Immaculato.

We learned how to employ elaborate locutions in *opera*

seria style in order to say the most trivial things. It was a giddy private joke that we dared to pull out only for ourselves, over drinks and candlelit dinners here in Todd's apartment. (Even in those days he could afford luxury.) By dessert time, we were usually convulsed in fits of laughter, a laughter that sometimes dissolved into tears. We cried because we were so funny, and because we had found each other, and out of the sheer joy of having learned to carry on. By the end of that summer we were taking our drama out of the closet, at least far enough out to "perform" at parties where we would amuse our fellow graduate students, who mistook it all for just so much cleverness. It was after one of those parties that Chris whispered to me, "Charles, we're doing The Summer of the Closet Scholars," and that became the title for our first summer together.

Next came The Summer of Botticelli, not a reference to the painter or our Italian affinities, but to the guessing game called Botticelli, which we found ourselves frequently playing that second summer while waiting for a civilized hour to dine. The unspoken rule is No Two Summers Alike. Presumably, that's why no one is showing much interest in the round of Botticelli we're playing now.

"Were you known for your famous sexual escapades with many of nineteenth-century Europe's most illustrious men?" Jimmy is asking Todd. He takes a drag on his cigarette. The youngest among us, Jimmy is the only one who smokes. ("All attitude," Russell says.) When he exhales, Jimmy exhales the satisfaction of having stumped his new lover.

"No, I am *not* Lola Montez," Todd says. He counters Jimmy's cigarette routine with a bit of his own stage business: a bored little sip of his daiquiri as if to say, Don't mess with me, girl.

I can see that the honeymoon—they've been together six months—is wearing thin. But oh, do I want this one to last. Jimmy is Todd's fourth lover ("fourth poopsie," Russell says), and I'm not sure I could take another summer of divorce counseling. That was the third summer, The Summer We Counseled Todd, the third summer and the first lover.

Brown and beefy, Chris is smiling at Todd, I suppose out of admiration for his ability to pull such exquisite trivia from his head. I have to admit, Todd's knowing about Lola Montez is pretty impressive. We've all come to expect Jimmy to know about the Lola Montezes of the world. (He's got a collection of over fifty coffeetable books on subjects ranging from movie starlets to the queens of Europe.) But Todd, tall, blond Todd, so cool, so aloof, keeps his knowledge a secret until the crucial moment when he flips it out like a trump card.

Jimmy will have to learn not to even try to outdo Todd. Todd's the best cook among us, the most stylish dresser, the one with the most vicious tongue. Of the original foursome, Todd was the only one with the foresight to have pulled out of his Ph.D. program and switched to law school. (Russell says that for Todd the glamour of the liberal arts, like the glamour of homosexuality, wore thin early on.) Todd has always wanted to be the arbiter of our taste, and this apartment is the salon where he's tried to instruct us. His large, cool abstracts on gray walls; the Federal period furniture upholstered in silk of Wedgwood blue; his bedroom with its elegant and seductive Japanese futon in shades of apricot; even these daiquiris—it's all part of Todd's statement to us.

"But what exactly is he trying to say?" Russell asked me last week.

"That he loves us," I told him.

And that's why I think this will become our Summer of the Daiquiri. Each of us has taken up these pastel drinks as a way of saying to Todd, We love you, too.

The reason we've again taken up Botticelli is less clear. Perhaps out of nostalgia for simpler summers; perhaps because we're introducing someone new into the group. Whatever the reason, Chris, Todd, Jimmy, and this new guy, a black Irish dreamboat named Kevin, have been trying for twenty minutes to find out who "M" is. Then there's Russell—Russell the Reader—my wonderful, maddening, bookish Russell, sitting on the sofa next to the new guy, lost in *The Hound of the Baskervilles*. Even though he's reading, I can tell that Russell is also keeping track of the game. And I guess I'm playing, too, but a lot of other things are going through my head these days, so I mainly just sit back and listen.

"Okay," says Chris, trying to salvage the game. "Let's review what we know." He gets up and walks around the living room, ticking off the facts we've so far gleaned.

"A non-American . . . born before nineteen hundred . . . not involved in science or the arts . . ."

When he gets behind the chair—a wingback—that Todd is slouched in, he wraps his arms around Todd's neck:

". . . or politics."

Chris, short for Christofero because he was born on Columbus Day, is the Italian teddy bear among us. He's dark and chunky, but without any flab, and his eyes are like two black olives.

Jimmy yells, "Come on, Todd. Play fair." At first I think he's accusing him of coming on to Chris. But then he says, "This is going to turn out to be someone totally obscure."

"No more obscure than Lola Montez," Todd says, delivering Jimmy a cool, bitchy grin.

"We don't even know if it's a man or a woman," Kevin, our newcomer, offers. "Todd, are you male or female?"

"Come over here and find out for yourself," Todd teases.

"Saints preserve us!" Kevin gasps.

Everyone laughs. Kevin is new to Botticelli. An Irishman and a priest, he is over here for a year of graduate theological study in pastoral care. Chris cruised him at Mass two Sundays ago, and now he is already our adoptee for the summer. (I suppose this could become our Summer of the Irish Priest, but it's not clear yet how big a part we're going to let Kevin play in our lives.)

"Kevin," I explain, "to earn the right to ask a question

about M, you must first stump Todd with a biographical question about any famous person whose name begins with M. Once you've done that, you can then ask a direct yes-no question about who Todd's person is."

"Good gracious, Charles," Kevin says. "All that just to find out if he's a bloody boy or girl!"

I like Kevin. He's beginning to relax with us and show us some of his Irish humor. I wonder if he fully understands what kind of humor we're showing him. I wonder if we do.

But now the game is becoming tedious. Chris, who's been massaging Todd's shoulders, goes over to the windows and twists the Levolor rods so that only tiny pencils of late afternoon light fall into the apartment.

"Lola Montez. Lola Montez. Where are you now?" Chris says. "Oh, Madonna Mia, do I need a sexual escapade!"

"Saints preserve us!" Kevin exclaims again. This has to be in jest. But then again, we've only known him two weeks, so maybe he truly is shocked. Jimmy, bless his heart, just automatically assumes that Kevin is being ironic, so he tries to heighten the campiness.

"It's Kevin who should be having the sexual escapade," he says, raising his eyebrows and squeezing a long, exaggerated *Ooo!* through a puckered kisser that screams for lipstick. Our resident Carmen Miranda.

Kevin laughs. I guess he feels safe with Jimmy.

"Kevin dear, stay celibate," Todd says in his dramatically languid way. "It's much simpler." He takes another sip of his daiquiri.

"What!" Jimmy says. "Am I sharing this gorgeous body with a man who . . ."

Jimmy is skating on thin ice here. Todd, who is at least ten years older than Jimmy (he refuses to tell us exactly how young Jimmy is), is really the one with the gorgeous body. He and Jimmy are both lean and tall and blond, but Todd has worked himself into the hot, chiseled look, while Jimmy's build is just cute and boyish.

"Jimmy," Todd says, "that 'gorgeous body' of yours could use a bit of toning." Seated opposite each other in those silk-upholstered wingbacks, Jimmy and Todd are like two spatting dowagers.

Escalating the snit, Jimmy folds his arms and crosses one leg over the other, so that his body turns toward Father Kevin, shutting Todd out. "Kevin, I simply cannot imagine how anyone who is celibate copes," Jimmy says. "My God, all that sexual energy and nowhere to . . . to *put* it!"

"Well . . ." Kevin says, giving us all an equivocal shrug of the shoulders, which could mean either "That's what we gay priests deal with" or "I can't imagine either how anyone who is celibate copes."

I'd love to steer the conversation toward this topic—priests and sex—but Todd is already grilling Chris about the escapade he wants.

"Your lover goes away for a week," Todd says, craning his head back to look at Chris, who's moved behind Todd's wingback again, "and already you're up for a new partner?"

"Who said anything about a new partner?" Chris says. "It's just that in Michael's absence I've become insatiably horny." He ambles behind the sofa now and starts teasingly rubbing Russell's and Kevin's necks. Russell, of course, keeps his eyes on the book he's reading; Kevin looks up at Chris and gives him a big, nervous smile.

"Chris, if we were as honest as you," Jimmy says, "we'd all admit that we were inscrutably horny."

Jimmy's malapropism bursts the tension. We all laugh, leaving him totally bemused. What a gorgeous fluffhead he is. I wonder if at this moment Todd can love him as much as I do.

Jimmy remains undaunted. "So," he says. (Jimmy loves starting sentences with *so*. He punctuates all his stories with them: *So, he says . . . so then, she goes . . .* Jimmy's a believer in the What Happens Next School of narration: all plot and suspense.) "So," he says, "Michael comes home Tuesday night. That gives you two more days plus tonight for your sexual escapade."

Russell momentarily looks up from his book. I can tell he's as curious as I am about this newfound enthusiasm of Jimmy's for other men's philandering. Todd takes another sip of his drink; Chris just keeps rubbing Kevin's neck.

"So, where will you go?" Jimmy pursues. "Who've you got in mind? So, what's your first step?"

"This is not a ballet and you are not about to choreograph Chris Sabatini's weekend for him," Todd scolds.

"*Choreograph?* I dunno nothin' bout no choreographin'," Jimmy wails in falsetto. "Who do you think I am, George Balanchine?"

"No, darling," says Todd. "We've already established that you're Lola Montez, Queen of the Sexual Escapades."

Everyone goes silent as Jimmy delivers Todd an icy stare. But Father Kevin is not about to let this thing drop. From the way his eyes have been darting from Jimmy to Todd to Chris, I know that he is totally captivated. Of course, he is still too shy or polite or inexperienced to say much himself. So I guess it's my turn to explain. I'm beginning to understand that there are more than just theological reasons for Kevin's calling me "little brother."

"Kevin," I say, "I detect a certain foreigner's curiosity about our quaint American customs of sexual prowling. It's time to teach you some facts. First of all, what Chris is about to do, or about not to do"—I quickly add—"is called tricking. Your church would call it adultery if it recognized Chris's relationship with his lover. Ten years ago tricking was practically the gay sporting event. Now, well, there are complications. Let's say we're all older and wiser."

"*Some* of us are older and wiser," Todd interrupts.

"It used to be," I continue, "that the traditional venues for picking up a trick were what I call The Four Bs: the bars, baths, bushes, and beaches. The baths, of course, have all been closed. And of the other three, the bushes are too dangerous. It's supposed to rain tomorrow, so that rules out the beaches. Which leaves Chris with the last, but hardly least, of the four options, the bars. The bars, in fact, are where we all began, Kevin."

"Where *some* of us began," Todd calls out.

"I have *nev-er* been to the bushes!" Jimmy says, at last uncrossing his arms and legs. Jimmy's stage set should always include a wingback. He looks and sounds terrific in one. Still, I can't tell whether he means for us to catch the outrageousness of this claim, or is so embarrassed by his having failed ever to romp in the Fens that he wants us to believe he's lying.

"Oh, God," Chris says. He turns away from all of us, as if it's easier to say this to the abstracts on Todd's wall. "One week a year I get without Michael, and what happens? Nothing. A little variety, that's all I'm asking for. A new face, a new body, just for one night. Something, anything different." He turns back and touches Kevin again.

"Read a good book," Russell mumbles without looking up from Sherlock Holmes.

"So, why don't we all go out for dinner?" Jimmy proposes. "Maybe Chris can cruise one of the waiters at Calypso." Thoroughly taken by his own idea, he gives us all (all except Todd, that is) a big smile.

"Add another B to the list," Russell says, still reading. "The bistros."

"Oh, I like that," Jimmy giggles.

"I am not going to a bistro," Chris says. "I am not going to a bar. And if you all don't leave me alone, I'm going to take myself to a movie—alone."

"That's another B," Jimmy announces with that delightful uncouthness of his. "The balconies!"

"You could find me ten Bs if you wanted," Chris says, "but it wouldn't do any good. God, everytime I even try to imagine tricking out, it just ends up feeling . . . I mean, what's the point? What do I think I'm looking for?" He chuckles, remembering something: "If two years in therapy have taught me anything, it's that loneliness—with or without Michael—is the universal human condition. Man's solitude," he says, and I can hear the scoffing disappointment in his voice. "It's just that I'm so . . ."

Chris falters, and the others jump to the occasion.

"Lonely," Todd says.

"Horny," Jimmy says.

"Bored," Russell says, turning a page.

"Why don't we just say you're 'in need'?" Father Kevin, ever the pastoral counselor, gently suggests.

"So that means we're right back where we started from," Jimmy says. "Chris is in need of a sexual adventure. I can sympathize with that perfectly." He shoots a quick, testy look at Todd. "Chris, I think that as long as you're careful and have an understanding with Michael about these things . . ." Now it's Jimmy's turn to falter. "Well, there's no reason why when he's away you shouldn't . . ."

He looks at me now, and this time there's anxiety on his face, as if he's not sure he wants to take the conversation this far. I sit there blankly, waiting to hear what he'll come up with.

". . . why you shouldn't . . . *indulge*." He smiles at me, and I give him a weak little smile in return.

All of a sudden, Russell throws down the Sherlock Holmes. It makes a muffled thud against the Wedgwood blue cushion.

"Indulge, Jimmy?" Russell says, fixing him with a solemn stare. "Indulge what, exactly?"

Knowing Russell as well as I do, I can tell that he is winding up for one of his Oxford don routines. But there's real impatience in his voice, too.

"Loneliness? Boredom? Cupidity?" Russell says, laying the pedagogical voice on thick. "Which is it? Strange how we all heard Mr. Sabatini say the same thing and yet we each find such different words to translate it to ourselves. Understanding the sex drive, gentlemen, is a little like the blind men describing the elephant. We've each got our fingers on a piece of it, don't we? And yet it's really too terribly big for any of us." He picks up his *Hound of the Baskervilles* again and taps the cover with his fingers. "Sex—ah, sex, gentlemen—is like the Great Grimpen Mire: vast, mysterious, deep."

I've got to hand it to Russell: occasionally, his Oxford

don number does strike a responsive chord. We all sit there in silence, the afternoon light waning behind the blinds. Todd is the first to move: he reaches over to turn on the brass floor lamp near his chair, but he can't quite reach it until Chris guides his hand over to the knob. When the light comes on, Chris turns it down, low.

"Why is everybody being so weird?" Jimmy says. "We're just talking about fantasies."

"And what are *your* fantasies, Jimmy?" Kevin asks. At first his question strikes me as uncharacteristically forward, but then I realize that Kevin is gaining confidence in this seminar we're giving him called "How to Talk Gay."

"In front of Todd?" Jimmy says, giving Todd a blushing smile. All of a sudden, he seems to want to reestablish friendly feelings with this boyfriend of his.

"Come now," Kevin says, "what secrets can you keep from your lover?"

"Yes, I'd like to know what secrets you keep from your lover, too," Todd says. He's still glaring.

But Jimmy's too out of it to notice. The three daiquiris he's consumed are beginning to show their effect.

"Oh, Kevin," he says, "I'd have to be drunker than this." He turns his empty glass upside down.

"More daiquiris for everyone?" Chris asks, looking at Todd. He collects our glasses on a tray and disappears down the hall to Todd's kitchen.

Todd calls after Chris. "Sabatini, let me help." He gets up from his wingback. "Excuse me, but perhaps Jimmy will feel more comfortable sharing his *fantasies* if his lover is absent." He follows Chris to the kitchen.

For a moment, the rest of us—Jimmy, Kevin, Russell, and I—go silent again. It's during this silence that I remember those first daiquiris Todd made us:

We were on a hoot about the colors. "Chartreuse! Fuchsia! Flamingo!" we were shouting. "*Qué colores magníficos*," Chris pronounced, and I thought he was about to launch us into The Summer of the Zarzuelas. I was laughing. We were all laughing. Then something happened. For one brief moment I saw those daiquiris for what they were: pure objects—without our clever references or self-consciousness getting in the way. In that moment, they ceased to be tokens of reassurance that we were smart and witty and oh so terribly sophisticated. Instead, they simply became beautiful in themselves. Beautiful for what they were. *Because* they were. And then I started laughing harder than anyone else, one of those laughs that go all teary on you, like the times that first summer when we all laughed for the sheer joy of being together.

I can hear Todd and Chris dropping ice cubes into the blender, talking sotto voce. There's a little hurt expression on Jimmy's face. I look at Kevin, and he sees it, too. Russell, of course, is back to ignoring everything but his book.

"So, Kevin," Jimmy begins, "you want to know what my fantasies are? For a long time my fantasies were all about men's bodies. My original type was the dark, muscle man. The three Hs, Kevin: handsome, hairy, and hot. I think Todd was the first blond I ever really turned on to. At first I couldn't believe I was falling in love with him. He was so not-my-type. But I was fascinated by his very definite opinions about things: furniture, art, people. Todd knew what he wanted, knew what he hated, knew who to know and who not to bother getting to know. It seemed as if he had made up his mind about everything. I was terribly impressed. He seemed so . . . so grownup. And I wanted to be like that. That was my real fantasy. To be grownup. With Todd it suddenly felt as if I could have that."

I look at Kevin, to see if he understands, but it seems that he's so caught up in the charm of Jimmy's story that he doesn't hear what's beneath it. It's Russell who brings Kevin back to earth. He closes his book and this time lays it very deliberately on the floor. Then, he twists around on the sofa so that he's facing Kevin, his arm extended out behind the priest's neck.

"Little brother," he says, "Jimmy has only told you Chapter One, which is a fairy tale. Chapter Two is in *verismo* style: harsh, bitter reality. Isn't it, Jimmy?"

"Oh, I'm not so innocent," Kevin says. "I can see things aren't quite like that right now." He lowers his voice to keep from being heard by Todd, who I guess is still in the kitchen helping Chris, though I can't hear them talking anymore.

"Bitter reality for sure," Jimmy says. "Chapter Two, Kevin, is only for the confessional." He winks.

Now this is an interesting tack. Why, I wonder, is Jimmy being so coy? Russell and I have heard Jimmy's Love Saga with Todd at least three times already this summer. He can hardly have left out any details. So why now this confessional stuff? Jesus! Is he coming on to Kevin? If so, it works.

"Confess, confess," Kevin is saying. He leans forward, cupping an ear in Jimmy's direction.

Jimmy looks nervously toward the kitchen. This, too, seems coy to me because the last time Jimmy told us his woes, Todd was again just within earshot. (Russell says that Jimmy really does want Todd to overhear him because he's too embarrassed to confront Todd directly.)

Russell gets up and stretches. "I'll go see about drinks," he says and strolls out the room and down the hall. He seems restless, which is unusual for Russell, but perhaps he's just tired of hearing Jimmy's confessions.

That leaves Kevin, Jimmy, and me. Kevin gets up, walks behind Jimmy's wingback and starts the same sort of neck-rub business. His graduate studies program must subscribe to the touchy-feely school. When Russell returns with the tray of fresh daiquiris, Jimmy tells him, "You haven't missed anything, Russell." Kevin sits down again. Is he insulted, or just embarrassed now that another observer is in the room?

"*Thaaat's goood,*" Russell says, in a way that tells me he's paying more attention to gingerly laying down the drinks than he is to Jimmy or Kevin. But then he gives me a quick, serious look that suggests there's something else he's gingerly laying down.

Jimmy picks up his daiquiri and takes a long sip. "Lovely," he says. His eyes are closed.

He's a believer in loveliness, Jimmy is. A believer in romance and the innocence of romance. How this squares with his wanting to be an adult—or his titillation over Chris's tricking out—I don't know. Each of us in the group has had, in his own way, to deal with these contradictions; each of us, in his own way, is still dealing with them.

"Yes," Jimmy is saying, his eyes open now, "Todd knows how to set limits: when to decline invitations, when to leave a party, when to say no." His voice is wandering, as if he's trying to reach the bottom of that drink, as if there he could find a world where all invitations can be accepted, where no one needs ever to say no to anything.

I feel Russell looking at me. When I look up, sure enough, he's got me fixed in a hard, sad stare. I recognize this look. He's trying to tell me something, and it's not that Jimmy's had too much to drink.

Kevin distracts my attention. He says something about Jimmy and Todd being good for each other because they seem like opposites.

Ah, the comforting myth of opposites. I look at Russell again to give him a knowing smile, but Russell isn't smiling, and then I figure it out, why Russell brought the drinks out instead of Chris and Todd.

"It's just that Todd is *so* stable," Jimmy is saying. "Just like Chris said—there's never anything new, never any surprises."

"What do you want?" Kevin asks with his calm, pastoral concern.

Jimmy flinches under the directness of the question. I guess none of us has ever framed it so unambiguously before. *What do you want?* It's such a pure question, like the pure moment of those daiquiris. Jimmy sighs.

"I want to be in love."

Kevin looks to me for help. His confused, foolish, gorgeous face is asking me to come to the rescue. But this is his baby now. He asked the question, and he can damn well come up with the answer himself. Dammit, I feel like screaming at him, So how does your fucking clinical-pastoral education deal with that? And I want to scream at Jimmy, Grow up! I want to scream at those two now in Todd's cool apricot bedroom, You can't do this! And I want to scream at Russell, though with him I can never find the right words for that combination of rage and affection he always brings out in me.

Instead, I don't say anything. But then, how I feel the ache of wanting to give him something, of wanting to give something to each one of these men, *these men*, of wanting to give something to myself: something sharp and certain, the knowledge of our needs.

SAYING THE TRUTH

MESA VERDE, CAN-
yon Lands, Monument Valley . . ." Tigh poked at the road
map that was spread out on his kitchen table, landing here
and there with his finger and calling out names. "Canyon
de Chelly. The Rio Grande."

Michael's eyes skipped along, trying to follow the ran-
dom trail his friend was tracing. The names meant nothing
to him, just a collection of western-sounding places. But
the images they conjured up—valleys, mesas, canyons, na-
tional parks—they were like the images Michael remembered of boy scouting when he was a kid: vast, unsettled
spaces you could get lost in.

"The Grand Canyon!" Tigh pronounced, his finger
making a circle around the spot on the map. "Da Big Ma-
looka!" He was doing his imitation big, dumb bruiser voice,
as if he'd just struck the jackpot on a slot machine.

Michael laughed. "Yeah, man," he said, punching his

right fist into the palm of his other hand. "The Big Ma-looka."

Michael Ziminsky was thirty-four, a Slavic languages cataloguer for one of the university libraries in town. He was fluent in Polish and Russian; when he needed to, he could make his way through Czech and Serbo-Croatian as well. He loved languages, and he loved Europe, where he had traveled every third year since his graduate school days. He kept a closet of neatly stacked slide trays, organized according to themes: churches (subdivided into Roman-esque, Gothic, baroque), castles, chateaux, Roman ruins. He had diaries that chronicled each day of each trip. He had scrapbooks.

"Utah!" Tigh said. *"You-taw!"*

For Michael, Tigh was all the things those Boy Scouts had not been: gentle and funny and intelligent. And though his sandy hair was thinning, and though he'd recently lost too much weight, Tigh still retained his all-American good looks, the kind of looks of someone who could handle the West.

They had been to Europe three times together, and would have been going again this year, too, had Tigh not gotten sick. It was to have been Austria and Hungary, Hapsburg and Esterhazy country, but in the spring, after his diagnosis, Tigh said he'd feel more comfortable traveling in the States, in easy reach of American medical facilities. "Besides," he'd added, "I've never seen my own country," not adding, though Michael understood anyway, that there might not be another time to see his own country. And so three weeks were cut to ten days; and the Hapsburg Empire became the Southwest.

"Let's get serious here," Tigh now said, pulling the map closer. "Here's Phoenix." He put his finger down again.

The plan was for them to fly to Phoenix around the middle of June, before the tourist season got underway. There they would rent a car and head north to the Grand

Canyon. Then to southeastern Utah, southwestern Colorado, and down into New Mexico. The Four Corners trip, they called it.

"Even if we leave Phoenix in the afternoon," Tigh explained, "we can still make the Grand Canyon by nightfall."

Michael watched him tracing the route. "I'd sort of hoped we could spend some time in Phoenix," he said.

"*Sort of?*" Tigh looked at him dubiously: eyes wide, eyebrows raised high.

"I was hoping to see Phoenix," Michael corrected. Then he tried again: "I *want* to see Phoenix."

They were practicing "saying the truth." It was Tigh's idea. "I want this trip to be about saying the truth," he'd told Michael when they were first making plans. "Saying the truth" meant that they'd tell each other everything, exactly what they were feeling, exactly what they wanted, every step of the way. "No withholding," Tigh had said. (It was something he was learning in his support group.) And Michael had agreed. He wanted to give Tigh whatever he needed.

"Exactly how much time do you want to spend in Phoenix?" Tigh now asked.

Michael hesitated. He was still not comfortable talking like this. Sometimes it just felt like selfishness. "A day?"

Michael was a Catholic—he still went to Mass, at the parish that served the university, though more out of a nostalgic devotion to the boy choir than out of any deep faith—and the thing about Tigh's newfound truth saying that sometimes got to him was how secular it seemed. It was as if saying the truth had been liberated from the realm of the Baltimore Catechism, the Ten Commandments, the possibility of eternal damnation: all those other things Michael remembered from his childhood. Tigh had explained that saying the truth was simply what you did to make sure you were heard. He was some sort of lapsed Protestant; his parents had been divorced; he'd gone to a fancy prep school in Connecticut and then to Dartmouth. Support group or not, it all seemed to fit.

"A day, huh?" Tigh said. "Michael, I'm not sure I want this trip to be about cities."

"So what *is* this trip about?" Michael asked. If, right now, he could say the truth, he'd have to say that it was beginning to feel like there wasn't anything in this trip for him.

Tigh said he wanted country: open vistas, majestic scenery. "I want to see things that I won't be able to find words for," he said.

Michael nodded his understanding. When he first found out about Tigh's diagnosis, the only word he'd been able to utter was no. Over and over again—no, no, no—all the way home from the hospital. He thought now of all those scrapbooks and journals he'd kept on previous trips, full of words and gathering dust on his bookshelves. An accumulation of words. Every morning, over coffee and rolls (those charming European breakfasts), he used to write up the previous day's events, then read it to Tigh: in the Piazza San Marco, at that little table under the lindens in Vienna, in Madrid, in Brussels—and not one of them, not one single word, any good anymore. Not for Tigh. *No, no, no*.

"I want this trip to be a spiritual experience," Tigh continued.

And Michael nodded again.

Tigh Jennings and Michael Ziminsky had known each other since graduate school, since the October night during their first semester when they'd met at the library checkout desk. Tigh, who was hefting a stack of books a foot tall, made a joke about how they must have been the only two guys without a date. It was a Friday night. Michael laughed. He was covering up the nervousness he felt. He didn't want this guy, this sandy-haired, blue-eyed, athletic type, to suspect that he never had a date on a Friday night. He didn't want this guy, this guy with his hearty, basketball court voice, to see the brightness he felt in being talked to. He didn't want this guy—what really got Michael's attention was his nose, one of those classically chiseled noses, unlike the Polish ski slope that Michael sported—he didn't want him to get too close.

That was the extent of their exchange, though when Michael took up his books and walked away from the counter, saying, "Take it easy," something he never said, he sensed that the guy was following him with his eyes.

The following Monday they passed each other on campus.

"Hey, how's it going?" the guy called out. He was with someone else and looked to be hurrying to class. Along with his voice, he had a hearty, athletic stride. He looked genuinely pleased to see Michael again.

The third time they met, a Friday night again, again at the checkout desk, they went out for coffee. They exchanged names and degree programs and past histories: hometowns, where they'd gone to college, what they'd majored in. Michael kept lowering his eyes to his cup of coffee. But when he'd drained his cup and the talk ceased momentarily, he felt an ominous pause, as if there were a decision to be made. He looked up.

"So what do you like to do?" Tigh asked.

"You mean culturally?" As soon as it was out, Michael realized what an awkward, bumbling response this was. "I mean," he said, trying to recover, "you mean, what do I like to do outside of graduate work?"

Tigh leaned back, rocking on the back legs of the cafe chair. He put his hands behind his head and stretched. "Yeah."

"Oh, concerts, plays . . ." Michael paused, trying to gauge how this was registering. "Probably the kind of stuff most eggheads here go for."

Tigh stretched again. Michael watched his Adam's apple appear above the collar of his pullover sweater. "So, do you want to do something next Friday night?" Tigh asked. He leaned forward, bringing the front chair legs back down to the floor.

"Sure. Like what?"

Like what turned out to be pizza and a movie. And then to Tigh's apartment where they drank Scotch, sitting on his couch, a commodious thing covered with a down comforter, and listened to jazz. Toward midnight, Michael announced that he probably should get going. They both rose from the couch.

"How do you say 'probably' in Polish?" Tigh asked.

"*Prawdopodobnie*. Why?"

Tigh put his hands on Michael's shoulders and shook him.

"Because you say it a lot." Then he pulled Michael back down onto the couch and started kissing him.

The next morning, they talked about all the things they hadn't talked about on that coffee break, at the pizza parlor, after the movie. They talked about when they first suspected the other of being gay. (Tigh said he knew about Michael that first night at the checkout desk; Michael said he wasn't sure right up to when Tigh pulled him down onto the couch.) They talked about the other half of their past histories, the part they'd withheld. They talked about the kinds of men they were attracted to. It soon became clear, from everything Tigh said, that Michael was not in the running as a potential boyfriend. In fact, it seemed that Tigh was not looking for a boyfriend at all. Period. *Absolutnie*.

Still, they became friends. Tigh introduced him to other gay men on campus. They did things together: movies, concerts, the discos. That summer they went to Europe, two weeks in Germany and Poland. Michael translated, Tigh found them the gay bars and cruising areas. They were twenty-four.

■   ■   ■

Day Nine, he wrote.

They were driving south out of Taos, through scrub country. Sagebrush and chamiza tufted the dry, powdery ground. Michael jotted down in his diary that it reminded him of central Spain, La Mancha. He rested the pen in the crease of the diary and let the pages flip by his thumb. He was keeping this journal more out of habit than through any strong desire to write. What there was to say seemed weightier, more dangerous than any of the words he could manage on paper.

"It's been a great trip," he'd written last night. That was true enough. All of it—the camping, the weather, the food. And the scenery. The sheer scale of it, and the eons it took to form: canyons, buttes, arches, massive upheavals of rock. He'd written entries about all of that.

And the Grand Canyon. The largest objects Michael had ever seen were the great cathedrals: Seville, Cologne, York. But none of them had prepared him for the immensity, and beauty, of the Grand Canyon. The Big Malooka, indeed. Tigh wasn't kidding. They had arrived in the late afternoon, in time to watch, from an observation point along the South Rim, the sunset. It stained the walls of the canyon—but even the word *canyon* seemed ridiculously inadequate to describe this thing that took up his entire field of vision—in oranges and reds and purples. There must have been forty or fifty tourists gathered on that terrace. No one had spoken. He'd written about all that, too.

After the Grand Canyon, he'd thought that everything else would be a disappointment, like seeing Chartres before you'd seen any other cathedral. But every day there had been something equally magnificent: other vistas, other colors, other landscapes. He'd dutifully recorded it all. And yet.

They were passing the junction for Ranchos de Taos.

"There's a famous church there," Michael said, consulting the guidebook. "It says it's the most picturesque in all of Spanish New Mexico."

"Do you want to turn back and see it?" Tigh asked. It was the first exchange they'd had since leaving Taos. Michael thought he heard an impatience in Tigh's voice.

"I guess not," he said.

Tigh turned to him, his lips tight. He was wearing sunglasses.

"No," Michael said, more decisively. "We've only got a day left, and I want to get in as much of Santa Fe as possible."

He was getting better at this business of saying the truth. At the Grand Canyon he'd been able to say that, no, he didn't want to take an extra day to drive all the way around to the North Rim. And in Moab, he'd told Tigh that he wanted at least one nice dinner out, that campsite food for ten days was not acceptable.

He'd said the truth about more important things, too: long conversations on those long, straight western roads about romances and boyfriends over the years; about his disappointment in not having a lover; and about how he had to admit that he wasn't exactly getting out there and looking very hard for one either.

"Maybe you really don't want a lover," Tigh suggested. "Maybe you just think you want one." Michael had to admit that that was probably—he grinned when he said it—*probably* true as well. And once again, he discovered what it was he loved about Tigh: how he could pin down what was really the case about things.

He'd talked, too, about the feeling he got standing on those railingless promontories in the hot, dry southwestern wind, an eerie, disquieting feeling of being in the presence of God.

"The vastness, the silence: it's like a sacrament," he'd said, looking to Tigh for confirmation, waiting for Tigh to open up about the spiritual experience the trip was supposed to be for him. But about these things—about God, about spiritual experiences, about the disease that would eventually wrack his body—Tigh had remained, for the past nine days, silent.

■ ■ ■

During his childhood—Michael told Tigh this story, too—
his grandmother had lived with the family. She was his
mother's mother, a fat, peasanty woman who ran the
kitchen and refused to speak English. When she wasn't
cooking, Babunia Krystyna would teach Michael and his
sisters Polish fairy tales and folksongs. And one day—he
had been home from school, recovering from the flu—she
showed him where the Virgin Mary lived.

"Look," she said, *"Najświętsza Panna,* the Holy
Mother." She pointed to the kitchen light. It was a round,
fluorescent fixture, the tube as thick and curved as a kiel-
basa. In the center, shimmering on the polished chrome
plate, amidst all the warped reflections of the kitchen furnishings, was the image of the Virgin.

Michael was old enough—eight, nine—to know this
was an optical illusion: a reflection of the table, perhaps,
bent and twisted as in a funhouse mirror so that it resembled
the face and robes and veil of Mary. Yet he indulged his
grandmother, arching his neck and exclaiming as she
pointed to the silvery icon.

"See how she's smiling," Babunia said. "Isn't she beautiful? She watches over us."

Later, when Babunia had left the kitchen, Michael had
returned for a second look. The image was still there. He
walked around the light fixture, trying to get an angle where
it would dissolve into a different image. But no matter where
he stood, the miniature Virgin continued to smile down on
him.

They drove on. The road climbed, up into the hills, past
villages with Spanish names: Placitas, Vadita, Peñasco. At
Las Trampas they passed an adobe mission church. Its walls
were brilliant in the midday brightness.

"It says," Michael read, "that these villages are so re-
mote that the people still use Spanish words from the sev-
enteenth century." He looked over at Tigh, who was

concentrating on the road and saying nothing. "Do you want to be spelled a while?" Tigh shook his head.

During the entire trip, Michael had done most of the driving: three-, four-, five-hour stretches at times. They hadn't planned it that way; it just happened. Besides, Tigh had always been good at reading maps, navigating. But this morning, he'd climbed into the driver's seat.

"Do you want to hear what I wrote about yesterday?" Michael asked.

"Not now."

Michael opened the guidebook and tried to read, but the heat and Tigh's brooding silence made it difficult for him to concentrate. Okay, he argued with himself, so maybe the truth is he doesn't need to talk, about this, about it, about anything. Okay.

At last they began to descend, into the valley of the Santa Cruz River. They passed Truchas and Cordova. As Michael was locating their position on the map, he heard Tigh's pill box beeper going off: a discreet little peeping sound that served as a reminder that it was time to swallow another capsule. Every four hours, day and night—during that sunset at the Grand Canyon, under the stars in Durango, crossing the Rio Grande gorge—the beeper had sounded. It was another thing they hadn't talked about.

With one hand on the wheel, Tigh reached into his shirt pocket, shut off the beeper, and pulled out a pill. He usually took the capsule without water, just popped it into his mouth and swallowed, a quick, deft, uncommented-upon gesture. But now Michael felt a strong need to acknowledge what he was doing.

"You want something to drink?" He reached for the plastic quart bottle of spring water that lay at his feet.

With a wave of his hand, Tigh declined. Michael wrenched off the cap and took a sip—*na złość*, for spite, his grandmother would have said—then replaced the cap with a firm smack and set the container down at his feet again.

"You know," he said, trying to regain some composure, "it does seem a shame that we haven't stopped at all along the High Road. I wouldn't mind snapping some photos of one of these old mission churches."

"All you have to do is say what you need," Tigh said.

"So, I'm saying," Michael began, checking the rising anger in his voice, "that I'd like to stop at this next town coming up. There's supposed to be a good example of the Spanish adobe mission style there. Besides, it's hot." There was the briefest pause before he added the truth: "And we're both getting cranky."

They entered the town and made their way to the parking lot next to the church. It was now almost noon. The sun was blazing in a clear blue sky. The car kicked up dust. Tigh pulled into one of the last spaces and turned off the engine. In the distance rose the mountains, the Sangre de Cristos, green above the arid foothills. The guidebook said that at sunset they turned red, the color of the blood of Christ.

All around—in the parking lot, on the dry hard-packed ground about the church, within the adobe-walled church-yard—people were roaming. Michael recognized it as the same kind of movement he'd seen around the churches and cathedrals of Europe: the half-purposeful, half-aimless roaming of tourists. A little ways off stood a separate build-ing, a gift shop, and people were spilling in and out of that, too.

He opened the car door and got out. Tigh followed him across the parking lot.

"Let me get a shot of this," Michael said.

They were standing just outside the churchyard. In front of them was an archway, crudely built into the adobe wall. It was framed in wood, which, over the years, had been bleached and cracked by the sun. A pair of gates—paneled doors, really, with a row of wooden spindles in the top partition—hung on ancient iron hinges. The archway framed a rough-hewn wooden cross, planted in a slab in the courtyard. It was an excellent photo composition, but even with his eye to the viewfinder, Michael could tell that

Tigh was impatient to move on. He snapped quickly. The camera buzzed, and the film advanced automatically.

Inside, it was as the guidebook had described: the whitewashed walls, the beamed ceiling, the painted side altar screens. And, at the altar end, in all the colors of the Southwest—ochres and oranges, golds and yellows and turquoise—the most elaborate screen of all. With its tiers and balustraded niches and central proscenium, it looked like a stage set for some festive Spanish puppet show. But inhabiting the central opening were not marionettes but a six-foot tall crucifix.

"Listen to this," Michael said, and read to them from the guidebook.

" 'On Good Friday, 1810, the head of an important local family saw a stream of light coming from a spot in the ground near where the present church stands. Digging in the soil, he uncovered a crucifix, whose touch miraculously cured him of a lingering illness. In a fervent procession, the populace brought the miraculous object to the Santa Cruz church, nine miles away, for veneration. But mysteriously the cross reappeared at its original burial site. Three times the crucifix was taken to Santa Cruz, and three times it returned, a sign that a new church was to be built on the site of its discovery. To this day, the hole where the crucifix was unearthed has provided' "—he hesitated, caught in a sentence he did not want to finish—" 'healing clay for thousands of the faithful.' "

"That the crucifix?" Tigh asked dully.

"An 'enlarged reproduction' of it," Michael said, consulting the guidebook again. "Apparently, the real one is off in some little side room." He looked up. To the left of the altar was a small opening in the thick, whitewashed adobe wall. "Over there," he whispered.

As they walked down the aisle, Michael began to see that the church was not, in fact, just as the guidebook had described. Everywhere—on the ledges of the side screens, on the altar, on little tables set up here and there—were mementos and offerings donated by the faithful: plastic flowers, rosary beads, devotion cards, an Infant of Prague doll dressed in lace. Cheap, sentimental trinkets brought here—dumped, it seemed—as a way of contributing to the decoration of the Santuario. He avoided looking at Tigh, embarrassed that *this*, apart from Phoenix, was the one stop he'd insisted upon.

They remained in front of the altar screen for a minute or two. The wooden Christ hanging on the cross was, like so many Michael had seen in countless churches throughout Europe, a sad, tragic figure. Spanish artists in particular, he reflected, seemed to dwell on the goriest aspects of the crucifixion. Here was a body, stretched, bruised, broken. A body wracked and scourged. Images from the Good Friday service crowded Michael's thoughts. The nails, the sponge dipped in vinegar and gall, the lance that pierced Christ's side. He thought of Tigh, not three months ago, lying in the hospital: the night sweats, the coughing, the oxygen mask. He thought of the next bout. When would it come—for it would come—tomorrow? next week? six months from now?

Whatever you ask in my Name, it shall be given you. Tigh, he thought, make Tigh well. But he knew that this was only a thought, a wish—not a true, believing prayer.

"You want to check out that little room?" Tigh asked in the same dull, disinterested tone.

They ducked their heads as they left the main church and entered the side room. Michael was immediately struck by the rise in the temperature. The room, a small, low annex, was stifling: hundreds of votive candles, set up in racks and shelves, flickered in the hot darkness. Tourists milled about, many of them with the dark, swarthy features of Hispanics. They were examining the tables and shelves, again cluttered with more devotional objects—cards, figurines, scraps of paper on which had been written, mostly in Spanish, ejaculations of thanksgiving for prayers answered.

At one end of the room was an even smaller, lower door, and through it many of the tourists were entering and exiting. Michael opened his guidebook.

"That's where the *pozito* is, the hole where they found the crucifix." He tried to sound disinterested too, in case Tigh did not want to see it, but Tigh moved forward.

They ducked in. The room was no bigger than a closet. It was dark and stank of hot wax, sweat, and dust. Seven or eight people were crowded around a scooped-out place in the ground. Several were kneeling, gathering up handfuls of the powdery soil, which they funneled into envelopes and small paper lunch bags. Michael saw one man put a pinch of the dirt on his tongue.

Lourdes, Fatima, Czenstochowa—he'd avoided them all, these places of miracles, these places to which the faithful journeyed, on palsied limbs, in wheelchairs, to see, to taste, to touch. Surely this was the most grotesque of all: groveling in the dirt, eating it. Dirt that the priests replenished each evening, from God knows where, so that the hole would not be enlarged. And yet.

He was aware of Tigh standing next to him, quietly, almost reverently, observing the pilgrims taking the dirt. What was going through *his* mind, Michael wondered. He thought of all those scraps of paper, testimonies to the efficacy of this place. Was Tigh thinking about that, too? He thought of the light that had emanated from the ground, the cross, its three-times transposition back to the original site. "Without human assistance" the guidebook had said. But already Tigh was turning away, ready to leave.

Now, right there, in front of Tigh, Michael thought, I could kneel down and take a scoop of the miraculous dirt. Not even a scoop, a pinch, a grain. I could humble myself, show Tigh the way.

For hadn't he learned—all those stories from Sunday school, from his grandmother—that this is how miracles happened: not in grand events, but in lowly, unassuming, even embarrassing ways? The simple faith of peasants.

Wasn't it for this moment that the whole of their trip, so unexpected just a few months before, and this detour, a last-minute decision—wasn't it toward this moment, here at the grubby little *pozito*, that they had been traveling? God may have been in those sunsets, but if Tigh was to be cured, this is where God—Michael knew His name in eight languages—where He would work His miracle.

And then he thought of that Madonna in the fluorescent kitchen light. A trick of polished metal, if you wanted to say the truth. He thought of the suggestion of skepticism in the guidebook's report: that the "discoverer" of the crucifix had been petitioning for years to build a church here. He thought about all the healing services he'd attended for other friends, stricken like Tigh, and now dead. And already he, too, was turning to leave.

They walked back down the aisle. With each step he took, Michael felt the weight of betrayal, of refusal, tugging at his shoulders. How many saints had, at first, made a similar refusal, then heeded that inner voice that said, Turn back. What would it take? Say the truth, he thought.

Outside, the noontime light blinded him. They walked back to the car in silence.

"Sorry about that," Michael said when they'd gotten in and Tigh was turning over the engine.

"About what?"

"Didn't you see it? All that tackiness. Jesus, those plastic flowers made me want to puke. It reminded me of that little church outside Florence—remember?—the one with the bare lightbulbs strung over the altar?"

"I don't know," Tigh said, easing the car back onto the main road now. "I thought this place was kind of interesting."

"*Interesting?* Tigh, it was disgusting. That lovely carved altar screen and then all those schlocky knickknacks strewn about?"

Tigh looked over at him. He wasn't wearing his sunglasses now.

"You angry about something?"

"No, I'm not angry about something," Michael snapped back. He paused, trying to find the right word. It was this: "I'm offended." But he felt a need to explain. "I mean, here you have a perfectly beautiful church, and they have to trash it up with all that . . ."

He turned away in frustration, staring out the window, watching the cars coming from the opposite direction. They all seemed on their way to the Santuario, each carrying someone with an impossible petition or a gaudy trinket to lay down.

"I mean," he tried again, turning back toward Tigh, "you'd think someone would have some control over what goes on in these places. Did you see that guy eating the dirt?"

"It's part of their culture, Michael."

"It's embarrassing, is what it is," Michael insisted. "I'm embarrassed for them."

Tigh glanced over at him. He looked as if he were waiting for something more.

"All right, all right," Michael said, "I'm angry. Is that what you want me to say?" He kept his eyes fixed on Tigh, daring him, even when Tigh looked back to the road, not to be satisfied. "Angry, okay?"

"Michael, I don't *want* you to say anything. The only thing I want you to say . . ."

"Is what? The truth?" Michael scoffed. "Is that what you want? Well, how's this for the truth, buddy boy?" So, he thought, this is how it comes out. "The truth, Tigh, is that you're dying and you're scared, and you're not saying a goddam thing about it. Okay? That's the truth, if you really want to say it. That's what you came out here to face, and you're not. You're not dealing with it at all." The pressure on his shoulders, which he'd felt since leaving the church, had transferred to his stomach.

Tigh turned to him again.

"What?" Michael snapped.

"You're right," Tigh said.

Michael could see his eyes, those blue eyes he'd immediately noticed when they'd first met, looking at him with something that resembled relief and compassion.

"You bet I'm right!"

They passed a road sign: Santa Fe, sixteen miles. Michael watched it blankly, sourly. They might as well have been driving through the remotest outback. The sign gave him no comfort or sense of orientation. It was just words.

For a while, neither of them spoke. Babunia Krystyna once told him that such silences meant angels were passing. But it reminded Michael of that Friday night back in graduate school when they'd first gone out for coffee and he had suddenly become aware that they were both holding back. Tigh had gone first then.

"You bet I'm right," Michael repeated, but there was no longer any comfort in these words either. With his fists, he came down hard on the dashboard. "And dammit, I don't want you to die." There, he'd finally said it. He brought his right hand up to his forehead and closed his eyes.

Then Tigh was touching him, rubbing his left arm. It was as if he were saying, "Thank you" or "I'm here" or "Yes." It was as if he were saying, "Rest now, you've said the hardest thing."

But there was more: "And I wish," Michael continued, taking his hand away from his face, opening his eyes, "I wish that I could believe in that dirt, that I could make you believe in that dirt." Out of the corner of his eye, he could see Tigh nodding, yes, yes.

And more: "And sometimes"—he was looking at Tigh now—"sometimes I feel guilty that you got sick and I didn't." When Tigh nodded again, Michael thought of the priests, the way they used to nod their acknowledgment behind the screen in the confessional, just taking it all in, perfect ears for whatever you had to tell them.

And more still: "And I'm really glad we took this trip

together." He reached over and rubbed the hand that was rubbing his arm. "And"—God, could there still be more?— "and I think I've always been in love with you."

He couldn't see now, but he knew that Tigh was still nodding, still hearing him. "And even though we're not lovers," Michael was saying as their fingers interlocked, the sweat of their palms merging, "I'll be there for you. And . . ." All right, he'd lay it all down, every last, little withheld bit of it, even this hardest truth of all. "And Tigh, I'm scared, too."

BODY WORK

IF HENRY WERE THE kind of guy who paid attention to these things—the kind of guy he knows plenty of but just can't seem to be—he would be able to come up with the name of the flick he has in mind right now. He'd know the name of the actress, the year the picture was made, the leading man, the supporting cast. He'd be able to rattle off all those famous bitchy lines. Henry's lover, Dane—and even Henry's older brother, George, formerly a priest and not out of the closet until he was thirty-three—even they can give you all the best lines from the films of Bette Davis and Joan Crawford. But Henry, out when he was nineteen and now pushing forty, hasn't a clue.

"You turn in your gay membership card this minute," George once teased his brother when Henry confessed that he had never even seen *All About Eve*.

When George teases Henry this way, Henry just scoffs, tells his brother that there's a lot more to life than being up on the camp classics. And, in turn, his brother always looks at him with that dumb expression from when they were both kids, the look that says, Duh, tell us another brilliant one, Einstein.

That's Henry: he never quite gets it. He never quite gets when he's supposed to be serious and earnest, and when he's supposed to be witty and gay. Take parties: if he tries talking music—which, for someone who works in medical records, he knows a lot about—he usually gauges the situation all wrong, so that he ends up saying erudite things to people who don't know the first thing about music, even about the greats like Beethoven, and trite or silly things to someone who turns out to be the conductor of a civic symphony.

Right now, while the chicken is roasting in the oven and a bowlful of fiddlehead ferns is soaking in the sink, while he waits for Dane to come home from his after-work swim, Henry would like to call up his brother in Hartford, to describe the movie, but he's afraid George will just go flabbergasted on him. "You don't know *that* one!" he'll say. "Henry, who *are* you?"

It's a thirties picture. That much Henry knows. Since he doesn't go to those film retrospectives in Harvard Square, he must have seen it on TV, and the scene he remembers goes something like this: The leading lady is getting a massage. She's probably just out of the steam room and her hair is done up in a huge, artfully twisted terrycloth towel. She's lying on a table, a sheet discreetly covering her midsection, and some ravishing guy is giving her a rubdown. It hurts, but she's letting him go to it, because she's depressed. It's got something to do with her boyfriend. She's telling this hunk of a masseur—is it Cary Grant?—what a creep her beau is, what insensitive lousy louts all guys are. And here's this Adonis with his hands all over her. She doesn't pick up on what's going on, though she keeps oohing and ahing and directing him to rub "a little lower here, a little higher there."

Henry can't remember whether or not she catches on that the masseur has the hots for her. He can't remember whether they end up in bed—or however people having an affair in thirties movies ended up. And he still can't remember the name of the picture. All he knows is that it's one of those flicks that give his brother, and Dane, and a lot of Henry's friends, a real hoot.

But he also knows why it's on his mind tonight: he's about to go for his first massage. It's a legitimate massage— or supposed to be anyway—not like the ones Henry has seen listed in the back-page classifieds of the gay newspapers. In fact, it's the kind of massage where your body "becomes receptive to spiritual energy." That's how Brian, the masseur, described it to Henry the other day.

It sounded good to him: a little work on the body, a little work on the soul. Henry thinks he could use some of both. He's got a body that, while not out of shape, isn't exactly prime cruising material in the shower rooms anymore: small upper arms, soft tummy, thinning brown hair. Even though he swims two or three times a week, Henry can't seem to shake the approaching-forty look. And the state of his spiritual life—well, it's got an approaching-forty flabbiness, too. What Brian was offering, this massage with "spiritual overtones," sounded real good.

On the other hand, if Brian was offering something else as well, if he's interested in Henry's body for more than just spiritual reasons, Henry doesn't want to end up like that dame on the table: totally missing the point. He doesn't want to end up, once again, feeling like a chump.

It wouldn't take much, either—to end up feeling like a chump. Brian's about fifteen years younger than Henry, somewhere in his mid-twenties. He has curly, sandy-colored hair, blue eyes, and a smile that, when Henry tries to describe it, brings up words like *radiant* and *wholesome*. Words that people in those hard-edged pictures from the thirties would only use in ironic, catty ways.

With his looks, and a name like Brian, it's hard to

believe he's Italian, but when Henry looks at Brian's face he can detect something Mediterranean: a *glow*, he wants to call it.

Henry is a sucker for "glow." He's a sucker for "radiant" and "wholesome." And for young and cute and sandy-colored. On top of all that, Brian's got one of those bodies where everything fits together perfectly: well-toned upper arms, solid shoulders, a nicely defined torso. It's the kind of body Henry is usually intimidated by, but the first time they met—at coffee hour after Mass—when Brian smiled at him, it made Henry feel trusting, as if he could completely hand himself over to this guy: soul and body.

Being so trusting: there is a kind of chumpiness in that, too, Henry realizes. That's what his lover, Dane, keeps telling him. "Foolish, lovable, heart-on-a-string Henry" is the way Dane puts it—"just too willing to let people take you for a ride."

"Then why do you put up with me? Why do you put up with these crazy infatuations of mine?" Henry once asked Dane. They had been having a teasing, playful conversation, but now Henry really wanted a straight answer. "I mean, don't I embarrass you sometimes?"

"I think," Dane said, "that I've actually fallen in love with the way you embarrass yourself. I'm almost in awe of it, Henry. It's so Catholic."

Catholic, Henry now thinks, as he drains the bowl of fiddlehead ferns into the sink. Catholic. And he wonders if *that's* the root of all the times he's missed the point. That's sure what George would say.

George, being an ex-priest, being Henry's older brother, just being George, gives Henry a lot of grief about his still going to Mass.

"George, it's not a regular Mass," Henry tried to explain last month. "I mean, it's a real Mass, but for queer Catholics."

"Why are you going to Mass *at all*?" George had asked. He's a lobbyist for leftist causes in Hartford now and is constantly reminding Henry that he, Henry, is the least liberated gay man he knows.

"Shall I turn in my gay membership card?" Henry tried to joke, but George just sighed. "I'm going to Mass," Henry told him, "because I want a spiritual dimension in my life."

"Henry, you are so earnest," George had said.

So, as he starts to trim the fiddleheads—for years it's been a springtime tradition for him and Dane to have fiddleheads and roast chicken—Henry thinks about all of this: about being so earnest and chumpy and Catholic, about being so susceptible to blue-eyed Italian cuties with a good line about spiritual energy. About never quite knowing what's up and what's down, about being such an enigma to George, and about being loved by Dane in spite of it all, even because of it all. He thinks about all of this and about his still not having told his lover that tomorrow he's going for his first massage.

There's a pile of fiddleheads on the table now. When Henry looks down on them they look like a jumble of little green question marks.

"Why are we having such a fancy wine tonight?" Dane asks halfway through dinner.

Henry looks at his lover. Dane is dark—dark eyes, black hair, a dark, bushy mustache—the opposite of the man who tomorrow will have his hands all over him, the man Henry was just getting around to mentioning.

"What's fancy about this?" Henry asks, tilting the bottle so that he can get a better look at the label. Looking at the label is easier than looking at Dane. "I thought when you bought it you said it would go really well with chicken."

"I meant company chicken. Not just us chicken."

"Well, what's the matter with *us*?" Henry asks. "Aren't we worth it? Can't we be good to ourselves, too?" Being good to oneself is a phrase Brian used when he described his work to Henry.

Henry and Dane have been a couple ten years, and the domestic pattern of their life together hasn't varied much in the last five, not since they moved to the house in Watertown and Henry got his job in Medical Records at Mount Auburn Hospital. Mondays and Wednesdays Henry cooks while Dane swims his half-mile at the pool; Tuesdays and Thursdays it's the other way around. And, no matter who cooks, they don't drink "fancy" wine—anything over five dollars a bottle—when it's just the two of them at dinner. Not unless they're celebrating something.

Henry keeps looking at the label. He's on the verge of the nervous gigglies. This conversation, the wine—it's getting to him. It's beginning to sound like a setup, a prologue to "Dear, I have something to tell you." And it's not. The selection of the wine was a totally innocent gesture. But now, just when he was about to say something, Henry can't bring up Brian, because now it would seem like a setup.

"So how was swimming?" he manages to get out.

Dane's a graduate of the Harvard Dental School—he specializes in making kids' teeth straight—and a dental school diploma gives him privileges at the Harvard athletic facilities. They share the swim card, pass it back and forth from day to day, so that twice or three times a week, Henry becomes Dane Dulong, D.M.D. He assuages his Catholic guilt about this by telling himself that using Dane's card is just a privilege any normal spouse would get. That's what George would say. Tomorrow is supposed to be Henry's turn to get the card, but he won't be using it because he'll be at the massage.

"Swimming was great," Dane tells him. "I pushed myself and did an extra quarter-mile."

Dane is older than Henry by a few years, but he's in better shape: trimmer, tighter. He "pushes" himself. In fact, everything about him seems in better shape: his body, his job, the way he's able to resist the appeal of cute guys.

"Any cuties in the shower room today?" Henry teases.

They both enjoy those Harvard swim types, but seeing those guys in the shower doesn't seem to throw Dane off the way it does Henry. For Dane it's just a passing show, nothing more than watching one of those amusing thirties flicks.

"Remind me to give you the swim card," Dane says as he pours them both some more of the wine that Henry is now wishing he'd never selected.

"Oh, I almost forgot," Henry says, watching the pale liquid fill his glass. He wants this to sound real casual. "I can't use the swim card tomorrow. You can have it."

If this were a thirties movie, and Henry were directing, he'd probably tell Dane to hold the bottle right there in midair, to put in some little gesture that would hint at suspicion, that would serve as the cue to a bitchy line. But this is the eighties, the decade when pulling off one of those great, campy lines seems to have lost its oomph, the decade he and Dane have been through together. A massage by a curly-haired, blue-eyed kid that Henry met at Mass? Dane isn't going to be a bit surprised by any of this. He won't even, as the saying goes, blink an eyelash.

And he doesn't, even after Henry tells him the whole story, even after he calls the massage "body work." Even after Henry reiterates all the stuff Brian has told him— about how we abuse our bodies, either by ignoring them or becoming slaves to them, about how we can put our bodies into the service of higher consciousness, "even-mindedness" is the word Brian used. Even after Henry tells him about Brian's yoga-trained approach: to relax the body, slow down the breathing, so that you can be open to the presence of God. Even after all that, Dane just keeps listening.

The next morning, just as they do every morning except when they're having a fight, Henry gives Dane a good-bye hug just behind the front door. Since they both leave the house at the same time and take the same trackless trolley down Mount Auburn Street, this "good-bye"—their last intimate moment together before they return home in the evening—takes place a good twenty minutes before they actually part, when Henry gets off at Mount Auburn Hospital. (Occasionally, on the trolley, if they get seats together, Henry will secretly scratch at Dane's leg, but usually they spend the trolley time reading, hands to themselves.)

Today Henry is careful not to put anything extra into his good-bye hug, no longer than the usual holding, no extra hard squeeze. In no way does he want Dane to think there is special import in today's good-bye. After all, he's just going for a massage. For his part, Dane doesn't say anything, doesn't tease Henry or ask what time he'll be home. As they leave the house, Henry wonders if Dane even remembers that he's going for this massage. But then he sees that Dane is toting his swim bag, the swim bag he wouldn't normally be carrying on Thursdays.

"Who's going to make supper tonight?" Henry asks after they've been on the trolley a few minutes. He's been trying to concentrate on a book called *Autobiography of a Yogi* that Brian had recommended, but this question of who will be responsible for supper has kept intruding throughout the chapter on Kriya Yoga, or Union with the Infinite.

"Well, I'm going for a swim and you're off doing your thing . . ." Dane says.

"Thing" makes Henry feel foolish, and he knows Dane knows that, too. "Thing" is carrying the weight of Henry's personal history on its sorry, slumped shoulders, the weight of every one of Henry's infatuations. "Thing" refers to Steven the nurse with whom Henry had a brief affair seven years ago; and Ray the architect, who, Henry once tried to convince himself, was just a guy to go to jazz concerts with, since Dane hated jazz; and Ralph the graduate student in theology, and David the poet, and John the window dresser. Except for Steven ("pre-AIDS Era Steven," Dane calls him), Henry never went to bed with any of these guys, but he knows, and he knows Dane knows, that this was just a consequence of the guilt, fear, timidity, and just plain missing the point—that singular combination—which it is his distinction to possess.

A technicality, really, not sleeping with them. You fall

for someone and you might as well: your lover is the body next to yours in bed, but these guys ravish your dreams. And now there's the possibility that Brian just might be into ravishing his body, too.

"Maybe we should do dinner separately tonight," Henry says. "I mean, I don't know how long my massage will take." Henry's on the verge of the nervous gigglies again. Thanks to their sitting side by side on the trolley, he doesn't have to look his lover in the eye.

"Is that what you want?" Dane says.

What Henry wants is to tell Dane that this one is different, that Brian—despite the good looks Henry still hasn't mentioned—is serious and intelligent and legitimate. That there's a brotherly quality to their relationship, a caring for the spiritual growth of the other. Henry wants to tell Dane the story he's just read in the *Autobiography* about the apprentice yogi whose guru invited him into his bed . . . solely to share the experience of divine tranquility.

"It's not what I want, necessarily," Henry tells him, rising to make his stop. "It's just that I can't predict how long it's going to take." And then he looks straight at Dane, trying to look divinely tranquil.

Brian works out of an old apartment building turned office space in Porter Square. It used to be a working-class building in a working-class neighborhood of Cambridge, but the extension of the subway—and the yuppies—from Harvard Square, a mile to the south, has given the whole area an upscale feel. Across the street, even the old Sears Roebuck store is being rehabbed with postmodern accoutrements.

An organization called the Center for Wholistic Health Awareness occupies the second floor of the apartment building. Brian has explained to Henry that he rents space from them, a room where he does his body work. Henry wonders what Dane, or George, would say about a place that spells holistic with a "W."

As he climbs the stairs for his five-thirty appointment, a woman about Henry's age is descending. She's wearing a denim skirt with an overalls bib and a tie-dyed cotton T-shirt. There's a beatific smile on her face. She doesn't seem to notice Henry.

The staircase takes a turn at the second-floor landing. Ahead, in a room that looks for all the world like a Mom and Pop grocery store, are two large showcases of holistic health goods: displays of crystals; baskets of dried fruits, roots, and barks; books, silk scarves, mats, contoured sandals; posters depicting holy scenes from the lives of Oriental saints. There's a fireplace mantle against one wall—probably this was the parlor of the old apartment—and taped to the oval mirror is a mandala. Two or three people are sitting cross-legged on the floor, filling plastic pouches with scoopfuls of herbs.

"Hi, Henry!"

It's Brian, at the other end of the hallway, giving him that radiant, glowing smile. A smile that Henry knows, just knows, even in the easily suckered foolishness of his heart, is honest and good.

Brian shows Henry the way to his massage room, what was probably once a small bedroom of the apartment. Now it has the quiet feel of a doctor's consultation room, though cozier. The floors have been sanded and polyurethaned, the walls are white. On a small table, there is a gilt statue of an Indian deity, maybe Shiva. A long padded table occupies the center of the room.

Brian explains that this is where they'll work, that he'll start with Henry on his stomach and eventually move to Henry on his back. He explains everything in a manner that sounds very professional to Henry, but what Henry really wants to know is why the Shiva. Why the yoga stuff? And how Brian Tagliaferro, a nice gay Catholic Italian boy from East Boston, got to be a person with such an unorthodox spirituality.

Brian hands Henry a clipboard with a form to fill out. There are the usual questions—name, address, birthdate— and questions about his medical history: serious illnesses, allergies, conditions for which he is currently being treated. Henry ticks off all the boxes marked "None."

"So," Brian says, taking the clipboard and giving the form a perfunctory glance, "I'll let you get undressed now. You can take everything off, or, if you'd be more comfortable, you can keep your underpants on. I'll leave you alone for a minute." He goes out of the little room, shutting the door behind him.

Henry loves the way Brian says "underpants" instead of shorts or briefs. It's so offhand, so unaffected, so cute— just like him. This, however, doesn't solve the problem of whether—whatever they're called—Henry is going to keep them on or take them off. He wonders if that's why Brian made such a big point of explaining that Henry would be starting off on his stomach. The more modest position first?

All day at work he wondered about getting an erection. It seems an inevitability, but he doesn't want to give himself away, doesn't want to reveal any horniness for Brian if that's not what Brian is up for. Not with Shiva looking down on them. Henry wants to take this all very seriously, this preparing the body for spiritual awareness. He wants to be a good little yogi, the best apprentice Brian's ever had. If that's what Brian wants.

When Brian returns, smiling again, Henry is out of his clothes and standing there, on the verge of shivering, in his jockeys, sucking in his gut. He looks for some sign of disappointment in Brian's face, some hint that he's already missed the point, that when you're invited to take your clothes off you take them all off.

"Okay, Henry," Brian says, giving him clear, step-by-step instructions, "whenever you're ready we can begin."

Henry listens for double entendres in everything Brian says: whenever you're ready . . . we can begin. Is there anything *behind* these phrases? That's what George would want to know.

From the end of the table, Brian pulls out a padded object that looks a little like a face mask on a stick.

"This is a face rest," Brian explains, draping the four little pads with clean tissues. "This way, you can rest your face straight down and breathe normally while I work on you."

Work on you, Henry thinks.

When Brian reattaches the face rest to the end of the table, Henry scoots his body up and fits his face into the contraption.

"Comfortable?" Brian asks.

"Yes," says Henry, talking to the floor. He closes his eyes. For a few seconds nothing happens; then he becomes aware of Brian standing over him, breathing—deep and regular—collecting himself, "centering," he guesses it's called. Finally, Brian takes in a long, deep breath, holds it, then lets it out.

"Pay attention to your body," Brian tells him. "To the way your knees touch the table. Your thighs. Your stomach." He says everything slowly and deliberately, pausing between sentences. "Feel your chest on the table." Henry feels it. "Try to be aware of your breathing," Brian says. "Of your inhalations." Henry breathes in. "And your exhalations." Henry breathes out. "Good," Brian tells him. "And now . . ." Brian's hands touch his shoulders. "Try to feel gratitude for your body. Gratitude for this gift you are about to give yourself." Henry inhales again. "Be grateful for this hour you have given yourself, for this time that is just for you."

Then he begins. He massages Henry's shoulders and back, kneading his fingers into Henry's flesh. Henry wants to let out a little groan of pleasure, but pleasure doesn't seem like the point. There's something solemn about this. Brian's movements are slow, deliberate, almost ritualistic, as if he is trying to initiate Henry into something new. You can work on me forever, Henry thinks.

Brian runs his hands down the length of Henry's arms, bearing into what little muscle there is, right down to the fingertips, as if he could squeeze out all the impurities and tensions. He does the same on Henry's legs, starting at each thigh, slowly pressing down and pushing on the muscles. Henry can feel them rippling and rolling under the flat of Brian's palm, being squeezed like pasta dough through a spaghetti machine. He wonders if his body is a disappointment to Brian. He wonders if Brian has to put up with a lot of this: out-of-shape guys who are just looking for a cheap thrill. He wonders if he's one of those guys.

"Henry." Brian's voice gently breaks the silence. "I'm going to slip your waistband down a little. Okay?"

Henry feels Brian's fingers slip under the elastic of his jockey shorts, slowly pulling them down, over his hip bone, halfway over his buttocks. This is it, Henry thinks. Suddenly, he's no longer doubting his body. But that's as far as Brian goes, and then he just resumes the massage, working now on Henry's lower back.

Henry wants to know what that was all about, but he's afraid he already knows. Brian is just being professional, doing what a nurse or doctor might do: tell the patient what's going to happen next, step by step, so he won't get freaked out. Doctors can't afford any misunderstandings. Maybe masseurs can't either.

Henry also thinks this: that there is every reason in the world for him to have a hard-on now—and why doesn't he? He sure doesn't feel all that spiritually advanced. What's happening, he decides, is that this damn feeling of being in a doctor's office, of being in professional hands, is getting in the way. When the time comes for Brian to flip him over and do his other side, won't he be surprised not to find much of a bulge down there? Or will he?

"Good," says Brian when Henry heaves a sigh.

After about a half-hour, Brian quietly asks Henry to turn over. Henry figures that this is the last opportunity. If something is going to happen, it will happen now. He eases himself onto his back, arms at his sides, the whole front of his body open and exposed, the pathetic pouch under his jockey shorts collapsed there like a spent balloon. He assumes that Brian will not make any overtures until he sees some sign of arousal on Henry's part. But Henry can't get the damn thing up. He tries willing an erection, thinking about those guys he sees at the pool, about Steven the nurse and David the poet, anyone—but it just won't come. From time to time, Brian rubs a little body oil into his hands, warming the liquid before he applies it to Henry's body, and this, that foreplay feel of oil on skin—something he and Dane haven't done in years—is the closest Henry comes to getting turned on. Here he is, finally ready to get the point, ready to *show* that he gets the point—if, dammit, there's a point to be gotten—and all he can do is lie here looking like some chump getting a massage.

And so, for over an hour, Henry just lies there, trying to feel gratitude for this mysterious, unpredictable body of his.

Three days later, at the weekly Mass for queer Catholics, Henry is sitting in his usual row, on one of the metal folding chairs they set up in the basement of a downtown Unitarian church, their renegade home. It's a shabby parish hall kind of place, with a small stage at one end that's probably used for pageants—if Unitarians even have pageants—and a kitchen to the side. The floor is beat-up linoleum, and wrapped pipes run across the ceiling. The whole place needs paint and sunlight. "The Catacombs" some of the members call it.

Henry looks around for Brian, quickly, because he doesn't want to look like he's cruising, even though some of that does go on during Mass, but Brian hasn't arrived. He twists around and a stabbing pain flares up just under his shoulder blade. It's been there, on and off, since Friday morning. Henry can't tell whether it's a sign that the massage is working or not.

Then one of the leaders gets up and invites them all to rise for the opening hymn: one of those invigorating, post-Vatican II songs from the sixties or seventies, accompanied by three guitars. At first, Henry feels a little silly belting out these sappy, catchy tunes. They remind him of all those heterosexual hootenannies he had to endure as a teenager. "Unrelentingly wholesome" is what George would call them. But, despite himself, despite his love of classical music, Henry always quickly falls under the thrill of these songs, and today is no exception.

Sing to the mountains, sing to the sea/Raise your voices, lift your hearts/This is the day the Lord has made/Let all the earth rejoice.

Down the aisle, if aisle is what you call the space between rows of folding chairs in a Unitarian basement, comes a man holding aloft a Bible, then a man and a woman carrying a plate of pita bread and a couple of carafes of wine. More vestiges of the sixties, Henry knows. He thinks of that denim-clad woman at the Wholistic Health Center; he thinks of Brian, *born* in the sixties Brian. He thinks of himself, degree in mathematics, head of medical records, reading a book about yogis levitating. *Henry, who are you?* George asks him.

After the acolytes comes the priest, a good-looking guy about Henry's age in red vestments. Henry loves this priest, Father Tom they call him. He loves Father Tom's ardent, intelligent, funny sermons, always so full of encouragement and good sense; he loves the way Father Tom reminds them that Christ came to break oppression and that the Holy Spirit gives us the freedom and the power to do so; he loves the way Father Tom wears street clothes, jeans, and sneakers, under his vestments. Henry has often wondered if Father Tom has a sex life, if the freedom the Holy Spirit gives extends that far.

It's Pentecost Sunday, and the readings—Isaiah, Acts, John—all emphasize the outpouring of the Spirit. Henry listens to the words: "In the days to come—it is Yahweh who speaks—I will pour out my spirit on all humankind." At these liturgies, they try to use words like Yahweh and humankind, instead of Lord and mankind, because they want to be a community that is "inclusive." The women, even though there aren't a lot of them at these Masses, always read one of the lessons and distribute the chalice.

Everyone laughs at the place in Acts where the skeptics

mock the speaking in tongues, claiming the disciples "have been drinking too much new wine." Henry laughs too. He knows what kind of ridicule those disciples must have had to endure.

And he laughs because of the happy camaraderie of this group. "Inclusive" is the word all right. He remembers Father Tom once telling them that the Mass was a place where one could bring everything that he or she is, bring all that stuff and dump it "before the Lord." Henry wishes he could get George to drive up from Hartford some Sunday and come to Mass with him, just once. He's tried to get Dane to come, too, but Dane's a lapsed Congregationalist and doesn't much take to all the hocus pocus of the Mass. Besides, what would it be like to have his lover here, in the same room with the guy who gives him a massage? Does he want his life to be that inclusive? And where is Brian anyway?

The sermon is not one of Father Tom's better ones. Rather than read from a prepared text, Tom is ad-libbing it, trying to make the homily sound relaxed and natural, but, in fact, it's pretty stiff. Every sentence is full of filler language, and, despite all the usual passion and ardor, underneath it's a halting, confused mess. Henry realizes that Father Tom hasn't a clue as to where he's going with this thing. He tries sending *Relax* vibrations Tom's way, anything to rescue him from this humiliation.

"And because Yahweh, the God of Abraham, Isaac and Jacob, pours his Spirit over all humankind . . ." Father Tom thrusts out his robed arms in a gesture of all-inclusiveness. "*All* humankind, black and white, rich and poor, gay and straight, and not just once at that Pentecost event, but continually, every day, because of this faithfulness, this radical faithfulness which . . ."

Get to the end of the sentence, Henry thinks. He is sure that if he ever got George to come to church again this would be exactly the kind of sermon they'd get that Sunday: a tripping, stumbling, flying-on-a-wing-and-a-prayer sermon. Henry can just picture the look George would give him. George, it's not always like this, Henry thinks.

Father Tom drones on. It sounds like he knows he's in trouble and he tries to tell a joke, but the thing doesn't quite come off. It's getting to be an embarrassment.

And you, Brian, Henry thinks. Where the hell are *you*? How do you come to get out of this? What do you know that I don't? Am I an embarrassment, too? Is that it? Taking my clothes off for you, asking you to give me something, expecting you to put it all together for me, body and soul? Where are *you*, dammit?

Mercifully, Father Tom concludes the sermon and they begin the Prayers of the Faithful, petitions offered up to God for personal and corporate intentions. Someone asks the prayers of the community for a friend struggling with alcoholism, another asks his "brothers and sisters" to pray for an end to the fighting in Central America, a third seeks the blessing of the Lord upon his newborn niece.

After each petition Henry repeats with the rest of the community, the words "Lord, hear our prayer." (Even the all-inclusive people let "Lord" stand here.) There are a lot of petitions today. Some of them—for friends with AIDS, for peace around the world—Henry has heard week after week for months.

During the petitions, Henry keeps his eyes closed. It helps him to concentrate. But now, in the dark theater of his head, it's Thursday morning again and he's on that trolley, sitting next to Dane, telling his lover, "It's just that I can't predict how long it's going to take." Dane, Henry now thinks, *you've* always known that, haven't you: that we never know how long any of this is going to take.

Then, without his even meaning to, while the petitions go on and on, Henry just starts repeating one word, privately, silently, over and over again. *You. You. You*, Henry is saying—You Lord, Yahweh, Shiva, or whatever Your goddamn all-inclusive name is—what's taking *You* so long? Who are *You* that I always end up the guy who never quite gets it? Why don't *You* do something about getting this mess of a body, this mess of a person, back into shape?

His shoulder is aching again, throbbing. He's so exhausted he could practically crawl up onto the white-draped altar table and fall asleep. Or let himself be worked on. Worked on and worked over by someone he can't quite figure, but who, Henry firmly believes, is as gorgeous and attentive as that actor whose name he still hasn't got.

THE WORDS

WHENEVER DONNY got depressed," I tell Ellen, "he'd buy himself a new shirt. The week we finalized our breakup, we spent one afternoon separating shirts, his and mine—they'd gotten mixed up in the two years we were together. He had one hundred forty-seven, as opposed to my eight. We counted them all out, one by one."

"*Who* counted them, Matt?" Ellen says, breaking eggs into a bowl. (By the looks of the pie shell on her kitchen counter, I can tell she's making quiche for supper.) She follows this up with a look, timed perfectly to coincide with the cracking of the last egg, signifying: If you want me on your side, first explain how *you* could live for two years with only eight shirts.

"Okay," I say, "so I enjoyed his collection, but the point is . . ."

She doesn't let me get away with even this much.

"*Enjoyed!*" Ellen cackles in a way that's both amused

and scolding. "*Enjoyed!*" She twists the syllables of that word until they sound like a pair of new sneakers squealing across her freshly waxed floor. "Matt Cooper, *enjoyed?*" And then she just bursts into laughter.

"All right, all right. I may have taken advantage of it," I confess.

"May have!"

Every Thursday night she and Mike have me over. But supper's just the excuse Ellen and I use to get together for heart-to-hearts. Even with her kids underfoot—Andy, the three-year-old, is playing trucks on the kitchen floor—we can be very honest with each other.

(I once introduced Ellen as "my best friend at work"—together we administer a day care center. "At work?" she laughed. "At work? I want to be your best friend, period!")

"Will you let me get to the point?" I say. "I admit it: we were very young. Both of us, Ellen. I was twenty-three and Donny was twenty-one when we split up. But what are you supposed to do with a guy who has an uncontrollable urge to buy new clothes every time he feels down in the dumps? He had no idea how many shirts he even owned. That's why, yes, *I* insisted on counting them. Someone had to show him how messed up he was. What was he going to do, spend his life buying shirts? And before you go saying anything," I add, "yes, I was also trying to humiliate him. I admit that, too."

"Dump truck!" says Andy, wheeling one of his Tonka toys up to my chair leg. "Andy go down in the dumps?"

"No, Andy," I tell him, "you're not down in the dumps." But Ellen's giving me another one of her looks; she thinks I'm down in the dumps.

"You think this time I want to put Brad through that kind of humiliation. Is that it? I don't, believe me, but there are some things he needs to hear."

"What do you want to tell him?" Ellen asks me. She fills the quiche shell with the egg and cheese mixture.

"God, what *don't* I want to tell him!"

"One thing, Matt," Ellen says, soothingly. "Choose one thing for right now."

Even Ellen's features are soothing: her eyes are brown, but not the dark, Mediterranean brown that's supposed to be so stunning on women. Same with her hair, which she wears in a clean-looking cut that doesn't call attention to itself. In general, Ellen's features don't call attention—her lips, her cheeks, her nose—but I love looking at her because the total effect is so soothing.

"One thing, Matt," she says again. In fact, Ellen can be so soothing that I sometimes lose patience with her.

"Now who's humiliating who?" I say. "You make me feel like one of the kids at choose time." At the day care we always have a few children who can't make up their minds what to do during their free, or choose, time.

"Choose," Andy echoes, and reaches up to where Ellen is slicing carrots. He grabs a couple of pieces.

"Andy, you may have one more slice before supper, and that's it," Ellen tells him.

When she's dealing with a recalcitrant child, Ellen's great at making her point without any physical show. It's all in her look and her voice. Very directed, like a laser beam. The kids know they can't dodge her.

"More," Andy demands.

"Andy, you heard me the first time: one more piece."

Andy's little hand, poised above the carrots, doesn't move. I watch him thinking. It's as if the message he's sent to his hand is on hold while he drums up a new way to justify his greed. But I can see that he's not coming up with anything. He knows this, too. A little twitch in his eyes tells me he's decided just to go for it. He grabs a fistful of carrot pieces.

Ellen's voice pounces. "Andy, go to your room!"

Andy's face collapses into a rubbery, featureless mass, like a sponge squeezing out tears. He drops the horde of carrots on the table and starts bawling.

"Andy, you know the rules," Ellen says. "Mommy told

you only one more piece, so now you have to go to your room."

I can't imagine this is sinking in, Andy is so convulsed in his wailing, but off he goes, a little lost soul, out of the kitchen and down the hall to his room. I look up at Ellen, as if we need to say something to restore peace, but she's already tossing the carrot slices into the salad bowl. Then she picks up a red onion and starts slicing it. I snitch a piece of carrot from the bowl and give her a cute grin.

"Look," I say, "I have one affair, one *minor*, two-week affair, and Brad gets incredibly self-righteous. You bet I have things to say to him."

"One thing, Matt," Ellen says.

"Like for starters, I'd like to tell him what life could be like without him."

Ellen suddenly raises her eyebrows and looks past me, an uneasy expression on her face. I turn around. Lindsay, Ellen and Mike's other child, is standing at the kitchen door, holding a piece of yellow school paper. She's seven and a pixie: Dutchboy haircut, Osh-Kosh jeans, and full of curiosity about what's been going on.

"Mom," she says, looking at me, "will you test me on my spelling words now?"

"Test you!" Ellen lets go with that cackle again, and Lindsay starts laughing guiltily. "Lindsay Alice, you have only been studying those words for five minutes. Are you sure you know them?" They give each other knowing smiles. I don't think anyone gets away with anything in this house.

"Well . . ." Lindsay says, stalling for time.

Ellen tells her to go back and study for another five minutes. "I'm talking to Uncle Matt right now."

Lindsay looks at me again. She lets out a huff, shrugs her shoulders very dramatically, and stomps—but not exactly stomps, paddles—back to her room, leaving in her wake the message: Unlike my naughty brother, Andrew, I am a dutiful and obedient child.

I wish I could reward her.

"Matt," Ellen says, "how do you see your life without Brad?" She is ripping lettuce now, very delicately, and adding it to the carrots and onions in the bowl.

We call these "hard questions." Whenever Ellen invites me over for supper, she says, "Bring some hard questions, Matt. I love hard questions."

"Life without Brad," I begin. "Life without Brad would be very different." I pause to let her object, but she just keeps working on that lettuce. "For starters," I say, "I'd have a lot more time for myself."

Ellen closes her eyes and murmurs something that sounds like assent.

"Look," I say, "is it such a big deal to want to go dancing occasionally? We never go dancing anymore. We never give parties. Sex is dull. Ellen, we've become stay-at-homes. Last Saturday night I baked bread and Brad practiced the piano. It's all getting a little too . . ." I watch Ellen start to butter a loaf of French bread with garlic spread. "Too domestic," I say, and check out how this goes over.

"Maybe that's who you are, Matt."

"Maybe it's *not* who I am!" I fire back.

This has been the gist of our Thursday conversations for years now. I've known Ellen long enough for me to become "Uncle" Matt to her kids, but who I am to me remains unsettled.

"In *Life Without Brad*," I try again, as if I'm making up the plot to a soap opera, "I'd move back to New York, I'd have lots of friends, we'd go out for dinner, stay up late, talk politics and philosophy and books. I'd give up this Ph.D. in sociology . . ."

She looks up from her buttering with an expression that says, I'm listening.

"Oh God, life without Brad," I say, and then I just leave it at that.

"It sounds lovely, Matt," she says.

I can't quite read this. It's as if she'll allow me, *but only me*, to have these fantasies. As if I haven't yet reached her standard of self-discipline, as if her strategy here is soothing patience rather than direct confrontation.

"Look, if you don't agree," I start to say, but then we hear a key turning in the lock, and Lindsay yells, "Daddy's home!" She runs out of her room and down the hall to the front door. Andy bounds out of his room, too.

"Matt," Ellen says, pushing the quiche into the oven, "I love having you here." Ellen could make a fricassee out of garbage.

In another minute, I can hear the kids clamoring for their father's attention. "Daddy, test me on my words," Lindsay says. "Daddy down in the dumps!" Andy says.

Mike shuffles into the kitchen, his jacket over his shoulder, loosening his tie. He's trying to make partner at his law firm. Even though he's exhausted, Mike's face shows the boyish good looks of Andy, the boyish looks of my first lover, Donny. I sometimes wonder what it would be like: Ellen and Mike, Matt and Donny. We'd each be celebrating eleven years together this year. It's a bizarre notion, but if Brad and I do stay together, we'll never be able to catch up with Ellen and Mike.

"Hello, Matt," Mike says, laying some enthusiasm over his weariness. He picks an olive out of the salad bowl.

"Me too, Daddy," Andy says, stretching to reach the bowl in the middle of the kitchen table.

"Here you go, Sport," Mike says, taking one out for Andy.

I give Ellen an amused look that's supposed to say: father's prerogative, huh? That's what it's supposed to say, but an impishness in me—the way I twist that grin at the last possible moment—turns it into something else, an invitation for Ellen to show me some disappointment. Okay, I think, after supper, since you like hard questions so much, how's about we tackle this one: What would life without Mike be like?

Mike pulls three glasses from the Hoosier cabinet he

refurbished into a kitchen cupboard. He sets them on the table. "Who's for a drink?" he asks.

"How about a hello kiss, first?" Ellen says.

"How about asking me my spelling words, first?" Lindsay asks, all little-girl huffy.

"A kiss for Mommy," Mike says, planting a quick peck on Ellen's lips, "and spelling words *later*." He taps Lindsay once on the nose.

I watch Mike open the freezer, pull out the ice bin, scoop up a fistful of cubes. Like a human dispensing machine, he passes his hand over the three glasses and drops some ice into each. It's the kind of deftness I wish I could develop, in anything—fixing drinks, playing tennis, arguing with Brad. To be able to "place" an ice cube, or a tennis ball, or a bitchy word, so perfectly that you win hands down.

From another shelf in the cupboard he gets out the Scotch and a package of cocktail nibblies in the shape of goldfish. (It's another part of the Thursday ritual.) He pours the goldfish into a bowl, sets it on the table, and sits down, looking as if he's now ready to face the family. I realize how much I'll miss these Thursday evenings if I move to Manhattan.

"Goldfish for Andy!" Andy says, still stretching his little arms across the table. Lindsay stations herself, like a dutiful sentinel, at Mike's side, waiting with that yellow word list still clutched in her hand for her father to pay attention.

"Goldfish for Andy!" Andy says, wiggling his fingers. Mike pushes the bowl further away from Andy's reach. Then he scoops up a handful, as deftly as he scoops ice from the bin, and deposits them in front of Andy.

Andy looks up at Mike as if his father is a god.

"Daddy, I want some too," Lindsay asks, in a squealy little whine.

"Help yourself," says Mike, offhandedly. He and Ellen look at each other. I've been around long enough to know this means, We know she's just vying for attention because

Andy's getting some, or It's important not to indulge the whining.

Lindsay reaches into the bowl, stops halfway, shrugs her shoulders, and withdraws her hand.

"I guess I don't want any."

Mike, Ellen, and I all look at each other.

"Daddy, will you ask me my spelling words now?"

"Later, sweetheart," Mike tells her. "Daddy wants to visit with Uncle Matt now."

"*Phooey!*" I can hear her mother's irony in Lindsay's voice. She turns to leave.

"Lindsay Alice, aren't we forgetting something?" Ellen calls out.

Lindsay paddles back, sheepishly. "What?" It's the clipped kind of *what* that says, I know what you want, but I'm going to try to get away with pretending I don't.

"You know," says Ellen in her no-nonsense day-care voice.

Lindsay looks at me, the regular Thursday guest.

"Uncle Matt is staying for supper, remember?" Ellen says, encouragingly. "You need to put out five plates."

When Lindsay goes to the pantry to get the plates, I say to Ellen, "Sometimes I wish you would tell *me* what to do."

Mike glances at me, then looks at Ellen. Their eyes meet, really meet, for the first time since he arrived home. And for a few seconds it looks like they're having a stare-down, but one that's full of eleven years of life together.

Eventually, Lindsay sets the table. The quiche and garlic bread come out of the oven. We sit down, take hands, and bow our heads for grace (another part of the Thursday ritual).

No one says anything, and all of a sudden I remember way back to elementary school, the inkling you get that, out of all the kids in the room, the teacher is going to call on you, and that's how I know Ellen's about to ask me to say grace. Which she does, of course.

I'm sitting between Ellen and Mike. Ellen's hand is soft, and she's squeezing my fingers ever so slightly, another one of her soothing, encouraging gestures. I squeeze back. Mike's fingers are thick and rough. Like Donny's, I think to myself, like Brad's. I don't squeeze Mike's hand, don't even dare move it for fear he'll misinterpret. How does one become deft at these things, I wonder.

"We give thanks for this day," I begin, "for this food, for our being together . . ." I stretch the catalog out: for the lovely spring weather, for good conversations (I give Ellen's hand another little squeeze), for dump trucks and goldfish and black olives. (Andy giggles.) This seems to put a cap on it, but into the darkness of my closed eyes and bowed head comes a remembered echo of Ellen's words: One thing, Matt.

There is nothing more I tell that voice, and say a loud *Amen*.

Ellen gives my hand a final squeeze. When I open my eyes, I don't look at her.

Mike cuts wedges of quiche, Ellen serves the salad. She is very careful that everyone gets the same number of black olives. Both Andy and Lindsay are crazy about olives and insist on a strictly equal apportionment.

"Three for Andy, three for Lindsay, three for Daddy, three for Uncle Matt, and three for Mommy," says Ellen.

"Four for Andy," Andy says, punctuating this with defiantly pursed lips.

"No, Andy, everyone gets three," Ellen tells him.

"Four!" Andy shouts, then looks around the table, smiling and giggling, ready to make one of us laugh with him. His own shouting has startled him, I think, and this is his way of undoing the shock.

"No, Andy," Lindsay pipes up, imitating the adults.

That does it. Andy stops laughing. He scowls at his sister and makes a grab for an olive on her plate.

"*No!*" Lindsay shrieks. She wrests the olive from his tight fingers just before he can shove it into his mouth. Andy raises a hand as if to strike her.

"No, Andy," Ellen says.

"Andy, no," Mike says.

Andy starts crying. Mike lets out a disgusted groan. Guiltily, I take a bite of the quiche. Ellen comes to the rescue. She calms Andy down, tells him that he may not take food from his sister's plate, reminds him of the equity in each person's receiving three olives. She says that we all have to share, asks him if he understands. Andy covers up his ears.

"You know what I'm saying," Ellen says, pulling his hands down. "We don't hurt each other, Andy." Andy covers up his ears again.

Then Mike pulls Andy's hands down. "Andy," he says, holding his arm tightly and talking right into the kid's face, "put one of your olives on Lindsay's plate." Andy obeys, and things seem to settle down.

While I eat, though, I watch Andy and the two remaining olives that Lindsay keeps tantalizingly on her plate. Andy sees me watching and turns this into a game, every now and then jerking his head in the direction of Lindsay's plate as if he's about to make for those last prizes. Ellen gives me a don't-encourage-him look.

"Eat your dinner," I tell Andy, in my sternest Uncle Matt voice.

Andy stuffs bits of crumbly quiche into his mouth.

"Mmm, good, Mommy," he says with such unaffected relish that I start chuckling. That sets Andy off, too. He giggles, and gobs of the egg custard fall from his mouth all over his chin onto the table.

I'm about to say, "He slays me," when Mike, with another disgusted groan, says, "Andy!" and tries to push the spewing morsels back into his mouth. Andy just laughs all the harder.

Lindsay echoes her father. "Andy!" she scolds, and then invites me to agree with her that "Andy is *so* messy."

Andy's face suddenly hardens. He reaches across the table to strike her. But he can't quite reach and flails at the air instead.

Ellen is about to chastise him, perhaps even gets out the first syllable of his name—it all happens so fast—when Andy interrupts her.

"The words, Mommy. Don't say the words." He's covering his ears again.

"Don't say the words," Ellen repeats. "Oh, you little monkey. You know what the words are, don't you?"

On nights when I'm over for supper, Mike puts the kids to bed. That way Ellen and I have more time to talk. We don't exclude Mike, but, to tell the truth, he usually seems impatient with the rambling ways of our conversations. There's an inefficiency about them that must drive a lawyer like Mike nuts. I think, too, that maybe he's embarrassed by the quality of girl talk that we sometimes fall into, especially when I get going on troubles with Brad.

It's the first warm evening of spring, so Ellen and I take ourselves out to the back porch. For a while we just sit, our feet up on the railing, and listen. The darkness, the faint traces of lilac in the air, the hushed and expectant air itself—all this makes me feel lightheaded, and reckless.

"Okay," I say, "ready for some hard questions?"

Ellen lets out a low, delicate moan as if she doesn't want to face it. It's the balmy evening, I guess, this promise of summer, its illusion of no responsibilities. My bringing up hard questions is pulling her away from her half-hour's respite from the family. I feel a momentary urge to back off. After all, compared to what Ellen's up against, the hard questions in my life seem like mere romantic indulgences. But this kind of thinking makes me feel foolish again, and *that* I don't want.

"Come on," I say. "Just now, what was in that little groan, Ellen? You sounded like Brad when I try to wake him in the morning. He hates to be roused from his dreams. Come on," I needle her, "what dreams are you hiding?"

"Dreams?" she asks distractedly.

"Don't play games with me, Ellen. No stalling." There's a rising hurtfulness in my voice that I didn't expect to be there, but I let it stay. "Tell me, now," I insist. "You'd just as soon get out of your present life, too, wouldn't you? What would life be like without Mike?"

"Matthew," she says. She sounds surprised—and hurt.

"Matthew nothing," I say. I'm riding on the crest of this ill will now, kind of enjoying the way it makes her squirm. "We know each other too well, Ellen. Come on, say it: you're jealous of me; you're jealous that I'm thinking about bailing out." Suddenly it seems very important that I get her to admit she's repressing things.

My eyes are getting used to the dark, and I can see her straining at me, trying to gauge exactly who it is she's talking to. She looks worried.

"Look," I say, backing off a little, trying to reassure her. "It's okay. I'll survive. I've done it before."

"You were twenty-three then, Matt," she says.

"What's that got to do with it?" I turn away from her, and for a minute we don't speak. But when I turn back, she's still giving me that how-can-I-reach-you look.

"It's this way," I tell her. "On the subway this morning, I overheard a guy saying that when he's in town he stays with his former boyfriend. Why did that strike me so, Ellen? It's these kids, they move in and out of relationships all the time, and still they remain friends. No trauma, no recriminations That's what I want, I want to be friends with Brad, even when it's over. And that's why I can't leave him, yet. I want to be sure we'll still be friends when we're no longer lovers. Dammit, Ellen, I want to be sure you and I will still be friends."

"Why shouldn't we be, Matt?"

"Because Brad knows things about me . . . he'll tell you things about me . . ." That sounds frightening, so I quickly explain, "Not horrible stuff. I mean, it's no big deal, but sometimes, sometimes I can be such a . . ."

Ellen lets out that pained little murmur again.

"You see?" I say. "You and I say so much to each other, even when we're hardly talking. You know what I'm thinking. You understand what I'm trying to say. We don't have to work at communicating. But with Brad, I keep feeling that he expects to hear things from me. Like I've got to spell it out for him all the time. Do you understand?"

And once more, Ellen softly groans. It's as if she's saying she understands only too well. I want to give her a reassuring grin, the kind I'm good at, the kind that will say, Okay, let's not make too much of all this, it really isn't a big deal, gay men break up all the time. But she's wise to these grins. Instead, I try looking out over the porch railing, out to the black silhouette of lilacs in the backyard, but again that old elementary school feeling that I'm about to be called on hits me. Before she can say anything, I turn back to Ellen.

"Matt, what does he need to hear from you?" she says.

I don't answer. The balmy air is beginning to feel oppressive. I try to focus on things I know, some incontrovertible fact: Donny *did* have one hundred forty-seven shirts!

"Come on, Matt," Ellen says. "The words. Say the words."

BABUSHKAS

RALPHIE, JEROME, and I sit on our fat asses, like three babushkas overseeing the party. The place is so packed that even though it's February someone has had to crack the windows open to let in some fresh air. Except for us, just about everyone else is standing. It's what I hate about cocktail parties—not just the congestion, but this obligatory standing. Really, can't anyone ever be tired for a change?

Then again, who wouldn't look tired next to Jerome's lover, Jeb? Jeb is one of those French-Canadian life-of-the-party types. Though he doesn't know any more of the guys here than I do, he keeps busy picking up drinks, dropping in on other people's conversations, "circulating." One minute he's delivering a critique of the latest film, and the next he's talking Bruins-Canadiens or the mayoral race or the Pope's visit to South America. Jeb can turn any party, gay or straight, into one big, happy *grande soiree.*

"How does he know so much about everything?" I ask

192

Jerome and motion toward Jeb, who's now talking deco-
rating to our host. The host's an architect and is using this
party to show off his newly renovated townhouse in the
South End.

"Jeb practices," Jerome tells me.

Jerome and Jeb have been lovers for three years. Sometimes I wonder how Jerome can be so comfortable with
Jeb's gregarious ways.

Ralphie and I, like the majority of the men here, don't
have lovers. We met last summer when we were huffing
and puffing our way through aerobics class together. Ralphie's still going, but I quit a while ago. In general, I guess
you'd have to say that Ralphie is more optimistic about
future prospects than I am. This evening, however, he's
not making the rounds, just seems content being babushkas
with Jerome and me. Last summer Ralphie had a brief thing
with our host, so maybe the whole scene—a cocktail party
for the architect's seventy-five closest friends—is a bit too
much for him right now. It would be for me.

"What do you mean *practices*?" Ralphie asks, leaning
across me to address Jerome.

Ralphie's still new to all of this, so he's always trying
to pick up some pointers.

"Well," says Jerome, and he pauses, as if he's got to
phrase this just right. "It's a combination of practice and
bluff. Jeb's pretty good at faking it, at least until he can
pick up enough to really know what he's talking about."

Until we all sat down together, I hadn't realized that
Ralphie and Jerome knew each other (as they hadn't realized
that I knew both of them), but then that's one of the charms
of gay life: we're all so interconnected through a hundred
ways I've finally learned not to inquire about. In my
younger days, when I was a little more naive, like Ralphie,
I used to ask dumb questions, too. "So how do you two
know each other?" I'd say. To which the response more
often than not was a series of awkward stares and blushes
and well . . . er . . . ums. You'd think I would have learned
the first time. So anyway, now, at this special age of thirty-

four, when I'm exactly twice as old as I am gay, I have finally learned not to ask.

Jerome tells me that after seventeen years being gay I should at least have learned how to mingle. He's coached me on how to open up conversations with strangers. His most useful tip: don't ask about work. "People either hate their jobs," he says, "in which case as soon as possible they'll turn the question back on you, or they'll talk your ear off about what incredibly fascinating things they do." Jerome says the idea is to drop in on a conversation and gradually ease into whatever is being talked about. The idea, Jerome says, is to impress without looking as if you're trying to impress.

"You see, Ralphie," I say, "you just have to be a big bluffer like Jeb."

But now I've pushed it too far, because Jerome comes to Jeb's rescue.

"Jeb is exuberant, that's all. He likes people and he likes to talk." Then he pauses and looks straight at me. "He likes *men*, Walter."

"Is it my fault I get tongue-tied in front of men?" I say. And turning to Ralphie, I add, "Even gay men. It's like being pee-shy, only worse. I mean, here we are, known the world over for being scintillating at parties, able to handle any topic with style and flair and grace, and what do I do? I clutch."

I'm not sure Ralphie's following this, but then Jerome says, "That's because you're still working on accepting yourself." I can tell he's saying this for Ralphie's benefit, too. (Contrary to what you might guess, Jerome is not a psychologist. He and I are both nurses at Boston City.)

"All right, already," I say. "So how do I learn to accept myself?"

"Stick with me, kid," Jerome says. "You'll get there."

"So here I am, sticking," I tell him.

A guy they call Mr. Safe Sex is here, passing out pamphlets. He's a kind of Crusader Rabbit type who's going around the country right now telling people how to do it safely. The architect has decided to combine showing off his house with a bit of consciousness raising. Somehow—how do these guys do it?—he succeeded in engaging this celebrity for his private party. You see what I mean? How can I have a good self-image when I wouldn't even know how to begin to contact someone like Mr. Safe Sex? I mean, he isn't exactly in the yellow pages.

Jeb comes bouncing over, flashing a safe sex pamphlet. "That's Mr. Safe Sex," he tells me, as if I'm his senile great aunt in need of a play-by-play commentary on the family picnic.

I look disinterestedly in the direction Jeb is pointing to. Which isn't exactly honest, since I've already checked out Mr. Safe Sex. He's actually cuter and less Marine Corps–looking than his publicity photos.

"That's his lover next to him." Jeb points to an older man, a rather stocky older man. "Isn't that wonderful!" he gushes.

"Isn't what wonderful?" I ask.

When Jeb's grin disintegrates, I realize he thinks I'm being bitchy. I'm not, it's just that I don't know what part he wants me to think is wonderful: that Mr. Safe Sex has a lover, that the lover is considerably older, or that he's less attractive. I don't know how deep into political correctness Jeb is inviting me to see.

"Well . . ." Jeb says, looking at Jerome for confirmation. "I . . . I think it's wonderful." Then he thrusts the pamphlet at me and dashes off.

Ralphie leans over to take a look.

"Here," I say, "you keep it."

Ralphie leafs through the pamphlet, which is full of information about what to avoid and how to enjoy what you can enjoy, then folds it up and stuffs it into the back pocket of his jeans.

"What does it mean to have a safe sex brochure sticking out of your left rear pocket?" Jerome asks, laughing at his own joke. "Oh God, remember the days of all those different colored handkerchiefs? Somewhere I still have a little chart I cut out of a magazine with all the color codes."

"Jerome," I say, "you sound like Hermione Gingold singing 'Liaisons, What Happened to Them?' Get over it, those days are gone." (This for Ralphie's benefit, too.)

Then I get up to get myself another orange juice.

Not that I don't enjoy alcohol, but somehow with Mr. Safe Sex here I feel an obligation to drink healthy. The pitcher of orange juice is on the buffet table, along with bottles of Poland Spring water. There are wonderfully chic munchies, too—fancy cheeses, crackers from places like Scotland and Norway, bite-sized quiches, a nice looking paté that's hardly been touched. I think about spreading some on the mini pumpernickel squares that have been tastefully arranged next to the mold. But then I wonder what everyone else knows about the paté that I don't. Maybe it spoils quickly. Maybe you can catch something awful from this paté.

It was my mother who taught me to put toilet paper on the seat before sitting down. I finally broke myself of this habit in nursing school—it was even more liberating than deciding to become a nurse—but lately I've noticed the practice has been coming back. Now, not only do I line toilet seats, but I generally avoid communal foods at parties. A lot of people do, I've noticed.

So I'm debating between just a chaste glass of o.j. and a morsel of something far more tempting when this tall, lean guy next to me says, "Didn't you run beside me in the Boston Marathon last year?"

At first I think he's making a tacky joke.

"With a body like this?" I say. I'm regretting wearing suspenders. They always make me look fatter than I am.

"What's the matter with your body?" he asks.

"I'm eleven pounds overweight for my height," I inform him.

He laughs and tells me I look fine to him, and then says, "Seriously, don't I look familiar?" and his body English invites me to peruse his physique, which is definitely of the marathon runner variety. He's got a nice face, too: cute and wholesome and slightly goofy-looking. Could he really be a city boy, I wonder.

"Oh, yes," I say, "now I remember. I waddled in, last place, and you planted the loser's wreath on my brow."

"Hey, why so cynical?" the guy says.

"Sorry," I tell him. "It's just that I have this incredibly poor self-image." He laughs, and this makes him seem so nice that I decide to try again. "The truth is, I'm uncomfortable at cocktail parties, especially gay ones."

Does he say, Hey, me too? Does he say, So let's get out of here and go someplace quiet? Does he say, Even if you don't run marathons I'm madly in love with you? Is the Pope Chinese?

What he says is, "Yeah, I saw you sitting over there with your lover looking pretty bored."

"That wasn't my lover," I tell him. Now what's this all about, I wonder. Is he trying to find out if I'm unattached?

All right, I remind myself. Whatever you do, don't ask about what he does for a living for at least five more minutes. And then I say:

"What do you do for a living?" It just pops out!

"Peter Frank," he says, extending his hand and smiling.

"That's what you do?" I say.

"That's my name," he says. "I usually introduce myself before answering personal questions." He smiles again, and that little bit of goofy in his face suddenly turns sexy. "What's yours?"

I can feel myself blushing as I pronounce Walter Mickieszewski. Don't ask how he knows the host, I tell myself.

"So," Peter Frank says, "now that we're introduced, you can ask me anything you like."

Out of the corner of my eye, I can see Jerome and Ralphie following this exchange intently. Even though they're too far away to hear what we're saying, they must pick up that "something" is happening.

"So, what *do* you do?"

"I'm a farmer," Peter says. I try not to look too charmed.

"You mean as in plow the soil, plant the seeds farmer?" I ask.

Peter laughs, tells me he raises rabbits in Vermont. He explains that rabbit yields more protein than equivalent amounts of any other meat, and that they consume far less grain to produce this protein. Apparently, if you have to eat meat, it is very ecologically correct to eat rabbit.

"But they're so cute," I say, putting on a cute voice myself.

"I know," says Peter. He gives me this knowing smile, but I pretend I don't know what it means.

"Well then, why do you do it?"

"Farming's in my blood," Peter tells me. He explains that his family has been farming in Vermont for a hundred and fifty years. He has apple orchards, too, but they aren't as profitable as raising rabbits. "You should see the apple blossoms in the spring," he says. "A whole hillside of them."

I glance back at the babushka corner. Ralphie and Jerome are gone.

"Have you tried the paté?" Peter asks. "It's rabbit paté. I made it myself." He spreads some on a cracker and hands it to me.

Okay, I think, down it goes, high protein, deadly germs and all.

"Delicious," I tell him.

"Thanks," Peter says and smiles again.

Jerome walks by and whispers in my ear: "Be still, my heart."

Peter gives me a quizzical look. "So, if he's not your lover, who is he?"

I tell him about Jerome, that he's my best friend, and that we work at the same hospital together.

"You're a doctor?" Peter says.

"No, just one of their humble handmaidens," I tell him. "I'm a nurse."

"In my book," Peter says, "nurses are more important

than doctors." He says this in such a nice way that it's not even patronizing. "Do you like your work?"

"At the moment, I like it more than anything else in my life," I tell him, and feel myself blushing more. "I mean, I like being involved in the healing process." Then, trying to keep the conversation going, I ask, "Are there many hospitals up where you are?" Though as soon as it's out, I realize what an embarrassing question that is.

"Sure are," says Peter, and gives me that look again.

Tuesdays Jerome and I are off from the hospital, and we usually meet for lunch. Half the time, we go to Burger King in Cambridge, my protest against health foods.

"Ralphie's in love," Jerome tells me after we've placed our orders. There are several people in line behind us, mostly working-class bruisers. I give Jerome a look that says, Wait till we're sitting down, but he goes right on talking. "Jeb introduced them at the party." Fortunately, the food comes right away. We take it to a booth and settle in.

"Who is he?" I ask.

"Some guy named Garrett—that's his first name— works at a bank downtown."

Jerome tells me all about Garrett, how he's not just a teller, but some important junior executive. How even with Mr. Safe Sex right at the party they still went home to Ralphie's and did it. "That very night," Jerome tells me.

"Well, let's hope Ralphie followed the guidelines on that pamphlet," I say, squeezing my packet of catsup onto the styrofoam tray.

"He did," Jerome tells me, very soberly. I look up. "He did."

This is one of the things I love about Jerome: he is never afraid to find out all the intimate details. I can just hear him asking Ralphie, "Did he use a condom?"

"Ah, romance," I say, and dip a french fry into my little glop of catsup.

"Spring's coming," Jerome says, and he doesn't take

his eyes off me, even when I keep dipping my fries into the catsup. It makes me uncomfortable, like he's trying to ferret out intimate details from me.

I look out the plate glass window onto the Burger King parking lot. It's one of those overcast late winter days, when everything is the color of lead. The asphalt, the bare branches of the trees, the sky. Even the music they're piping through the restaurant. This whole state, I think, feels gray like lead. Even the name: Massachusetts.

When I look back at Jerome, he's still staring at me, waiting.

"Jesus, Jerome," he makes me say at last, "if you want to know, ask, but don't just sit there staring at me."

"So who was he?" Jerome says.

"His name's Peter, he was the architect's houseguest, he raises rabbits in Vermont, and, no, we didn't go home and do it, safely or otherwise. We talked. At the party. That's all."

"That's incredibly romantic!" Jerome says. "I am so jealous."

Jerome wants to know more, but there is little else to tell besides the fact that Peter invited me to come up for a weekend, for apple picking.

"Apple picking! But that's months from now!" Jerome protests.

"I know," I say. "I think that was supposed to be a hint. I don't think he was as charmed with me after I told him about the cancer ward and bedpans."

"Oh, you poor dear," Jerome says. Then, to give me encouragement, he adds, "Maybe he just didn't want to come across as too forward."

So for two weeks I sit on that one: maybe Peter just didn't want to come across as too forward. I'm of two minds about this: part of me thinks that Peter's initiating the conversation was forward to begin with. So why should he have suddenly turned shy? On the other hand, someone had to start up the conversation, though inviting me up too soon, now that would have been forward. Then again, apple picking? At the very least he could have made it apple blossom time. But maybe that would have sounded too corny. After all, you don't want him acting like a lovesick cow, right?

"Call him," says Jerome, the following Tuesday at lunch.

"What do I say?"

To avoid Jerome's look, which says, Walter, sometimes I just don't know about you, I look down at my salad and push the tomatoes around. Because it's only March, they're still the tough, almost white kind.

"Jerome," I say at last, "I tell you, I'd clutch."

"Don't you see how romantic that is?" Jerome says. "I'd give anything to be that shy again. If he hears that shyness in your voice, he'll melt. Walter, the guy raises cuddly little rabbits. He's just your type!"

I start to smile, and Jerome pounces.

"Aha! I see that smile. Don't tell me you haven't dreamed about moving onto that farm in Vermont."

"Okay, okay, I'll give him a call, but it's hopeless."

"What's his number?" Jerome asks.

"What do you mean what's his number? You think I've memorized it?"

"Come on, Walter, what's his number?"

"Jerome," I say, returning his I-don't-know-about-you look, "I have not memorized his number."

"Come on, Walter," Jerome says. He sounds like a doctor coaxing a kid to "Come on and open wide, this won't hurt," and I start to laugh. "Come *aw-awn*," he says again.

"Jerome, I love you," I say, and recite it for him, area code and all.

The voice that answers the phone is not Peter's. "This is Mark," it says. "Can I take a message?"

I feel like slamming the phone down, but that seems excessively dramatic, so I say yes, that he can tell him Walter from Boston called.

"Do we know you?" Mark says, sounding like he's searching for a face.

"No," I say, and then I think to myself, what the hell, might as well be friendly. "I met Peter at a party down here a few weeks ago. We got to talking and he told me all about your farm."

Your farm, Peter and Mark's farm. Already I hate those two names: they sound so good together.

"Walter from Boston—oh, now I know," says Mark, suddenly putting together a name and a story, if not a face. "Peter's told me about you. How're you doing?"

I can't believe how genuine he sounds. Like it's no problem for him. This means only one thing: Mark—this Mark of Peter and Mark—feels no need to be jealous. I don't know whether to be happy or sad about this.

"Oh, I'm fine," I say. "Just thought I'd call to say hello."

Mark tells me Peter will be happy to hear that I called. He tells me I should come up some time to see the farm. He tells me a few more things, but I'm busy flipping through my little black book, crossing out *their* telephone number. If I'm lucky, I can unmemorize it, too.

"Damn," says Jerome when I tell him. "I was counting on this one."

"Yeah, I guess I was, too," I say.

Today it's the hospital cafeteria, and the head dietitian has given us each an extra large helping of the macaroni and cheese. She is the only person I know who says I look thin. She thinks every nurse should look robust: for the patients' sake.

"*You* wouldn't ever lead on someone you'd just met at a party, would you?" I ask Jerome.

He looks down at his plate. "After today," he says, "I'm going on a diet. Let's bring grapefruits for lunch from now on."

"*Jeroh-ohm*," I say. "Would you?" I raise my eyebrows,

the way my mother used to do when she just wouldn't put up with any of our nonsense.

"Look," he says, "according to Jeb, a little titillation every now and then is good for the soul."

"Jeb *would* say that."

"Walter," Jerome says—and I can tell he's hurt now—"Jeb isn't the trashola you think he is. He just happens to be incredibly exuberant."

That word again: *exuberant*. I turn it over and over in my mind. There are days when all these words we use seem so strange and imprecise, so unscientific. I mean, you take a throat culture to the lab, and it comes back either positive or negative. It's clearcut. But a guy with a lover in Vermont, coming on to me, of all people. What's clear about that? Where's the exuberance? And what else comes with that exuberance?

"Look," Jerome says, "the guy thought you were cute. He was down in Boston without his lover, and, well . . . Look, eventually you would either have become friends or drifted apart. Jeb calls it gay networking."

When I don't respond, Jerome tries another tack:

"So maybe he sensed that you were looking for something more. Or maybe he just got scared, I mean with Mr. Safe Sex around and all." Jerome must think I'm not buying any of this, because he takes a deep breath and, like it's the only thing left to say, he reminds me, "The guy *likes* you, Walter."

"And what am I supposed to do with that?" I ask him.

I stare at Jerome's abandoned plate of macaroni and cheese. Part of me wants to dump it all onto my plate and gobble it up, wants to get as fat as a babushka and be done once and for all with this hankering after romance.

"What you're supposed to do with that," Jerome begins, and then he just stops and looks at me. "Walter, if it's too painful . . ."

"It's painful all right," I tell him, and start picking at his plate.

For a minute, we don't say anything more. Jerome just keeps staring at me with his compassionate nurse's eyes, even when I look away. Then this Dr. Kildare type walks by, and out of the corner of my eye I see Jerome's attention drift over to him. When I'm sure Jerome isn't watching me anymore, I look up and take a glance, too. Suddenly I remember Jerome whispering to me at the party, Be still, my heart, and I start giggling. The kind of giggle cranky, stubborn patients sometimes give you when they finally have to admit they feel better.

Jerome turns back to me with a bemused look on his face, and this just sets me off even more: that I should be the one to let him in on a secret. I look at the gobs of macaroni on our plates and push them both away. Jerome watches me, but he still doesn't get it.

"Okay, okay," I tell him. "Tomorrow we'll have grapefruits. Grapefruits . . . and a teeny-weeny slice of paté."

THE LANGUAGE
WE USE UP HERE

B UNKIE AND I HAD
been dancing together for a good half-hour before we ever
spoke a word. I'm not sure I'd even asked him if he wanted
to dance; it was just a matter of giving this cute black kid
standing next to me a smile and a nod, and off we'd gone,
boogying our buns off. Actually, we said a lot to each other
that first night on the disco floor, but it was all through our
bodies. We played out an entire conversation in gestures
and looks, in the casual but deliberate movements of our
hips, and chests, and shoulders.

I said things like: I think you're very hot. And he said:
No one's ever told me that before. I said: I love the way
you move your ass. He said: I'm really pretty shy. I said:
Don't get me wrong, I'm not a trashy person. I can be shy,
too. And romantic, and funny, and kind. He said: I can
tell, that's why I'm dancing with you. I said: I'd like to get
to know you better. He said: Let's stop dancing.

As we moved off the disco floor, I ran my hand up and down his back and introduced myself.

"Pleased to meet you, Robert Garthside." He spoke with a Southern accent that I immediately found charming. Even the way he repeated my whole name seemed charming, and almost foreign, as if the nuances of the language, the language we use up here, weren't quite in his mastery yet. He shook my hand vigorously. "I'm Bunkie Williams. Bunkie with a i-e at the end." He pronounced the letters *ah-ee*.

"Bunkie," I repeated. I loved the way he wanted me to get the spelling right, and I wondered what he was telling me in that.

"It comes from my daddy," Bunkie went on. "Daddy being Thurnell Bunker Williams the *Third*. Thurnell Bunker was Daddy's daddy's name, and his daddy before that." He rattled off the genealogy, then giggled, a little stifled-cough sound at the back of this throat. "Yessir, Robert, I might have had quite some bodacious name: Thurnell Bunker Williams the Fourth."

"That would have been some name all right," I said, guiding him toward the railing that penned in the disco area. He seemed oblivious to everything but the story he was delivering, and for a minute I wondered if I'd misread his body English while we were dancing.

"Except that Daddy up and died," Bunkie continued. "Just before I was born. So that's when Mama got determined to break with the family tradition. Superstition, I guess. I suppose she didn't want no son of hers inheriting Daddy's misfortune along with his name. Yessir, she put a stop to me being the Fourth."

The way Bunkie went on and on, I guessed that maybe he was on speed. But when I learned that he was new to Boston—he interrupted himself to tell me he'd moved up at the end of the summer from a place called Dothan in Alabama—that seemed to explain it all. We stepped off the platform and into the crowd near the bar.

"I'm the only son," he said. "I've got six sisters, all

older than me. Naturally, everyone was waiting for a boy to come along"—and he laughed again—"so as to carry on the family name. Still, three previous generations of Thurnell Bunker Williamses, it sure is hard to ignore, and that's how Mama and my sisters they come to compromise on Bunkie. Bunkie's my actual baptized Christian name."

A broad grin plumped his cheeks and accentuated his tiny ears. I realized that Bunkie wasn't high at all. It was just that he was happy: happy to make my acquaintance. And unsuspicious, too, in the way that strangers to a new city often are, not yet knowing what's to be wary of. I think he would have been just as friendly to anyone that night. He was the indiscriminate friendly type, a type I find very sexy and—I can admit it now—a little threatening.

I looked at him. Sweat was tracing silver lines down his brown forehead, across his temples and down his neck. His close-cropped hair was glistening, too, from the perspiration and the gelled lights that kept altering the hues in his face: blue-black, red-brown, yellow. He looked exhilarated, almost too exhilarated for this place of choreographed poses. I think right then and there I started falling in love with him.

We smiled at each other, the way you do when the only thing to say next is too obvious, or too embarrassing, or both. And then I saw Bunkie's eyes move back to the dance floor. I looked. There, dancing like a couple of bleached-blond show girls, their bodies as loose as seaweed, were two queens. Young kids, about Bunkie's age—twenty, twenty-one—they wore blousy shirts fastened at the waist with cummerbunds, gaucho pants, and too much jewelry: chains and ear studs and rings on both hands, which they splayed out as if they were demonstrating the aftereffects in a liquid detergent commercial.

"Really," I said, in that way that's taken the place of: Give me a break.

Bunkie looked back at me. He seemed puzzled.

"Queens," I explained, figuring this was part of the vocabulary he'd not yet encountered.

"That's Ted and Jeremy," Bunkie said. "They're friends of my Uncle Carl."

"Uncle Carl?"

"My uncle I live with," Bunkie said.

And that's how I came to learn of Carl.

A lot of my friends have told me that it's just as well things didn't work out with Bunkie and me. They talk about the age difference, the fact that Bunkie was from the South, and once someone even brought up the black-white thing. But eventually they all get around to Uncle Carl.

Because I work for the city housing authority—I'm an administrative type—I've had plenty of experience with good-intentioned liberals. In fact, I guess you'd have to call me a liberal, too. I know how to recognize racism when I see it, enough to admit that I'm not altogether innocent there either. But what happened between Bunkie and me involved something else. Supposedly I was introducing him to the possibility of a dignified life, a dignified gay life. What could have been more politically correct than that?

And that's where, my friends tell me, Uncle Carl comes in.

"What did you expect," they say, "when the kid's only adult role model was someone like *her*?"

That first night—we'd ordered drinks and sat down at a table—Bunkie went on and on about Uncle Carl.

"My uncle's a chef at a big restaurant downtown," he told me, and then, typically, his story went off in several different directions: about how Ted and Jeremy were waiters at the restaurant where Uncle Carl cooked; about how he, Bunkie, had been in town only a few weeks, working days in a bakery and studying at one of the community colleges in the evening; how it was his uncle who'd found him the job and put him up rent-free; how Uncle Carl was his Mama's little brother.

"But Mama isn't speaking with him anymore," Bunkie

said. "Mama's been saying for years how Uncle Carl sold his soul in the North."

He told me how Carl had run off when he was twenty and made his way to Boston, where he eventually became a chef.

"Mama came up here to visit him once—I must have been about eleven—and when she came back she announced as how he'd been *intirely* corrupted. I remember she kept shaking her head, and my sisters, they all shook their heads, too. And then Mama said that he didn't seem to want to find himself a wife either, and everyone shook their heads again. It sure seemed peculiar to me."

"Peculiar until you started putting the facts into place, right?" I winked at him. "I mean, isn't that why you came North? Isn't that why you're living with your uncle?" I reached across the table and stroked his arm.

"To tell the truth, Robert, I hadn't much thought about coming North." Bunkie touched me back, a shy, friendly "An' how're you?" touch. "It was Miss Allyn who encouraged me to come up here."

"Who was Miss Allyn?" Bunkie was weaving so many strands into this tale, but I would have listened to an epic as long as it allowed me to keep talking to him.

Bunkie told me that Miss Allyn was his senior English teacher. A white woman and a New Englander, she apparently took quite a liking to Bunkie and pushed him to apply to schools up here.

"She'd have me over for tea," Bunkie explained, "and she and Miss Roberts—that was her lady friend that she lived with—they'd read through the catalogs with me and later helped me polish up the applications. She was the one that suggested I could come North and live with my uncle."

"What did Miss Allyn know about your uncle?" I asked.

"Oh, Mama gave her quite a earful," Bunkie said. "When Miss Allyn came to call one afternoon, Mama wanted nothing to do with any plans for my going to school up North and living with Uncle Carl. *Oo-ee!* It took quite a lot of convincing on Miss Allyn's part to get Mama to agree."

"She was a clever dyke, wasn't she" I said.

Bunkie shook the ice in his glass and gave me a confused look.

"Dyke?"

"Don't you see? Miss Allyn saw how it would all work out if you came North. She guessed that you were cut from the same cloth as she and your Uncle Carl. That you needed space to grow—gay space." I watched him for a reaction; I loved introducing Bunkie to these new phrases.

"But what's a dyke?" he said.

We were interrupted by the arrival of the two queens I'd seen on the dance floor, Ted and Jeremy.

"Bunkie!" they shouted practically in unison as they came rushing over to our table.

One of them—I didn't particularly care to learn which was which—gave me the once over, then turned his attention back to Bunkie. I was being written off. Maybe they were jealous of my hair being naturally blond, or maybe the understated preppie look turned them off. Who knows. I've heard all the theories about why queens and straight-appearing gays don't get along. I didn't care. They turned me off, too, and that's all that seemed to matter.

They hovered over Bunkie, spilling out gossipy little stories with manic energy, like a popcorn machine at climax. Even though they were Bunkie's age, it became clear as I listened that Ted and Jeremy were actually Uncle Carl's friends, that Bunkie was someone they'd met only a few times. I watched Bunkie reacting to them. He seemed amused, but awkward, too, and I realized he wasn't sure when he was supposed to laugh or how exactly to react to some of the outrageous tidbits they were throwing out. But with that indiscriminate friendliness of his he did his best to pick up the cues, to become conversant with their campy style.

Then, in a flutter, Ted and Jeremy were gone. Bunkie smiled again.

"Really," I said.

We didn't go home together that first night. Nor the second time we met. Something told me to go slow with Bunkie. It was hard to tell just how inexperienced he was. I wasn't even sure he'd ever slept with another guy; it was certainly difficult to imagine he could have done so under the watchful eye of his Mama and six sisters. But the more we talked—for we'd agreed to meet regularly at Flash for dancing and talk—the more I picked up that his Uncle Carl was taking Bunkie in hand. Carl had given him a tour of the discos during Bunkie's second week in town. He'd thrown a dinner party to introduce Bunkie to some of his friends. The last week in September, Carl had even taken a day off from work and the two of them made a day trip to Provincetown on the ferry.

"Your uncle sounds terrific," I told him. It was our third Friday night at Flash, our third Friday of dancing and conversation. I kept expecting that Bunkie would want to play the field, but he seemed perfectly happy just spending the whole evening with me. "I mean," I said, "it's got to be every gay man's dream: a gay uncle who'll show him the ropes."

Bunkie blushed.

"Uncle Carl even gave me the birds and bees talk," he said. "Not the regular one." He laughed. "You know, the other one, the gay one, and about how to do it safely." For the first time since we'd met, the look he gave me did not seem shy.

I reached across the cocktail table and ran my hand along his cheek.

"Robert," he said, "Robert Garthside. There's so much I don't understand."

"I know, Bunk," I told him. "There's a lot I don't understand either. Maybe all I'm saying is that it would be nice not to understand things together."

■ ■ ■

I still remember the first time I ever went home with another man. I was eighteen, which makes it a good fourteen years ago. It was the spring of my senior year in high school and I'd gone to town to buy records. As I was browsing through the bins—Mozart, Brahms, Ella Fitzgerald—I noticed this guy kept looking at me. At first I was scared, but then, when I figured out why he was staring, I just looked up at him and nodded my head. He took me to his apartment, somewhere in town, to a section I didn't know. What I most remember is not the sex, which I'd been imagining for quite some time, but the being in a strange neighborhood, a strange home, not my own. I kept looking at everything— the furniture, the appliances, the bed. It was all very different from the furnishings I'd grown up with, and yet familiar, too. And I got scared again.

That's why I agreed to go to Bunkie's house. I was trying to protect him from feeling overwhelmed the first time.

Bunkie directed me to a neighborhood in Dorchester.

"Turn right," he said after we'd driven a while down the main avenue. "Now right again. This is my street."

One block long, the street fanned out around both sides of an oval park that was lined with tall trees, even an elm or two. It still surprises me to find elms that the blight hasn't reached. Large Victorian houses, each with a front porch, circled the park, in the middle of which someone had planted a flower garden. Even though it was late October, marigolds and dahlias were still blooming.

"That's Uncle Carl's garden," Bunkie said. "I mean, he plants it and weeds it. He calls it his gift to the neighborhood. He's always doing stuff like that. And this"—he pointed—"is our house. Number twenty."

I parked the car, all the while thinking, Is this how it will be from now on, coming here on weekends, watching the progress of autumn, the leaves falling and these over-arching elms going bare, the garden collapsing with the first frost; Christmas here, too, and I bet the neighbors all put up lights, and then waking up some January morning with Bunkie next to me and finding it snowing outside; and probably Uncle Carl has planted bulbs, too, so that when spring comes crocus and daffodils will come up; and summers sitting on his porch and being lazy together. I thought about how normal all this was and how much I wanted that, for both of us.

"Twenty's my lucky number," Bunkie continued. "Twenty was how old Uncle Carl was when he came North, twenty is how old I am, and twenty is the number we live at. How about you, Robert? Anything twenty about you?"

"Only that sometimes I wish I were twenty again." As he led me up the front stairs I twisted my finger in his back.

He put his key in the lock, then turned around to me. "Why do you want to be twenty again?"

"Because it wasn't much fun the first time around. I'd like to go through all that stuff I went through at twenty but get it right this time."

"Seems to me you've gotten it all right," he said.

"You think so?" I said.

The house was dark except for a single table lamp in the hall, an overly dramatic thing in crystal and brass—the kind of piece decorators call a "statement." It cast a soft, boudoirlike light against the wall, which had been papered in paisley. Next to the lamp sat a cheap marble copy, about eighteen inches tall, of Michelangelo's David.

"A famous Italian artist made that," Bunkie said, acknowledging the statuette. "It's David. You know, from David and Goliath? Uncle Carl says the man that made this wanted to show how proud and brave David was. He has nothing to hide, that's what him wearing no clothes means."

Bunkie pulled a chain on the lamp and another light went on.

"Uncle Carl goes out with his friends after work on Friday nights. This is our special signal to each other: one light on means no one's home, two means one of us is home."

"And how do you signal that I'm here?"

Bunkie chuckled. "I don't know."

"I hope your uncle won't be too surprised," I told Bunkie. "I'm actually looking forward to meeting him."

"He wants to meet you too, Robert. I've told him a lot about you."

"Like what?"

"Like how similar you two are. You are, you know. You both know a lot; you're both fun to be with; you both like nice things, and you both care about other people."

"We care about you," I told him. "Except I care in a different way."

The living room was even more of a statement than the hallway. It was papered in gold and black vertical stripes, over which hung framed pages from *Très Parisien* and menus from famous steamliners of the twenties and thirties. There were gilded French Empire chairs and a Victorian love seat upholstered in purple velvet. Between them was a coffeetable carved from an enormous piece of driftwood, highly shellacked and polished, and under it an imitation bokhara in fire engine red. To the left and right of the mantel, a piece of ornate cabinetry that enclosed nothing but the heating grate, stood two tall Chinese vases stuffed with plumes of pampas grass. And on every available surface *objets d'art*: porcelain figurines, enameled ashtrays, a collection of sentimental bibelots. I thought about what Bunkie had said about his uncle and me "liking nice things," and decided that next week I'd show him my place.

He turned on the stereo system, took an album from the top of a pile on the floor, and put it on.

"I want you to hear something," he said. I sat down on the love seat.

As the needle came down on the disk, it picked up a lot of the surface noise on what must have been a well-played record. I put my head back and closed my eyes.

Then a timpani roll, a rush of strings, a chorus of *ahs*, and finally a choked-up voice singing "I'll follow the boys."

Dear Lord, I thought.

"Do you know who this is?" Bunkie asked.

I opened my eyes. He was looking at me full of happiness. I nodded my head wearily. "Another famous Italian artiste."

"Uncle Carl has all her albums."

"What a surprise," I told him.

He sat down next to me and stretched back. "Isn't she wonderful?"

"What do you like about her?" I asked him, putting my head on his shoulder.

Bunkie leaned forward suddenly. "Can't you feel it?" he said.

"What I'm feeling," I told him, running my fingers slowly down his cheek, "has nothing to do with Connie Francis."

We heard the front door open and close. From the hallway a falsetto voice joined Connie for the final refrain. Bunky jumped up from the sofa.

"That's Uncle Carl."

I turned around just as Carl appeared in the parlor entrance. He was an older version of Bunkie, just as lithe, with the same diminutive ears, the same button nose, but his hair was thin and peppered with gray. He was removing a tailored leather jacket trimmed around the collar in white rabbit's fur. He gave us both a broad grin just like Bunkie's.

"Well now," he said, tossing the jacket onto one of the Empire chairs with a certain studied flourish, "you must be my nephew's friend Robert. What a distinct pleasure to meet you."

He wore a Chinese red kimono shirt, cinctured at the waist, and baggy black pants. There were gold bracelets, a lot of them, around his wrists. His face, which was remarkably wrinkle-free considering his age, was highlighted with a blush of rouge on both cheeks, and a little diamond in each earlobe finished off the effect. He and the two bleached-blond numbers probably shopped together.

As I got up to shake his hand, he held his out, divalike.

"How do you do, Uncle Carl," I said. I tried putting some grip into my shake.

"Uncle!" he exclaimed, drawing back and touching his bejeweled right hand to his chest. "Please, just call me Carl. Sugar, I'm not the grandmother, you know." He looked over at Bunkie and winked.

Connie was now onto a perky castanet and electric mandolin arrangement of "Tonight's My Night." She sang about wanting to laugh, wanting to love, wanting to throw her cares away.

"I *love* this lady!" Carl said, swaying to Connie's rhythms. "*We* love this lady." He nodded to Bunkie, then sighed. "Key West. Ah, that spring of nineteen seventy-eight. Just before my fortieth birthday. That album. I listened to it every morning, sitting on my balcony, sipping fresh squeezed orange juice and watching the ocean. The man I was with gave me that album." He paused theatrically. "At least I still have the album."

He moved over to the stereo, his hands held slightly aloft, as if the bracelets would slip from his wrists if he dropped his arms to his sides. "But enough of this sad reminiscing." He picked the tone arm off the record as if he were picking a tea sandwich from a silver tray. "I don't want this child to grow up thinking all affairs end in sadness."

Throwing out his arms, Carl clasped Bunkie's head to his chest. "You remember that, child. There's plenty of goodness in this world, and lots of good folk." This last— "*Lots* of good folk!"—he repeated while he gave me a scrutinizing stare.

Bunkie seemed perfectly relaxed with his uncle. I thought about all the folks back home in Dothan—his mama, his sisters, and poor unsuspecting Miss Allyn—and wondered what they'd say right now. Carl motioned for us to sit.

"You know," I said, taking the sofa again, "I've eaten at Dolcissimo several times. What a coincidence that you should turn out to be a chef there."

"*The* chef," Carl corrected. "I've been head chef for

five years now." He raised his eyebrows. "I am, you know, one of the reigning stars of the restaurant world here."

I guessed he could be a first-class bitch when he needed to be. I could tell that he was studying me carefully, trying to decide whether I'd be admitted into his court. I was sure Ted and Jeremy had given him a bad report on me.

"Bunkie's told me a lot about you," Carl said, "but I still feel I don't know you very well." He'd crossed his legs in a studied pose that, along with the kimono shirt, made him look like a thirties actress at an informal photo session.

I glanced over at Bunkie. He was leaning forward in his chair, elbows on his knees, studying his uncle with keen fascination. I turned back to Carl.

"What do you want to know?"

"Oh, the usual," Carl said, suddenly putting on an exaggerated Brahmin accent. "Your lineage, where you prepped, what clubs you belong to."

"I'm afraid you've got me pegged wrong," I told him. "That's not my scene."

Carl broke into a hearty cackle, and Bunkie laughed, too.

"Sugar, relax," Carl said. "Ah ain't gonna bite cha." He had switched to a mock Aunt Jemima dialect. He looked at Bunkie. "*Mmm-mm.* Yessir, a lot of people want to see this child do well. A lot of people tryin' to teach him 'bout the world. But you know what ah thinks, Mr. Robert? I thinks he gotta learn it on his own."

In the morning, when I woke up, Bunkie was not in bed, but I could smell bacon frying and heard the whir of a blender. It felt late, maybe as late as noontime.

I found a bathrobe, white terrycloth with a royal blue C monogrammed on the breast pocket, and went in search of the kitchen: down the stairs and past the hideous David again.

Standing over the stove was Uncle Carl. He was wearing a Japanese cotton robe in shades of indigo and blue, and rush sandals. The kitchen radio was playing a Broadway showtune.

"Mornin'," he said, pushing strips of bacon around the skillet and sleepily humming to the song. "Orange juice is on the table." He turned from the stove and nodded over to the kitchen table.

"Thanks," I said. I poured myself a glass and sat down, pulling the terrycloth robe closer together over my chest. "Where's Bunkie?"

Carl turned around and gave me a stare, the kind that says, What's the matter with my company?

"Taking his bubble bath."

"Bubble bath!"

"Relax, sugar. He's out buying muffins for his overnight guest. How you like your bacon, crispy or fatty?"

"I don't eat bacon," I told him. "It's bad stuff."

"Lordy, Lordy." Carl was into his Aunt Jemima act again. "You mighty careful, ain'tcha? Every once in a while's not gonna kill you, sugar. You gotta learn to relax." He laughed, an older, sarcastic version of Bunkie's back-of-the-throat laugh.

Bunkie came into the kitchen carrying a bakery bag and a dozen flaming pink gladiolas.

"Hi!" he said, smiling and winking at me.

"Child, what have we here?" Uncle Carl exclaimed. He set down the long-handled fork and put his hands on his hips. "My, my. You takin' after your Uncle Carl, bringin' all these pretty flowers home." He looked at me. "What you think about that, Mr. Robert? Bunkie's gonna grow up to be just like his Uncle Carl."

Bunkie was standing between us, the bunch of glads in his arms, beaming first at Carl, then at me. When Carl took the bouquet, I got up from the table and gave Bunkie a kiss and a long embrace.

"I love you," I whispered into his ear. I had not said that to him during the night, even during the most passionate moments of our lovemaking. In two years I had not said "I love you" to anyone, but I felt I had to say it now.

▮ ▮ ▮

The rest of the story—the part about how it didn't work out with Bunkie and me—well, I've told you my friends' theories: how the end was practically predetermined by the differences between us—race and age and all—and by Bunkie's being under the influence of Uncle Carl. I saw all that, but I told myself that we could overcome those differences and that, as far as Uncle Carl went, what I had to offer Bunkie he'd come to recognize in time.

And so we saw each other the rest of the fall and into the winter, gradually weaning ourselves away from Flash, and Uncle Carl. We spent most weekends just the two of us, taking drives into the country, hiking, and, when it got too cold, going to museums. In the evenings, we went to the movies and once in a while to the theater. Bunkie loved the theater and was considering transferring to a four-year college where he could major in drama. When we slept together, it was now at my place.

Then, one Saturday in February, Bunkie and I decided to go skating. He had to spend the morning studying, so I agreed to pick him up after lunch. When I rang the bell, Carl answered the door.

"Well, Happy New Year, sugar," he said. "You been hidin' from Uncle Carl?" He was holding a silk scarf, threaded with gold, which he demurely held up to his chest. Then, extending it out, he ushered me inside.

It was almost Valentine's Day, and, on the entrance hall table, he'd placed a large red cardboard heart edged in lace behind the statuette of David. I followed Carl into the living room. Seated on the purple velvet loveseat were Ted and Jeremy puffing on cigarettes and listening to one of Carl's Connie Francis albums.

"Hi, Robert," one of them said and wiggled his fingers at me.

"Is Bunkie ready?" I asked Carl.

"Not quite. You know how long these bubble baths take."

Ted and Jeremy giggled. I was being mocked.

"So what do you fellows have planned for this afternoon?" I asked, trying to keep the conversation innocuous.

"Sugar, we's goin' skatin' wich you."

The boys giggled again. Apparently they found his Aunt Jemima routine quite amusing.

Bunkie came running down the hall stairs and into the living room. He was wearing the new Brooks Brothers sweater I'd given him for Christmas.

"Child, you look divine," Carl said. Holding the silk scarf by the ends, he cast it around Bunkie's neck and roped him for a kiss on the forehead. When he let go, the silk scarf was still around Bunkie's neck.

Bunkie looked at me. It was that same half-amused, half-uncertain look I'd seen him give Ted and Jeremy the night we met at Flash. I figured it was now or never.

"Look," I said, pulling the scarf off Bunkie and throwing it back at Carl. "How about easing up on the queeny stuff?"

Ted and Jeremy made little outraged squealy noises.

"And that ridiculous Aunt Jemima act. Christ, don't you have any self-respect?"

Carl gave me an amused look. I turned directly to Bunkie.

"I'm sorry, Bunkie, but there are things you need to learn. Things you have to be made to see."

And then I just let it out:

"You uncle's a queen, Bunkie. Do you know what that is?" I grabbed him by the shoulders. "A queen." I was trying to sear it into his brain. "You've got to learn these words. It's the language we use up here."

He looked at me, then past me, at his uncle.

"I know he's family," I said. "I know he's been good to you, but there's a bigger family out there. It doesn't have to be all this . . ." I tossed my head over to where the vases of pampas grass stood. "All this froufrou, all this self-mockery. Think of Miss Allyn, think of *me*. There's another world out there, Bunkie."

By now I was kneading my thumbs hard into his shoulders. I stared right into Bunkie's eyes. Whatever else happened I didn't want to catch sight of Carl's amused grin again. Or to see Ted and Jeremy, sitting side by side like a couple of doves and now very quiet. There was pain in Bunkie's eyes.

Pain, I thought. Why does growing up have to involve so much pain? Here you have someone with everything going for him: intelligence, beauty, talent, energy. And still there are things he has to learn the hard way. He'd cut himself off from all that bullshit in Dothan, only to buy into more bullshit up here.

"Stereotypes, Bunkie. Ah, now there's another word for you." I looked back at Carl and glared. "They're no good, Bunkie. You've been a victim of them all your life. Take your mother, for instance: her notions about the North, they're all stereotypes. And her ridiculous fears about you living with . . ."

I caught myself, but not before Bunkie's eyes widened. For a second he looked panicked.

I must have started to correct myself, but he interrupted me.

"No, Robert," he said, "I hear you." There was still all that wonderful generosity in his voice, but something else now, too. Something I'm still trying to put a name to: anger maybe, a sense of betrayal. Or maybe just clarity.

He shrugged my hands off his shoulders and with his finger started tracing circles around my heart. "I get it. Stereotypes." The pressure increased—his fingers were digging into the terrycloth—and then he looked over at Uncle Carl. "Yes, that's a good word, Robert. Now I see what you're telling me."

PALLBEARER

WHEN HIS UNCLE
Jerry died—"from old age," as Michael's mother put it, not
mentioning the shingles—Michael Vivace was asked to be
one of the pallbearers. The invitation came from his cousin
Sal, Uncle Jerry's son, but it was relayed by Michael's
mother because, she told him over the phone, "Sal didn't
know how to reach you."

This was family language. Michael was hardly un-
reachable. Though he lived in Boston, he was less than
fifteen miles from the town where he had grown up and
where most of his family still lived. He sent Christmas cards
every year to all his uncles and aunts and cousins; he had
a phone with an answering machine. Sal could easily have
"reached" him. What his mother really meant was something like this: that it was just less awkward—*meno difficile*,
she might have said had she tried to explain—less of a hassle
for her to do the calling.

Sal and Michael were first cousins, but, like all of Michael's first cousins, Sal was considerably older, by over twenty years. It was a consequence of Michael's being the youngest child of his mother, herself the youngest of five. Sal had played on the championship football team his senior year; Michael had been president of the madrigal singers. Sal had married his high school sweetheart, opened a dental practice in the hometown, done some things in town politics. Michael worked for an agency that brought forty-minute versions of the great operas into the city's elementary schools. "Factotum" he called himself: a combination booking agent, manager, librarian, office boy, and placater of prima donnas. He owned a two-bedroom apartment on Beacon Hill with another man. And it was something like that, too, that Mrs. Vivace must have meant.

"Sal's also asking your brother Steven," his mother told him. "And Raphie."

There were two Raphies in the family, but Michael knew which one she meant: Raphie Santangelo, another cousin, again on his mother's side. He was a big husky fellow with the same Santangelo nose—they called it a Roman nose, though the Santangelos were from Naples—that Michael had also inherited. Raphie, too, had married a hometown girl, but in the last year rumors had started circulating that he and his wife were not getting along. And then, about a month ago, Raphie's mother—why was it always the mothers who spread the news?—announced that he and Cindy were getting a divorce.

"Did you hear about the divorce?" Michael's mother now asked him.

"Ma, you told me last month." He wanted to get off the phone and back to the study guide to *Carmen* that he was preparing. He was staring at the screen of his word processor, watching the cursor flashing.

"So, what do you think?" she said, ignoring his peevishness.

"What's there to think?"

"The divorce," his mother said. "It's a shame." Michael knew she was annoyed about having to explain the obvious.

"Divorces happen," he said. "Life goes on."

"Michael, sometimes you can be so peculiar." She used the Italian word, *curioso*, as if no other language could possibly get to him.

"Well, love is *curioso*." He looked at the last sentence he'd written, the sentence where the cursor was blinking: In the Seguidilla Carmen flirts with Don José.

"Eh," she said, an expression all the Santangelos used that carried a multiplicity of meanings, and here signified something like, So what else is new? And then her tone changed to something more conspiratorial. "You know, they say Cindy used to run around."

"Ma," he snapped back, but she was off and running, repeating all the rumors Michael already knew. It was the stuff of a cheap Italian soap opera: bad mother, *mala femmina*, *putana*.

"You know," he told her when she'd finished the litany of Cindy's sins, "it's never one person's fault."

"What do you mean? You think Raphie was running around too?" She was ready for more innuendos.

"Ma, that's not my point." He heard Clark's key in the door. "It's just that you think everyone in our family is a saint." The door slammed shut. "Look, I've gotta go."

"This will be the first divorce in the family," she continued. "They're not even going to try to get the marriage annulled."

"Yoohoo. Did you hear me? I've got to hang up now."

"Why? What's your hurry? You got to drain spaghetti or something?" She was teasing him.

"Yeah," he laughed, "something like that."

"That could only have been your mother," Clark said, coming into the small study that served as Michael's office. He gave Michael a quick massage on the shoulders, then plopped himself into the easy chair. Michael continued staring at the screen of his word processor.

"How do I explain to a bunch of eleven-year-olds what *Carmen* is all about?" He diddled impatiently with the cursor key—backward, forward—then flipped off the computer and looked up at Clark, slumped in the chair. This was the first time in two days that they'd made eye contact. "Uncle Jerry died."

"I'm sorry."

"They want me to be one of the pallbearers."

Clark nodded slowly. Even looking as tired as he did, Clark was strikingly handsome, with a finely chiseled face, slicked-back black hair, and blue eyes that he highlighted with tinted contact lenses. The first time Michael met him he had thought to himself: model. Clark was a lawyer.

"They'll probably expect you at the funeral, too," Michael told him.

"Yes, I suppose so."

"Will you go?"

Clark shrugged his shoulders. He looked profoundly sad. They stared at each other, without speaking, for over a minute.

"So," Clark said at last. "How's the tenor?"

The tenor also had blue eyes—blue eyes and blond hair—though Clark didn't know any of these details yet. He'd only found out about the tenor two days ago.

Michael sighed. "Okay. His name is Robert, we've been sleeping together for a couple months now, and, to answer your question of two days ago, yes, I'm in love with him."

Clark nodded his understanding. "So where does that leave us?"

Michael slowly brought the palm of his right hand up to his forehead. "Does it leave us anywhere different from where we've been for the last year?"

Sex, good sex, had ended a year ago, a year that began when they had taken to sleeping separately—Clark in "Clark's room" (really their room); Michael in "Michael's room" (really the guest room)—on those occasions when Clark had to get up early and needed a good night's sleep.

Michael was a clinger and cuddler in bed, and Clark said he couldn't get his complete rest with his lover all over him. That had led, tacitly, to their sleeping apart every weeknight and then, when Clark's lack of interest and Michael's resentment became so strong that even weekend sex was no good, to a permanent, though undeclared, separation.

"You made me feel totally undesirable," Michael continued.

"And you," Clark said, "made me feel that nothing I gave you was enough." There was exhaustion in both of their voices.

"When it became nothing, of course it wasn't enough."

"Michael, it didn't become nothing until you started to withdraw."

"Withdraw!"

"Don't start yelling," Clark said, closing his eyes.

"When you spend five nights a week at the office until nine, and then accuse me of withdrawing, I do start yelling."

Clark opened his eyes.

"It was never five nights a week, Michael, and maybe if you had a regular job like most . . ."

"Oh, so this is now the fault of my job?"

"Is it the fault of *mine*?" Clark said.

"It's the fault . . ." Michael stopped and buried his forehead in his palm again. Maybe that's what the eleven-year-olds needed to learn, that in matters of the heart faults were not the point. "What about passion, Clark?" Michael listened to the resignation in his voice: he could not imagine passion between them anymore. "What about passion?"

"And what about companionship?" Clark said. He, too, sounded resigned. "What about affection? What about the comfort of a nice home?"

Michael thought about how proud his mother had been when he had announced that he was buying a condo on Beacon Hill. "Of course, the only way I can swing it," he'd told her, "is to go fifty-fifty with someone else." That's who Clark had been these four years, his business partner.

"That's not enough," Michael said. "Even real husbands and real wives need more than that." He studied Clark's tie, his white button-down, his clean shave.

"I don't suppose there's any point to seeing a counsellor," Clark said.

"My parents," Michael replied, "were married for thirty-six years. Although they had their fights and yelling matches, when my father died they were still very much in love. Not once, not once did they ever go to a counsellor. You know what Dad would have said about marriage counsellors? *God forbid*. That's what he would have said. God forbid."

Michael knew the words in Italian, too, but he was crying now, and so was Clark.

The evening of the wake, a mild April evening, Michael drove out to his old hometown. The family had engaged the funeral home they'd used for all the family funerals, Donohue's, an elegant old mansion on Beebe Avenue, recently dressed up with vinyl siding. Michael knew that the siding was supposed to give the place a well-maintained, reassuring presence, but to him it was unforgivable, the way they had covered up the ornate shingle work he remembered from his childhood.

Inside there were more unforgivable modernizations: the rooms were paneled over, there was wall-to-wall carpeting (even in the fireplaces), and the original windows had been replaced with fake diamond-pane. Crucifixes hung in each of the rooms and inspirational paintings, misty mountain ranges and forest glades in spring, adorned the area above the mantles. His friends on Beacon Hill, his friends in the opera world, his lover—his former lover—Clark: they would all have gagged.

From the foyer, Michael could see the anteroom and the viewing room, both crowded with callers. People had come from all over. After the Massachusetts side of the family, the largest contingent came from Long Island, followed by relatives from Connecticut, New Jersey, D.C. Even Buddy Montello, Uncle Jerry's brother's son, was there, all the way from Florida. Buddy was a hairdresser. He owned three shops in Fort Lauderdale, which, according to Michael's mother, did quite well.

She came up to him now.

"Michael dear. When did you arrive?" She held out her cheek for him, and he kissed her, not sure whether this was supposed to be an affectionate, filial kiss or a kiss of consolation to a member of the bereaved family. Uncle Jerry had been her brother-in-law.

Rita Vivace was in her late sixties, though she looked no older than fifty, the result of fashionable dressing, weekly color jobs at the hairdresser's, and good Santangelo genes. She was fond of telling the story of how the sales ladies at Bloomingdale's would call her *dear* until they saw her last name on the charge plate. "They thought I was Jewish," she'd say, amused and full of pride. This evening she was wearing a black wool skirt and a silk blouse, also black, with a cascade of frills down the front that managed to be simultaneously jaunty and subdued. She took Michael's hand and held it fast.

"Where's Clark?"

"He's coming tomorrow," Michael said, trying to sound as nonchalant as possible. Under normal circumstances Clark would have come to the wake as well.

"There are so many people here," she told him. Under his mother's grief, Michael could hear a thrill in her voice. "So many people from out of town. I want them all to meet you."

"Ma."

"Hey," she said, pouncing on his reluctance, "now don't start. Let me be proud."

"You're too proud."

"There's no such thing when it comes to my boys," she told him.

By "boys" Michael knew she meant not only him and his brother, Steven, but Steven's twin sons, her grandsons, Peter and Jimmy. Her pride in them all was unrelenting. And though this sometimes irked him, Michael had to admit that he admired it, too, this way she had of loving them—at least the family members by blood—unconditionally.

She no longer asked him when he was going to get married, no longer asked when he would start making the contribution that the family expected each one of them to make: children, grandchildren, more cousins, *more family*. Being asked to meet all those far-flung relatives, being asked to help carry Uncle Jerry's casket, even in Sal's roundabout way—it made Michael feel, at age thirty-eight, forgiven.

"So who's here?" he asked.

She rattled off a list of names: relatives, friends, business associates, the old men in Uncle Jerry's club.

"Raphie's here, too."

He knew she wanted a reaction, something that would draw him into intimacy with her, a conversation that they could build on, mother-and-son-like. Instead, he pretended that what she'd said didn't warrant a reply. He looked around the funeral home, as if he'd absentmindedly slipped from their conversation. When he turned back to her, she was giving him a puzzled look, searching his face with the same expression she might give to one of her cakes, her time-tested sponge cake for instance, when, one time out of fifty, it wouldn't "come good."

"I'm going to pay my respects to Zia," he told her.

In the viewing room, most of the older callers were sitting on folding chairs facing the open casket. The men stood at the back, their arms folded across their chests or clasped behind their backs, talking. A couple of women were gathered around Zi'Antonetta, Uncle Jerry's widow, who was seated off to one side. Despite the fact that Zi'Antonetta and his mother were sisters, Zia, as the family affectionately called her, looked a generation older. With the death of Michael's grandmother a few years before, she had taken on, both in mannerisms and facial features, the cut of the family matriarch.

"Zia," Michael said, taking her hand. "I'm so sorry."

"Oh, Michael." She looked at him with sorrowful, bewildered eyes, then moved her head slowly toward the casket. "Doesn't Uncle Jerry look good? The undertakers did a beautiful job, no?"

Michael looked over at the coffin. He could only see the tip of Uncle Jerry's nose and his chin. But the flowers—there were close to thirty baskets: bursting sprays of gladiolas, mums, carnations, roses—were spectacular. Because Uncle Jerry had been in the flower business, people had made sure to send expensive baskets, not just the kind that looked expensive. When he looked back at Zi'Antonetta, he realized he was holding her hand in the same bracing, reassuring way his mother had done when he'd arrived.

"He was such a good man, Michael," Zi'Antonetta told him. "Such a good father." The lines in her eighty-five-year-old face were sharp and deep. She looked pale, exhausted, worn down by the fifteen months of Uncle Jerry's final illness. "Here, sit here."

Still holding Zi'Antonetta's hand, Michael sat down.

"Your Uncle Jerry," she continued, "he never even raised a hand to me, not once, in all the years we were married." And her eyes, pale and watery, began to widen. "*Figurati!* Imagine. Every morning, for sixty-two years, Michael, I made your uncle breakfast. Even when he had to get up at four-thirty to go to the flower market in Boston." She looked hard into his eyes and repeated the time—"four-thirty."

"That's wonderful, Zia."

"And never once," she went on, ignoring him, "never once did I let him see me in a bathrobe. I always got up early, washed my face, did up my hair, and put on a nice dress for him."

Michael thought of all the times he had spent the day in front of his word processor in a baggy pair of chinos and a sweatshirt; how many times Clark had found him that way—still unshaven, even—when he returned home in the evening. In recent months, the only days he had taken care to dress were when he had to check on something at the company's rehearsal studio, especially if Robert, the tenor, were there.

"Ah me," she said. There was a little groan in her voice, the Santangelo groan, a mixture of *Life is hard* and *What are you gonna do*. "Did you hear about Raphie?" she asked, suddenly as conspiratorial as her sister.

When he told her yes and she asked him what he thought of it, Michael had to stifle a smile. The two sisters were so much alike. He shrugged his shoulders.

"Sixty-two years Uncle Jerry and I were married," she said, lapsing into her reminiscences. "Married people today . . ." She didn't finished her sentence, for now Sal had come over.

"Thank you for coming, Michael." With his wavy, silvery hair, he looked like the successful dentist he was.

"He's a good boy, this Michael," Zi'Antonetta told her son.

But sitting knee to knee with his aunt, still holding her hand, Michael only felt awkward, feminine, part of the world of sewing circles and gossipy Italian nonnas. No wonder Sal hadn't called him directly.

"Ma, the priest wants to say the rosary," Sal told his mother.

"All right, Sal," she said. Michael could hear that it was some comfort to her to be told what to do next.

When Sal moved to help his mother, putting his hand under one of her arms, Michael did the same. They eased her up and she hobbled one step forward.

"Oo, I'm stiff from all that sitting," she said, laughing at herself. It was great, Michael thought, how she could still find something amusing in all this sorrow. That was a family trait, too.

The next morning, a heavily overcast one, Michael tried making small talk with Clark on the way to the funeral home. He recounted Zi'Antonetta's story, the one about her never wearing a bathrobe in front of Uncle Jerry.

"I loved that," he concluded.

Although he had kept his eyes on the road the entire time he was talking, he was aware that Clark, who was driving, kept looking over at him, staring intently. Now he shot Clark a quick look in return.

"What?" Michael asked. "You think I feel guilty, is that it?" Clark didn't say anything. "It was a charming story," Michael insisted. "That's all."

"It was a charming story," Clark agreed. He spoke softly, deliberately.

Michael felt as if he were being led into a trap.

"Dammit, Clark, what do you want me to say? The days of sixty-year marriages are over, you know. Maybe they weren't happy at all; maybe they just tolerated each other. That's what we were doing toward the end—wasn't it?—tolerating each other?"

"What I was thinking," Clark said—he was maintaining that calm control in his voice, even though Michael's had become highstrung—"what I was thinking is how much I'm going to miss your family, how much I'm going to miss all those stories people like Zi'Antonetta and your mother tell."

Michael swallowed hard, but his eyes were welling up with tears again. And then he chuckled.

"You know," he said, trying to summon up some of that good old Santangelo humor, "it's a good thing it's a funeral we're going to and not a wedding."

"Here are your sunglasses," Clark said, pulling them out of his breast pocket. "You left them on the hall table."

"It's going to rain," Michael said.

"That's not what they're for," Clark told him.

At the funeral home, the mood was somber. The chattiness of the previous evening had given way to a hushed expectancy. His mother greeted them with a quiet "Good morning, boys" and a kiss on the cheek for each. Michael realized that, had he not cried on the way, he might have broken down right now. Clark immediately went into the viewing room, a move, Michael was sure, as much to be alone as to pay his final respects.

As Michael talked to his mother, killing time before the funeral cortege assembled, he kept an eye on Clark. Clark stood in front of the casket, looking down on Uncle Jerry—even Clark had called him Uncle Jerry. He did not make the sign of the cross, or kneel at the prie-dieu. These were Catholic gestures, and Clark came from a good Swedish Lutheran family. How overwhelming the family must have been for Clark during these four years they'd been together: all the rituals, the Italian ones, the Catholic ones, the ones peculiar to the Vivaces and Santangelos, all the expressions, the customs, the ways of behaving. Clark had given them his best shot. And now, once more, with the stoic dignity of *his* people, he was giving it one last best shot. *Did we give each other our best shot?* That's what Michael wanted to ask him.

The priest led them in a few final prayers, and when that was over the funeral director asked everyone to assemble in their cars. Some people moved out quickly; others lingered, knowing these were the final moments to view Uncle Jerry. Michael watched as Zi'Antonetta made the sign of the cross, kissed her fingers, and touched them to the waxy, rouged lips of Uncle Jerry. Then she turned and hobbled off under the arm of Sal.

Michael helped his mother put on her coat. She was already wearing her sunglasses.

"You're going with the morticians, so I've asked Clark to drive me in his car."

"Fine," he told her. Even through the sunglasses he could see her eyes. She looked concerned.

"Are you all right?" she asked.

"Hey, Ma, it's a sad day. What do you want?" He could tell she wasn't quite buying it.

He rode with two of the other pallbearers: his brother, Steven, and Raphie.

"Long time, guys," Raphie said. "What have you been up to?"

Steven said "not much," then proceeded to tell Raphie all about the twins, who'd started Little League this year, and the new rumpus room he was building in his basement. Michael knew—it was another family trait—that Steven was chatting out of nervousness, but whether nervousness over the funeral or over the fact of Raphie's divorce he couldn't tell. Raphie lit up a cigarette.

"Uncle Jerry looked good, didn't he?" Raphie asked. He took a deep drag.

"What do we do when we get to the church?" Steven asked. "Raphie, do you know what we're supposed to do?"

"These guys'll show us," Raphie said, motioning his head toward the undertakers in the front seat.

"Have you ever done this before?" Michael asked, just to be part of the conversation.

"Yeah, there's not much to it," Raphie told him. He stubbed out his cigarette. "You guys mind if I smoke?" And when they told him no, he lit up another.

"Raphie," Michael said, "I don't know if it's appropriate to say this, but I was sorry to hear about you and . . ."

Raphie interrupted him by simultaneously shaking his head, waving out his match, and exhaling his first puff. He coughed once.

"I appreciate your saying that, Steven."

"I'm Michael," said Michael.

"I mean Michael," Raphie said. "But it's really not anything to be sorry for. In the end it's going to be the best for both of us."

Michael nodded his head. "I'm sure it will."

When they got to the church, the funeral directors instructed them on what to do: carry the casket up the steps, settle it on the roller, then follow it along, down the aisle, until you reached the altar. Reverse the procedure on the way out.

Michael was surprised at how little the casket weighed. He felt that he was hardly lifting his fair share. Had Uncle Jerry lost that much weight during his final illness? Or was it that the solid, highly glossed wood was really lighter than it looked?

The Mass was well attended. Michael estimated that there were well over two hundred people there, and he knew that this would please Zi'Antonetta. He sat with Steven and Raphie in the section reserved for the pallbearers; Clark sat with Michael's mother a few rows behind them. He wondered what they'd spoken about in the car. He wondered, too, if his mother would love Robert as much as she'd come to love Clark.

By the time they got to the cemetery, the rain was coming down hard. People tried to park as close to the grave site as possible. Car doors slammed, umbrellas were popped open. The way they were moving, Michael could tell everyone wanted to get this over with.

He got out of the undertaker's car and went around to the hearse to lift the casket out, but the funeral home people were taking charge now, already moving it onto the lowering device. Others were unloading the flower baskets, this time piling them up—heaping them—onto the mound of dirt by the side of the hole. The dirt and the surrounding area had been covered with Astroturf. The air was chilly.

Michael's mother and Clark came up to him. They were each carrying an umbrella.

"Michael, Steven, Raphie," she called out, "get under these umbrellas."

Steven dipped underneath his mother's umbrella and huddled close to her, wrapping his arm around her waist. It was the dutiful, protective gesture of the elder son. Raphie shook his head no.

"Go ahead," he said to Michael, "you take it," motioning toward Clark's umbrella. Automatically, Michael went over to Clark.

"How're you doing?" he whispered.

"Your mother asked me if something was wrong," Clark said.

"What did you tell her?"

The priest began reading the words of commitment. Clark motioned for Michael to be quiet. Under the gray, heavy downpour, everyone bowed their heads. When the priest had finished, he sprinkled the casket with holy water flung from a silver shaker. From where he was standing, Michael thought he felt a few drops of the holy water hit him, though it might have just been the rain. *Bless me, too, Father*, he thought. The undertakers began to lower the casket into the ground. Zi'Antonetta wept and Sal held her close.

"The family of Mr. Montello invites you all back to the house for a buffet luncheon," the undertaker announced to the crowd. Slowly, people turned and left.

"Mike, I'll take Mom back," Steven called out to him. For Michael there was something pleasing about the loud, take-charge manner his brother had now assumed. Life was already picking itself up again. He turned to Clark.

"So what did you tell my mother?"

"I told her she'd have to ask you now."

They stood there, both holding onto the umbrella, watching the flowers being pelted by the rain. Even the morticians were leaving. The grave fillers would not begin their work until the last mourner had left. Out of the corner of his eye, Michael caught sight of someone standing off to the right and just behind them, shoulders jerking, chest heaving. It was Raphie.

"Goddam!" he said, turning to them. "Why did it have to rain? You'd think he could at least have had a sunny day for the funeral. Look at this."

The flowers were breaking up in the intense downpour. Beaten down, flattened by the heavy drops of rain, they sat in soggy, muddy puddles.

Raphie bent down and picked up a basket of yellow

roses. He plucked one out, smelled it, kissed it, and tossed it into the grave.

"The last rose," he said, hardly able to speak through his sobbing.

Michael had never heard that expression, "the last rose," before. Was it a ritual, a family ritual perhaps, which he had missed, a custom he had failed to learn? He stood there, dumbly looking at Raphie, who was rubbing the tears away with the thick palm of his hand. Raphie plucked two more roses from the bouquet, handed one to Michael, one to Clark, then turned and walked to his car.

Michael tossed his rose onto the coffin. "This is my second divorce," he said.

"My third," said Clark, tossing his. "And it doesn't get any easier, does it?"

"The first was Tom," Michael said. They had started walking toward Clark's car. "Dad was still alive then. We lived together for two years, in an apartment in Cambridge. Mom and Dad thought we were such nice roommates. It was easy to be 'roommates' then, back in your twenties. They never said a thing when we split up."

"My first," Clark said, "was Lee. I've told you about him. I was the one who ended it, but that wasn't any easier either. It took me three years to get over him." They had arrived at the car, and Clark now opened the passenger door for Michael. Then he went around to his side, folded up the umbrella, and got in. "I didn't even date anyone else the whole first year after we'd split." They sat there a minute, staring at the rain on the windshield.

Tonight Michael would sleep at Robert's, where even amidst all this sadness they would engage in long, hungry lovemaking. Afterward they'd hold each other and, if the rain kept up, listen to the trickling outside the bedroom window. These things were back in his life again, pushing up like spring bulbs.

Michael took off his sunglasses. "Clark, I just didn't know how to reach you."

There was a pause. Michael could hear Clark breathing: one slow, focused intake and exhalation.

"Me neither," he said. Then he turned the ignition key. The car roared to life and the windshield wipers resumed the furious flapping they'd been making all the way to the cemetery.

FAMILY STORY

WHEN LARRY WALKS into the office, the women all look up, as if caught in the act. But the act of *what* Larry isn't sure. From the look on their faces, it's more than just lesson plan sharing or tales of classroom woes—a lot more. He'd love to be let in on the secret, love to be a part of the little circle that these three women—not that much younger than he—have formed this year. But he knows that he's not supposed to think of the office as one big happy family. After all, it's embarrassing enough for a man, even one as unthreatening as he is—slight of build and soft-spoken—to be running a department whose members are all women. Expecting them to confide in him, too? That would be too much. Larry knows they have stories he can't hear.

Contracts, he figures. Because it's February, the talk around the office has all been about contract renewals: who's getting rehired and who's being let go. The fact is, though, the headmaster hasn't fired anyone in five years. So the real issue is who's deciding to stay on another year.

As private schools go, it's a good one, and the faculty is fairly content. Teacher burnout is rarely the reason anyone leaves. When someone decides to leave—when a woman decides to leave—it's usually over babies.

Larry closes the door and gives them a knowing smile. Lisa, Susan, and Robin are all in their late twenties, married and childless. Lisa is the oldest and has been with the department the longest, three years. Susan and Robin came at the beginning of this year, to replace two other women who left to have children. It was risky, Larry knows, hiring these women. They're married to men with upscale careers, the kind that can singlehandedly support a family. But Susan and Robin were by far the best applicants. Besides, Larry also knows that you can't discriminate on the basis of what he calls the pregnancy factor. He's so clear on this point, he knows he can even joke about it.

"What's the huddle all about?" he says, dropping a pile of books and papers onto his already overcrowded desk. "I hope no one's going to up and get pregnant on me this year. You know, the fertility rate runs pretty high in this office."

Susan gives him a sick little smile, and for a moment Larry thinks she *is* sick, morning sickness sick.

"You all right?" he asks.

"Larry," Susan says, "just shut up and mark papers, will you?"

Larry likes this: the way Susan feels free to give him grief. He likes the easy give and take in the office, the way they all share ideas and methods, the way they tell each other where to get off.

With four in the office, they have to get along. It's an eight-by-sixteen-foot cinder-block cubicle, with picture windows on one of the long sides so that it overlooks Beechwood's playing fields—now buried under a foot of snow—and the woods beyond. The other long wall is shelved with metal braces and pine planks that sag under the weight of multiple copies of *A Separate Peace, To Kill a Mockingbird, Warriner's Grammar*. Standard junior high stuff. Other books, piles of them, are stacked on the floors along with confiscated hockey sticks, rolls of maps and charts drawn on oak tag, disheveled piles of term papers. Heavy velvet costumes in need of stitching lie in a heap on Lisa's desk (she doubles as the drama coach). Over Larry's desk is a poster, a portrait of Shakespeare.

Larry sits down. Amid the mess in front of him are two stacks of papers: a set of essays and a grammar exercise, participial phrases. He opts for the essays and begins to read the first one. An uncharacteristic silence has fallen on the office.

Too quiet. Larry finishes the first paragraph of the first essay, then noisily flips through the rest of the composition, counting off pages. "Twelve!" he shouts. "I ask the seventh grade to write a five-paragraph essay—an *essay*!—on What My Family Means to Me, and Phyllis Hanes gives me a twelve-page saga called Family Story. It's February, and she still doesn't know the difference between an essay and a story?"

He doesn't often give himself the luxury of carping like this. Part of setting a good example means not dumping on the kids. If anyone, it's Susan, first-year Susan, who does most of the ranting and raving about the students' writing. But now it's she who comes to the defense of defenseless Phyllis Hanes.

"Larry, get off your high horse," she tells him. "Sometimes a kid just needs to tell a story. Sometimes it just won't condense into one of your neat little five-paragraph expository essays."

Larry can see the beginnings of tears in her eyes, just before she slams her pencil down and rushes out of the office. And next thing he knows, Robin is up and out the door as well.

"What's going on?" Larry asks Lisa.

"This isn't quite the fertile office you think it is," she

says, swiveling her chair around to face him. "Robin's been trying to get pregnant for two years. Her tests came back yesterday."

Larry drops his head into his hands and rubs his face. "Oh, Lisa, I'm sorry. If I'd known . . ."

"It's okay, Larry, you didn't know. It was a legitimate mistake."

Larry continues to rub his forehead. He feels like a creep.

"Is it definite?"

"The test results are definite. There's still hope that some kind of medication will work."

Larry picks up a Rubik's cube, a long-ago confiscated item, and starts twisting the planes of little colored blocks. "Oh God, what a raw deal," he says. "What can I do?"

"Not much," Lisa tells him. "Just try to be understanding, Larry."

He wants to tell her that "understanding" is what he tries very hard to be all the time. For instance, he wants to say to her, it's because of him, because he fought like hell with the headmaster to let her go, that she'll attend the teacher's convention in New York this weekend. He argued with the headmaster that Lisa had demonstrated her loyalty to the school by staying on three years, and—"more to the point," that's the phrase he'd used with the headmaster— that it was important to get past the hierarchical structure that says only department heads go to conferences.

He'd like to tell her, too, that even though he's not married, even though he doesn't have kids, he thinks he understands what it's like not to be able to have children. He'd like to tell her all this, like to say, See? I'm on your side; I'm one of you. But he doesn't. Maybe he has stories she can't hear either.

"Well, there is one thing you can do," Lisa says, swiveling back toward him. "Under the circumstances, I don't think I should go to New York tomorrow. I want to be around for Robin."

What about me? Larry wants to ask. Can't I be around for Robin? Aren't I part of this office, too? Instead, he says sure, that it will be easy for him to go in her place. He can even stay with his friend Matthew who lives in Manhattan. And then he tries one last time to lighten up this whole mess of a conversation.

"Don't you think I'll make a swell Lisa Johnson?" he says. Though he stops right there, checking any impulse to flash her a campy, girlish gesture like patting his hair or batting his eyelashes.

During the winter term, the eighth grade does *Romeo and Juliet*, their first taste of Shakespeare. Larry always starts the unit with a few of the sonnets. It's his way of introducing the kids to the language and rhythms. They do "Shall I compare thee" and "That time of year" and "Like as the waves"—just a few of what Larry calls the "biggies," but enough to bring up themes he will later stress when they get to the play.

Larry begins today's lesson by reading aloud to the class last night's assignment, "Music to hear, why hearst thou music sadly." He'd asked the kids to write out a paraphrase, but he tells them to put it away for now and just enjoy the poem itself.

"This is so queer," Ethan Marquette says after Larry finishes. Ethan is a newcomer to Beechwood and still speaks with his parents' South Boston accent. He says *quee-ah*, and pronounces his own name *Mah-ket*. He's the school's hockey star, feisty, dirty-blond, and Catholic, the first in his family to go to private school, which means, in the language of the admissions committee, he brings "diversity" to Beechwood. Larry loves him.

"What's so queer about it?" Larry asks, emphasizing the *r* at the end of the word. Larry's still somewhat amused that in the nineties queer has again come to mean strange, weird, incomprehensible. He suspects that Ethan never even attempted the paraphrase, and that means an automatic detention. But Larry doesn't bring this up. He'd much rather encourage Ethan to try now. Larry's constantly going to bat for the kid.

"I don't get it," Ethan says.

"Is it the meanings of some of the words?" Larry asks, encouraging him to be a bit more specific. "Do you understand the general situation? The person the sonnet is written to is being addressed as *Music*." Larry always refers to the recipient of Shakespeare's sonnets as "the person" or "the friend." He doesn't think eighth graders need to know that a lot of the sonnets, including this one, were written to a man, but he doesn't want to be dishonest and use the feminine pronoun either.

"It's a metaphor," another student, Nicole Whitby, says. Metaphor was a term Larry introduced last week, and sharp, headed-toward-Harvard Nicole is the one he can always count on to see the connections between last week's lessons and this week's. "He's comparing a family to a well-tuned musical instrument," Nicole explains.

"Right," Larry says. He looks at Ethan, who seems totally baffled. "Ethan, can you find a line where Shakespeare uses music imagery?"

Ethan stares at the text as if it's a potato.

"The first one?" he asks.

"Well, yes. But are there others?" Larry coaxes. He wants Ethan to get this. Nicole and two or three other students have their hands up, but Larry waits—hopes—for Ethan. "How about line five?"

Ethan looks up at him, then down at the text.

"What does 'concord' mean?" Ethan asks.

"Here it means harmony," Larry tells him, and then, ignoring Nicole, whose hand is waving wildly, he leads Ethan, practically by the hand, through the second quatrain. "Now, what's harmony, Ethan?"

"It's like when two notes go together."

"Exactly!" Larry says, putting maximum enthusiasm into his voice. Ethan smiles. "Two notes," Larry tells the class, as if Ethan has just uttered the most profound exegesis. "Now," Larry continues, again focusing his voice on Ethan, "Shakespeare has just pointed out that the friend seems so sad, even when sweet music is playing. And here he asks the friend, If harmony offends your ears—do you see that, Ethan?—if harmony offends your ears, then maybe it's because you are single, like a single note without harmony."

Out of the corner of his eye, Larry can see Nicole staring at him. He wonders if it's too obvious that he's spoon feeding all this to Ethan, but he decides to risk another question.

"If you think of a guitar, Ethan, you know that you can play even more than two notes together. And in the final quatrain . . ." (Larry pauses to give Ethan time to find the final quatrain.) "Got it? In the final quatrain, Shakespeare creates a wonderful metaphor: if one string is a 'sweet husband' to another—and another word for husband is 'sire'—then three notes played together in harmony are like . . ." Larry is leaning over his desk, virtually dropping the answer onto Ethan's lap.

"Oh, I get it," Ethan says.

"What?" Larry asks, wanting Ethan to say the words.

"Like 'sire, and child, and happy mother.' Like a family."

"Bingo!" Larry says, and Ethan, the bully of the eighth grade, blushes with pleasure. "And so . . ." Larry winds up his voice for the coup de grace. "The point of the couplet is . . ."

Nicole's hand shoots up again. Larry decides that he should leave well enough alone. He nods to Nicole.

"To urge his friend to stop being single, to get married, and to have children."

Larry knows Nicole can't help being so competent. But he wishes she would—just once—not have the right answer.

"Right," Larry says, and he finishes up the lesson telling the class how important having children, having a family, was in Elizabethan times.

Early the next day, a Friday morning, Larry boards the train at South Station. Even though the train takes almost five hours, and he'll miss most of the opening day's sessions, he refuses to fly.

He loves the train. There's the scenery—he always takes a seat on the left side, the shore side through Connecticut—and it's easier to meet people. On a plane not even the stewardesses talk to him, which is silly because Larry treats them with respect and doesn't flirt. But on a train, he can walk the aisles, buy a drink in the club car, stand around and chat. That's how he met Matthew six years ago, on another trip to New York. It was a Sunday evening, Larry was beginning a weeklong vacation, and Matthew was returning from a weekend to Boston.

They'd nodded to each other as they stood in the club car, gently swaying back and forth, drinks in hand. Larry finally opened things up by offering to buy a second round, and they got to talking. In those days—Larry was twenty-four—he went for intellectual types. Matthew was wearing a white Oxford-cloth shirt, a wool tie, and tortoiseshell glasses. He looked like a graduate student. It turned out he was a teller at a bank in lower Manhattan, and looking for work as an actor. They had dinner together the next day, and slept together the rest of the week. But Matthew hated kids and wasn't a bit interested in Larry's stories about teaching at Beechwood. And after the initial excitement, Larry lost interest in Matthew's accounts of life in the theater. They called each other a few times that summer, dropped postcards once in a while, then let the romance die down. Nevertheless, six years later, Larry can still refer to Matthew as "a friend in Manhattan."

He tosses his coat and travel bag onto the luggage rack and sits down. The car is warm and cozy. A light snow is falling. He opens the book he's brought along, poems of Adrienne Rich.

A hefty, mid-fortyish woman, lugging a hefty suitcase, stops at Larry's seat.

"Would you mind helping me with this?" she asks him.

Larry immediately spots her for a teacher. There is something about the way she grooms herself—a sensible off-the-rack suit and a frilly-necked blouse—that gives her away. Half career woman, half playground supervisor. As he hoists her suitcase onto the rack, he realizes she means to sit with him. The train begins to move.

"Thanks," the woman says and plops herself down, sure enough, next to him. She's puffing hard. "Where are you going?" she asks. Everything about her is direct, no nonsense, to the point. A *public* school teacher, Larry guesses.

When he tells her New York, the woman says that New York is where she's going as well, to a teachers' convention. Guiltily, knowing he won't be able to conceal it forever, Larry lets her know that he's attending the convention too. He watches her eyes do a quick survey of his clothing: down jacket over an unironed white shirt, faded jeans, sneakers.

They are already halfway to Providence before they conclude the long litany of exchanged information—names and marital statuses, schools, subjects taught, do-you-knows, and what-looks-worth-attendings.

"Private school," Mary Catherine muses. "I have a friend who teaches in a private school. You people don't get tenure, do you?"

"No," Larry says, "but as long as you keep your nose clean and do a good job, you're pretty much guaranteed a renewed contract. At my school, the only people who leave are the women who get pregnant."

"Well then, they can count on you to stay, can't they?" Mary Catherine says. It's a corny joke, but Larry figures she's at least trying to be friendly. "Of course, we have to keep our noses clean, too," she tells him. "Last year . . ."

Larry guesses the story even before it's out. Misconduct isn't very interesting unless it involves child abuse. In

Mary Catherine's case, it involves a colleague who approached a boy during an overnight ski trip.

"Naturally the boy told," Mary Catherine continues, "and the teacher was gone on Monday. Out of the school on Monday, out of the state on Tuesday. No one had suspected a thing; he was such a nice, wholesome-seeming man."

Larry gives her his canned spiel: that statistically most child molestation is perpetrated by heterosexual men, that the gay men he knows are hardly into little boys. He watches for some sign of a reaction. Mary Catherine doesn't miss a beat.

"Oh, I know all that," she says in her direct, no-nonsense voice.

A couple of guys, whom Larry recognizes as nice, wholesome-seeming men, walk down the aisle toward the club car. He notices Mary Catherine noticing them too.

Larry opens his book again, but Mary Catherine wants to keep talking. And that's the end of Larry's reading. She goes on and on. Most of it's a lot of shop talk, stuff about discipline problems, the difficulties in finding good substitute teachers, her duties as faculty sponsor of the newspaper and yearbook. She sounds overworked.

When she finally stops a minute—opening her purse and offering him a butterscotch—Larry seizes the opportunity to get away.

"No thanks," he says. "I thought I'd get some breakfast in the club car." He knows Mary Catherine is the type to have already fortified herself with a good, wholesome breakfast before she left her house this morning. He hates being rude, but he needs some breathing room, some "gay space," as Matthew would put it.

But by New Haven, when he still hasn't met anyone in the club car, and they stop to switch to electric, Larry decides he should spend the final leg of the journey back in his seat with Mary Catherine.

"Had a nice breakfast?" she asks, peering over a pair

of reading glasses. She's hands him back his book, smiling knowingly.

As they travel the long, dark tunnel under Manhattan, Mary Catherine asks Larry if he's staying at the convention hotel and if he wants to share a cab. Larry tells her he's staying with a friend, but that he'll be happy to hail a cab for her.

In the station lobby, he spots Matthew, introduces him to Mary Catherine, explains the situation. Matthew grabs hold of Mary Catherine's bag and the three of them head for the street, Larry leading the way and the two others trailing behind, chatting. He can hear Mary Catherine grilling Matthew. She seems very curious about this Manhattan friend of his.

Although it's only two o'clock, the streets are already jammed with Friday traffic, and Larry has to stand at the curb a good ten minutes before he can get a taxi to pull over. All the while, Mary Catherine and Matthew are chatting it up. This is typical Matthew: loquacious, affable, charming. She's asking him all about the theater, about the shows he's been in. Most of the shows Matthew's been in, Larry knows, are not ones Mary Catherine is likely to have heard of: off-off Broadway things about phone sex and men dying of AIDS. Larry hears Matthew telling her the titles, and, when she presses him, delivering short, innocuous plot summaries. He's grateful for Matthew's discretion.

At last, they put her into a cab. Off she goes, and Larry hopes that's the end of it. It's a large convention, and there's no reason he should run into Mary Catherine again.

They take the subway to Chelsea, to Matthew's apartment. Once inside, fresh from a shower and with tea water boiling on the stove, Larry doesn't feel like schlepping all the way back to Midtown for the late afternoon speakers. He'd rather enjoy Matthew for a few hours, go out to dinner, perhaps catch his show, and later go for a drink. Matthew's life seems deliciously unencumbered by the kinds of responsibilities working with children has come to signify for Larry.

Wrapped in Matthew's forties-vintage rayon dressing gown, he lounges on the sofa, leafing through *The Village Voice*, while Matthew prepares the tea.

"I've got big news," Matthew announces, carrying a tray of tea things into the living room.

Larry gives him an expectant face. "Don't tell me your show's moving to Broadway?"

Matthew laughs.

"The show's closing next week. No, it's got nothing to do with the theater." He starts pouring their tea. "I'm going to be a father."

For a second Larry's confused. He knows what these words mean, but coming from Matthew—a guy who's prone to calling heterosexuals "breeders"—they must mean something else, some new gay expression Larry hasn't heard of yet.

"Well, not a real father," Matthew continues, moving the tea strainer to the other cup. "I mean, a lesbian woman I know wants to have a kid, so . . ."

Larry grabs the strainer out of Matthew's hand.

"Are you serious?"

"Of course, I'm serious," Matthew says. There's a tinge of annoyance in his voice.

Instantly, Larry fires a barrage of questions at him: is he marrying her (no); has he been tested for diseases (yes); how are they doing it (coitally); have they seen a lawyer?

"What do we need to see a lawyer for?" Matthew asks.

"Because it's a big responsibility," Larry informs him.

"Larry, you're always playing the schoolmarm. Doris and I *are* adults, you know. We've considered this very carefully."

"But having a kid," Larry insists. "Bringing him, her up!"

"Oh, that," says Matthew. "I'm not going to bring the kid up. Doris doesn't want that and neither do I. I'm just furnishing the Y chromosome. I'm not exactly the family type, you know."

"I can't believe you, Matthew!"

Larry feels ridiculous, having this conversation in an imitation silk dressing gown. It's so typical of what he hates about New York: this man he's had sex with but hardly knows, this man who is sort of a friend but not really, this man who breezes in and out of trendy shows about earnest subjects (or is it earnest shows about trendy subjects?), this man who can be so casual about siring children.

"What can't you believe?" Matthew says.

"*This!*" Larry yells, throwing out his arms. "All of this!" He hears himself blurting out something about people who are dying to have kids and can't, but it comes out all incoherent, and, in frustration, he realizes that he's not sure what he's trying to say.

"Doris is dying to have kids, too," Matthew tells him calmly. "Or don't you think lesbians are worthy of children?"

"Okay, okay," Larry says. "I guess I'm just saying it seems like such a big step. I'm not sure I could ever take it myself."

"Oh, you would if you were Doris," Matthew tells him. "She really wants a family." And then he adds, "Maybe for gay teachers their students are their family."

"Yeh," says Larry, turning over this cliché of an idea, trying to find something in it. "Yeh, maybe."

After the faces, it's the ring finger. Clothing is a neutral at these conferences: the men all wear jackets and ties. But the ring finger, that's the best bet. No ring and you can start making some assumptions. Though even here you have to be careful. There are exceptions: men who don't wear a wedding band, or take it off on long trips; and guys with lovers who do wear gold bands. So nothing's perfectly clear. Still, Larry looks for the ring finger.

During the Saturday morning coffee break he watches these men's hands, holding pencils, clasping styrofoam cups, punctuating the air to make a point. There are some extraordinarily beautiful hands at this conference: some with the exquisite proportions of classical sculpture, soft, hairless, the blue veins just hinted at; others are chunky, olive-complected, hirsute. Larry imagines his fingertips caressing these hands, feeling the smoothness, the coarseness, the bones and skin. He catches himself rubbing the place on his own left hand where a ring would be.

At lunch time, as he enters the Grand Ballroom, Larry sees Mary Catherine rushing over to join him. He pretends he doesn't see her and quickly finds a place at a table with only one unoccupied seat.

The guest speaker at lunch is the president of a distinguished women's college. Her topic is "Children Are the Future." She reminds them that the generation of children they are now teaching will determine the future of democracy and civilization. It's a speech that starts with startling, depressing facts and ends with a stirring, optimistic exhortation, the kind of speech that keeps the overworked Mary Catherines of the world going.

Larry gets caught up in it, too. As much as these conferences can be a bore, he does love all the grand words: future, civilization, democracy. It makes him feel part of a wonderful enterprise, another word the college president uses.

Toward the end of the address, a guy across the luncheon table catches Larry's attention and raises his eyes. What a pile of bullshit, he's saying, though Larry wonders if there isn't something else he's signaling, too. He glances at the guy's hands—no wedding ring—then shoots him a quick, friendly smile. But how to make that smile say two different things: *yes* to the flirtation; *no* to the guy's cynicism about the speech?

Then the address is over and everyone applauds. And when the applause grows and people begin to rise for a standing ovation, Larry rises, too. Everyone at his table does except the guy across from him, who sits there with his arms folded across his chest and slouches. It makes Larry wonder if he hasn't been duped by all the idealistic language. Matthew's talk about "breeders" may be a lot of political rhetoric, but maybe all these stirring thoughts about kids are no better. Maybe children—having children, having a family—are overrated.

He looks over toward Mary Catherine's table. She's applauding wildly, her arms raised in the air, her head shaking up and down as if she were at a pep rally. Then he looks back at the guy, who's rising now, gathering up his papers. Larry pulls together his own notes and publisher's catalogs and makes his way, as nonchalantly as possible, to the other side of the table.

"What did you think?" he asks in his best matter-of-fact voice. He doesn't want to come across as pursuing anything. Not yet.

The guy shrugs, an ambiguity Larry thinks he can hang on: at least there's an opening here, the possibility of a conversation.

"I dunno," Larry ventures again. "I wonder if we don't sometimes get overly romantic about children."

The guy is half paying attention, half scanning the fast-emptying ballroom. Cruising is what it looks like to Larry.

"My name's Larry," he tries a third time, holding out his hand.

"Mike," the guy says. He gives Larry a perfunctory smile and a quick handshake, then cranes his neck again out over the crowd.

"You know what I mean?" Larry says. "I mean . . ." Mike starts walking toward the door. "I mean, there are other family models—you know, besides mother, father, and two point five children—that have legitimacy, right?" Larry can't believe that this sentence has come out of his mouth. It sounds so finky, and he's sure he's lost Mike. "Would you like to go for a drink?" he asks, almost in desperation, just as Mary Catherine comes running up to them.

"Wasn't it wonderful!" she says, beaming at Larry. Mike keeps walking and Larry doesn't know what to do. He stops, looks at the fast-retreating Mike, looks again at Mary Catherine, who is flushed with enthusiasm. She looks at Mike, too, and when she turns back to Larry, Larry thinks he can detect—what on her face?—confusion? embarrassment? recognition?

"Oh, I'm sorry. I think I've interrupted something," she says.

"Hey, it's nice to see you!" he tells Mary Catherine. And he means it.

He spends the rest of the day with Mary Catherine. They attend a panel on word processing, another on sexism in children's literature. At five, they go out for the drink Larry's been craving since lunch.

In a quiet bar on the Upper East Side, Mary Catherine orders hot mulled wine; Larry gets a double bourbon. Suddenly, he's very grateful for the companionship of this overweight, motherly woman who wears clothes that are supposed to be fashionable but aren't quite, and he imagines her standing in front of her too large seventh-grade English class, tapping her feet crammed into high heels, while she runs yet another discussion of *The Pearl*. Hot mulled wine in a quiet bar on a Saturday night must seem a soldier's reward to her.

At the other end of the bar, a cocktail pianist is playing hushed torch songs. They listen to him for a few minutes. Larry wonders if Mary Catherine has noticed the three men, older wholesome-looking types, who are gathered around the piano. For the first time in a long time, he feels good about New York, about its cosmopolitan way of making a place for lots of different people all in the same bar.

"My poor husband," Mary Catherine says. She picks two modest peanuts out of the bowl in front of her and sets them down on her cocktail napkin. "He has to take the boys to hockey practice tonight. Usually I do it, but"—and, shrugging her shoulders, she looks up into the soft, recessed lighting—"here I am!" She giggles at him.

"How old are your kids?" Larry asks. He wants to know everything about her homey, unremarkable life.

She tells him about Skippy, age eight, and Philip, twelve. How Skippy's actually a better skater than his older brother. Philip is more cautious, more "cerebral," she says, the type who prefers reading books.

"What kinds of books?"

"Oh, just about anything he can get his hands on: history right now."

Larry loves the way she says "right now." She's the kind of mother who can go with the flow. He thinks about it and wonders if that's the kind of father he would have been.

"If I had a son," he tells Mary Catherine, "I'd name him Ethan." The bourbon is beginning to get to him.

Mary Catherine giggles again. A nervous giggle.

"What?" Larry asks, cocking his head at her.

"Oh, it just seems so funny, sitting in a bar with some-one other than my husband." She cups the mulled wine in her hands and looks around the room.

"Does it make you uncomfortable?"

Mary Catherine turns back to him. "Oh, no," she says quickly, too quickly.

"But it *is* unusual," Larry acknowledges. He's trying to let her know it's okay if she feels weird right now.

"In this day and age, oh . . ." Mary Catherine says, lingering on that oh, balancing it like a ball that could tip either way. "Do you really think so, Larry?"

"Well," he tells her, "I think I'm feeling a little un-comfortable." He takes his highball glass and twists it, first one way, then the other, into his napkin. When he looks up, Mary Catherine is giving him a puzzled, maybe even hurt, look.

"It's nothing to do with you," Larry says. "It's just that being single sometimes feels so decadent. I mean, when I go home at the end of the day, I don't have to deal with a husband and kids. I mean a wife and kids." He laughs at his own mistake, but he knows his face is flushed.

Mary Catherine laughs too. "Whatever," she says, toss-ing out her heavy arms in a carefree manner that reminds Larry of those remarkably dignified hippo ballerinas in Dis-ney's *Fantasia*.

"Let's face it," says Larry, trying to keep the laughter going, "you're doing twice as much for the future of democracy and civilization as I am."

"Well, any time you want to trade!" Mary Catherine tells him.

"Sure," Larry says. "How about next Saturday: I'll come by and take your kids to hockey practice. How's that?"

He means it as a continuation of the joking, but when he sees in Mary Catherine's face a hint of concern, Larry realizes she's not so sure she would entrust her children to him, to this man who reads lesbian poems and runs after other men at a teachers' conference.

"No thanks, I wouldn't want your life for anything," he says, trying to be reassuring, wondering if that's true. She laughs, too, but then she stops and just briefly touches his hand as if to call a halt to the joking.

"From my perspective," she says. There's a carefulness in her voice. Larry twists his glass some more, and it starts to tear into the soggy napkin. "From my perspective . . ." She stops again, so that he has to look at her. "I want to get this right, Larry, you know that? I mean, that teacher, the one I told you about on the train . . ."

"Oh that," he says. "Forget it. I've already put it out of my mind."

"But you were right. He is the exception. I mean, when you come right down to it, there isn't much difference between most of us, is there? We're all part of one human family."

He looks out over the lounge. One of the men at the piano is cruising him, and this time, when he turns back to Mary Catherine, she's giving him the kind of amused look that makes Larry realize he can be caught in the act sometimes, too.

"Family," he echoes, trying it out for size.

There is something about that word. Like a stirring phrase in a speech, or the perfect rhyme at the end of a sonnet. Something he'd like to hold onto. He'd like this whole weekend, this whole month, to come under the rubric of Family. He wants it to sum up everything; his relationship to the women in the office, to his students at Beechwood, to Matthew and Mary Catherine; and to the Dorises, too, the people he may never meet but knows are pulling in the same direction; even to all the people—all the *men*—who are still just promises of some connection; and maybe even to the Mikes of the world, the guys who won't let him get too sappy about any of this. He wants to be able to trust that it's all adding up to something, maybe to the future of civilization, though he'd settle for something a lot smaller.

He's holding her hands across the table now, his right thumb gently brushing her rings. "Family," he says. "It sounds like the title of a speech, doesn't it? Or an essay. An essay that really wants to be a story."